CHRISTMAS ON MAIN STREET

A SWEET SMALL TOWN CHRISTMAS ROMANCE
(SANTA'S SECRET HELPERS, BOOK 1)

LEEANNA MORGAN

ABOUT THIS BOOK

This Christmas, something magical is happening in Sapphire Bay.

Emma loves everything about living in Sapphire Bay. The scenery in the small Montana town is spectacular, her communications business is thriving, and her six-year-old twins are happy. When a Christmas Facebook post goes viral, Emma and her friends are swamped with people asking Santa for help. But it's her twins' Christmas wish that breaks her heart.

Jack Devlin finds missing people. When his brother asks him to locate Emma's ex-husband, he thinks it's going to be an easy case. But the more time he spends with Emma, the more complicated their relationship becomes.

With more than one heart on the line, will they go back to their old lives or risk everything for a once-in-a-lifetime kind of love?

CHRISTMAS ON MAIN STREET is the first novel in the Santa's Secret Helpers series and can easily be read as a standalone. Each of Leeanna's series are linked so you can find out what happens to your favorite characters in other books. For news of my latest releases, please visit leeannamorgan.com and sign up for my newsletter. Happy reading!

Other Novels by Leeanna Morgan:

Montana Brides:
Book 1: Forever Dreams (Gracie and Trent)
Book 2: Forever in Love (Amy and Nathan)
Book 3: Forever After (Nicky and Sam)
Book 4: Forever Wishes (Erin and Jake)
Book 5: Forever Santa (A Montana Brides Christmas Novella)
Book 6: Forever Cowboy (Emily and Alex)
Book 7: Forever Together (Kate and Dan)
Book 8: Forever and a Day (Sarah and Jordan)
Montana Brides Boxed Set: Books 1-3
Montana Brides Boxed Set: Books 4-6

The Bridesmaids Club:
Book 1: All of Me (Tess and Logan)
Book 2: Loving You (Annie and Dylan)
Book 3: Head Over Heels (Sally and Todd)
Book 4: Sweet on You (Molly and Jacob)
The Bridesmaids Club: Books 1-3

Emerald Lake Billionaires:
Book 1: Sealed with a Kiss (Rachel and John)
Book 2: Playing for Keeps (Sophie and Ryan)
Book 3: Crazy Love (Holly and Daniel)

Book 4: One And Only (Elizabeth and Blake)
Emerald Lake Billionaires: Books 1-3

The Protectors:
Book 1: Safe Haven (Hayley and Tank)
Book 2: Just Breathe (Kelly and Tanner)
Book 3: Always (Mallory and Grant)
Book 4: The Promise (Ashley and Matthew)
The Protectors Boxed Set: Books 1-3

Montana Promises:
Book 1: Coming Home (Mia and Stan)
Book 2: The Gift (Hannah and Brett)
Book 3: The Wish (Claire and Jason)
Book 4: Country Love (Becky and Sean)
Montana Promises Boxed Set: Books 1-3

Sapphire Bay:
Book 1: Falling For You (Natalie and Gabe)
Book 2: Once In A Lifetime (Sam and Caleb)
Book 3: A Christmas Wish (Megan and William)
Book 4: Before Today (Brooke and Levi)
Book 5: The Sweetest Thing (Cassie and Noah)
Book 6: Sweet Surrender (Willow and Zac)
Sapphire Bay Boxed Set: Books 1-3
Sapphire Bay Boxed Set: Books 4-6

Santa's Secret Helpers:
Book 1: Christmas On Main Street (Emma and Jack)
Book 2: Mistletoe Madness (Kylie and Ben)
Book 3: Silver Bells (Bailey and Steven)
Book 4: The Santa Express (Shelley and John)
Book 5: Endless Love (The Jones Family)
Santa's Secret Helpers Boxed Set: Books 1-3

Return To Sapphire Bay:
Book 1: The Lakeside Inn (Penny and Wyatt)
Book 2: Summer At Lakeside (Diana and Ethan)
Book 3: A Lakeside Thanksgiving (Barbara and Theo)
Book 4: Christmas At Lakeside (Katie and Peter)

The Cottages on Anchor Lane:
Book 1: The Flower Cottage (Jackie and Richard)
Book 2: The Starlight Café (Andrea and David)
Book 3: The Cozy Quilt Shop (Shona and Greg)
Book 4: A Stitch in Time (Laura and Joseph)

CHAPTER 1

*E*mma rushed into the meeting room at The Welcome Center. Pastor John and Willow were already there. "Sorry I'm late. My babysitter forgot she was looking after Molly and Dylan."

"You could have brought the twins with you," John said. "They would have been no trouble."

Emma took off her jacket and grinned at John. The single, forty-two-year-old pastor was the sweetest, kindest man she'd ever met. But he had no idea how mischievous her six-year-old twins could be, especially Molly. Dylan would have sat quietly with his pencils and paper, but Molly would have wanted to be part of the meeting. Especially since they were talking about the tiny home village.

"It's easier without Dylan and Molly. Have I missed anything?"

Willow shook her head. "We thought we'd wait until you arrived. Kylie can't leave her flower shop—someone ordered a dozen flower arrangements for a birthday party tomorrow afternoon."

"I'll visit her after the meeting and let her know what we

talked about." Emma was pleased she wasn't the only one who had trouble being here. Juggling her communications business, her volunteer work at The Welcome Center, and looking after the twins sometimes felt like a losing battle.

John handed Emma a folder. "Willow told me my list of fundraising ideas needed some work. So I sat down and came up with a different approach. What do you think?"

Emma glanced at Willow and tried not to smile. John's last list included hosting the Miss America pageant. Although the boost in tourist numbers would be appreciated, she knew that wasn't the reason he had included it.

She opened the folder and looked at the ideas. Ten months ago, Pastor John had decided to do something about the lack of affordable rental accommodation in Sapphire Bay. The small Montana town had the same problem as most cities and towns around the world. A growing number of people were living in their cars or with family and friends because they couldn't afford to live anywhere else. Others suffered from mental health and addiction issues, making it almost impossible to live independently or convince a landlord to rent their homes to them.

After investigating different options, John had worked with a team of architectural students at Montana State University. They'd designed affordable, tiny homes that would provide subsidized rental accommodation. So far, six homes had been built in an old steamboat museum and transported to a plot of land opposite the church.

The community's goal was to have twenty-five tiny homes built in the next twelve months. Raising the funds to build them was an ongoing project. And that's what Emma, Willow, and their friends were doing.

Emma leaned her elbows on the table. "A lot of these ideas have a Christmas theme."

Pastor John nodded. "It's mid-July. If we don't think about Christmas now, it will be too late to plan anything."

One of the projects made Emma frown. "Isn't the beginning of September a little early to have a Christmas parade on Main Street?"

John shrugged. "It's never too early for Christmas. Besides, if we involve the entire community, people will come from all over Montana to enjoy our Christmas events."

Willow sighed. "There's only one problem. Zac and I are getting married soon. Between planning the wedding and making sure my next photographic collection is ready, I don't have a lot of spare time."

"Don't worry," Emma reassured her. "You've already done an incredible amount of fundraising. You can help us when your life is a little less hectic."

John pulled out a sheet of paper from his folder. "I agree. You need to take care of yourself," he said, handing the sheet to Emma.

"What's this?"

"It's my plan B. I had a feeling Willow would be too busy to help, so I mentioned the tiny home village to Bailey Jones yesterday. She's talking to Zac about a job in his medical clinic."

Willow frowned. "Is that Sam's sister?"

John nodded. "She's wanted to move here for a long time. But it wasn't until she heard about Zac's clinic that she was able to seriously consider it."

"Why do you have a copy of her resumé?" Emma asked.

"If Bailey gets a job with Zac, she's offered to help with the fundraising projects for the tiny home village. She gave me a copy of her resumé to see if her skills match what we need."

Emma smiled. "I hope you told her we aren't picky. As long as she's happy to help, we'll find something for her to do." Her eyes widened when she read Bailey's qualifications. "Why does she want to live in Sapphire Bay? She could work anywhere in the world."

"It's probably because of Sam," Willow murmured. "They're a close family." She looked over Emma's shoulder and released a low whistle. "I don't know anything about being a family therapist, but having a degree from Harvard and working in the Mayo Clinic is impressive."

"When would Bailey move here?" Emma asked John.

"It depends on Zac. If he wants her to start next week, she could."

Emma's mind was racing through the events on John's list. They'd need all the help they could get if they were going to do half the things he'd planned. "Where is she staying while she's here?"

"For now, she's living with Sam and Caleb. If she gets the job with Zac, I'm not sure where she'll live." John looked at Emma and raised his eyebrows. "What do you think about a Christmas on Main Street event?"

"It sounds like fun," Emma said cautiously. "But there's too much on the list. We'll have to take out some things."

John looked at the list and sighed. "I guess that means the cross-country sleigh race and the pop-up North Pole village are out of the question?"

Emma laughed. "Maybe. You've given us the outline of what you'd like. How about I talk to Kylie? We'll look at how much work is involved in each idea, then come back to you with a program that works for everyone."

John sat back in his chair. "That sounds like a good plan. I can't wait to hear what you come up with."

Neither could Emma. Because regardless of what she'd said to John, Christmas was her favorite time of the year. Even if they were starting a little early.

JACK LIFTED his suitcase out of his brother's truck and took a moment to enjoy the view from Acorn Cottage. The clear blue water of Flathead Lake sat like a polished jewel against the towering mountain range on the far side of the bay. Pine, spruce, and oak trees added color and texture to the sheer cliffs, sheltering the land from the worst of the weather that tore across the lake.

"Do you ever get tired of this view?" he asked his brother.

Noah smiled. "It hasn't happened yet. Even in the middle of summer, each day is different. You could always live here, too."

Jack rolled his suitcase toward Acorn Cottage. "I wouldn't have enough work to do." Five years ago, he'd started his own private investigation company. Lost and Found specialized in reconnecting family and friends who had, for one reason or another, lost contact with each other.

He couldn't have grown the business into the success it was without the highly qualified team he'd recruited. Moving to the sleepy town of Sapphire Bay would be a huge stretch for any of them. Especially if they spent most of their time searching for missing cats and runaway children.

Noah opened the front door and handed Jack the key. "Cassie left some fresh milk and butter in the refrigerator. There's bread and enough cereal for a few days in the pantry. I'm heading into town in half an hour. If you need anything else, let me know."

"I stopped at the general store on my way through town and picked up a few groceries. If you and Cassie want to join me for dinner, I've got enough meat and salads for everyone."

"What time are you eating?"

"Six o'clock."

Noah nodded. "We'll be here."

"I'll call Granddad and invite him, too. How are the plans going for your birthday?" Turning forty was a big deal, not that you'd know it if you spoke to Noah. Jack was surprised his brother was having a party. Even before he'd moved to Sapphire Bay, Noah did everything he could to keep his personal life as low-key as possible.

"Everything's organized. When you see Granddad, remind him that he needs to be here by two o'clock tomorrow afternoon. Knowing him, he'll get so involved in building the tiny homes that he'll forget about the party."

Jack frowned. "I don't think that will happen."

"You might be surprised." Noah wrapped his arms around Jack and gave him a hug. "It's good to see you little brother. Thanks for coming all this way."

"You're welcome. I wouldn't have missed your birthday for anything."

Noah looked away, but not before Jack saw the worry in his brother's eyes. "What haven't you told me?"

"Everything's fine," Noah assured him. "The thought of turning forty is stressing me out."

Jack laughed. "You'd better get used to it. You've got one day left to enjoy being in your thirties. After that it's all downhill."

"I'd be careful what I said, if I were you. You're only two years younger than me." Noah checked his watch. "I need to get back to the cottage for a conference call. I'll see you later this afternoon."

Jack said goodbye and watched his brother walk across the yard. Thinking about getting older was the least of Jack's worries. Over the last year, he'd started thinking there was something wrong with him. While all his friends were finding the love of their lives and settling into parenthood, he was still making the same mistakes.

None of his relationships lasted more than a couple of

months. And once they ended, he never saw the woman again. If there was someone meant for him, he hadn't met her. And the most depressing thought of all was that maybe he never would.

EMMA OPENED the door to Blooming Lovely, Kylie's flower shop. As soon as she walked inside, she inhaled the gorgeous scent of roses, lilies, and sweet peas.

Kylie stood behind the front counter, adding some delicate white flowers to a vase. "Hi, Emma. I'm sorry I couldn't be at the meeting. How did it go?"

"Pastor John has some great fundraising ideas. I'm not sure if we'll be able to do everything on his list, though."

"That's John for you." Kylie turned the vase around. "What do you think?"

"It's beautiful."

"That's seven down with five left to go." Carefully, Kylie lifted the vase off the desk and headed toward the special refrigerator at the back of the store.

"I don't know how you go home each night. Your store always smells so wonderful."

"It's one of the reasons I became a florist. The color, shape, and scent of the flowers makes me happy."

Emma took Pastor John's list out of her bag. "I have something else that might make you happy. This is the list of events John is thinking about for the Christmas fundraising program."

While Kylie read through the list on the first sheet of paper, Emma placed another folder on the counter. "John photocopied a more detailed description of each program for both of us. I thought we could go through the ideas over the next day or two and decide which ones we can do."

"That sounds like a good plan. What does Willow think of the ideas?"

"She was glad John reduced the number of activities, but she won't be able to help us for a few months. She's too busy planning her wedding and getting her photographs ready for an exhibition. Pastor John talked to someone else who might be happy to help. If I have enough time, I'll visit her this afternoon before the babysitter goes home."

"Do you want to come to my house in two days' time for dinner? I'll make something Molly and Dylan will enjoy. We can decide what programs we'll start straight away and which ones will take more time to organize."

"Sounds good. You look tired. Do you want me to make you a cup of coffee before I leave?"

Kylie leaned against the counter and nodded. "That would be awesome. I've got another big order I need to get ready before tomorrow morning."

"Is there anything else I can do to help?"

"Not at the moment, but thanks for asking."

As Emma made Kylie a cup of coffee, she looked around the workroom and sighed. If she hadn't opened her website design and social media business, she would have loved being a florist. Instead of creating strategies that drove traffic to her clients' businesses, she could have created amazing bouquets and floral arrangements.

Emma frowned. Until now, Pastor John hadn't used social media to tell people about the tiny home village. What if they changed the way they communicated with the wider world? What if they created posts that were engaging and made people feel part of what they were doing?

Holding a hot cup of coffee, Emma walked back into the flower shop. Kylie was making another bouquet. "What if I design a Facebook post that asks everyone what events they want for Christmas? We could still look at John's events, but it would give us a better idea of what the community wants."

Kylie picked a yellow rose out of a container. "I think it's a great idea. But do you have time to put something together?"

"I'll make the time. If it generates enough interest, it will give us some ideas for when we get together again."

For the first time today, Emma was feeling more positive about the events John had suggested. The programs they chose had to create the greatest impact and make the most amount of money for the tiny home village. And the only way they would do that was to give the community programs they were excited about.

JACK STOOD under the shade of an oak tree watching Noah's friends enjoy the party.

A company from Polson had arrived early this morning to erect a large white marquee tent between Honeysuckle Cottage, where Noah and Cassie lived, and the vacation home where Jack was staying. Apart from the trees surrounding the property, the tent provided the only shelter from the late afternoon sun.

"Excuse me. Would you mind if I took this chair?"

He looked into an incredible pair of deep blue eyes. "Ah, sure. That's fine. No one's sitting…" He stopped talking, hoping she hadn't noticed how tongue-tied he'd become.

"Thanks. If you need the chair later, I'd be happy to return it."

"No, it's okay. You keep it." Jack was stunned by the woman's beauty. With blond hair falling around her shoulders, and a gentle smile on her lips, she took his breath away.

She bent down to move the chair.

He stepped forward. "Let me carry it for you."

"It's okay. I can manage." She picked up the chair, holding it close. "If you're not here with anyone else, you could join us at our table."

"Thanks for the offer, but I'm all right. I want to catch up with Noah before dinner."

"Okay. But if you change your mind, we're not far away."

"I'll remember. Enjoy the party." Jack watched her walk across to her friends. As soon as she sat down, she lifted a young boy onto her lap.

He looked at the people around her, wondering if she was here with a boyfriend or partner. Most of the people at the table were women. He recognized Cassie's friends, Megan and Willow.

He could ask Megan who—

"I thought you'd be behind the bar serving some of those fancy cocktails you enjoy." Patrick, Jack's eighty-one-year-old grandfather, stood beside him.

He pulled his attention away from the blond woman and smiled at his granddad. "I felt like taking a backseat today. Besides, the catering company Noah employed is doing a good job."

Pulling a wooden seat closer to his grandson, Patrick sat down. "I haven't seen Cassie. Do you know where she's gone?"

Jack had been wondering the same thing. "I haven't got a clue. I thought she might be inside the cottage."

"I've already looked. She's not there. It's not like her to be late to Noah's party."

"I'll see if I can get hold of her." Jack took his phone out of his pocket. The call went straight to voicemail. "She must have turned off her phone."

Patrick pulled himself out of the chair. "We should speak to Noah. He might know where she's gone."

Jack knew there was no point arguing with his grandfather. He loved Cassie as if she were his own daughter. If she were missing, he'd find her.

"There's Noah." Patrick pointed to a group of people standing in the marquee tent. "When did he change into a dinner suit?"

Jack followed his granddad across the backyard. "Beats me. The last time I saw him he was wearing a cotton shirt and trousers. I wonder if he realizes he's a little overdressed."

Patrick slowed his steps. "He looks so much like your father."

Jack smiled. "I think he looks like you."

"You need your eyes checked," came the gruff reply. "If I looked half as good as you two boys, your grandma would have had to chase all the girls away."

"I couldn't see Grandma doing that," Jack said with a sigh.

Patrick scanned the people inside the tent. "Don't you believe it. Your grandma was a Southern lady, but she could be a lioness if someone was up to no good with the people she loved. Cassie isn't here."

Jack nodded toward his brother. "Let's talk to Noah."

They were halfway across the tent when his brother tapped a teaspoon on the edge of a wine glass and invited everyone to join them.

Patrick sent Jack a questioning look.

"I don't know what he's up to, either," Jack whispered. Noah wouldn't thank everyone for coming without Cassie being here. And as for giving a speech, his brother enjoyed that almost as much as he enjoyed turning forty.

While Noah waited for everyone to move into the tent, his gaze connected with Jack's. Whatever he was about to do was anyone's guess. But Jack knew one thing, his brother was more nervous than he'd ever seen him.

When most people were inside the tent, Noah cleared his throat. "I'd like to thank everyone for coming here tonight.

The invitation you received was for my birthday, but we'll be celebrating something else, too. Cassie and I have decided to get married. Tonight. And we'd like you to be part of the ceremony."

For a few seconds, all the guests stood in stunned silence. Then everyone burst into applause.

Jack was shocked that his brother was getting married today. It wasn't like him to keep it a secret, especially when everything in his life was planned at least six months in advance.

"Did you know about this?" Patrick asked.

"I didn't have a clue."

Noah walked across to his grandfather. "You must be surprised."

"I am, but I'm also happy for you. I thought you were getting married in October?"

"We were, but Cassie has been invited to exhibit her jewelry in Milan at the same time. This was the only weekend when everyone would be together, so we decided to bring the wedding forward."

The staff Noah had employed walked into the tent carrying foldaway chairs. In next to no time, straight rows of chairs began to appear. When the rest of their family and friends saw what was happening, they pitched in to help.

Noah looked anxiously around the tent. "I hope Cassie's okay."

"Where is she?" Jack asked.

"With one of her friends." Noah checked his watch. "She should be here soon."

Patrick wrapped his arm around his grandson's shoulders. "She'll be fine. I imagine she's feeling exactly the same as you."

Jack looked around the tent, then back at his brother.

"We'd better help get everything ready. Otherwise, Cassie will be walking into chaos."

Noah took a deep breath. "At least moving chairs will stop me from panicking."

Jack wasn't sure anything would do that. Noah was about to change his life forever, and he looked as though he was going to be sick.

CHAPTER 2

*E*mma sat at the back of the tent, mesmerized by the unexpected wedding. Being here to celebrate Noah and Cassie's wedding, to be part of the next chapter of their lives, was so special it brought tears to her eyes.

After Noah told everyone what would be happening, the marquee tent was transformed into a lovely wedding venue. Emma was sure she recognized some of the flower arrangements from Kylie's flower shop. But her friend hadn't said anything, so she assumed she was as unaware of the wedding as everyone else.

As she looked at the guests, Emma's gaze lingered on the man she'd met under the oak tree. Megan had told her he was Jack Devlin, Noah's younger brother. He lived in Manhattan, visited Sapphire Bay every few months, and usually brought a different girlfriend to Montana on each visit.

When Emma had spoken to him, he didn't look as though he had anyone with him. And now, seeing him beside his grandfather, she was positive he'd come to Sapphire Bay alone. But, even if she was attracted to him, it didn't mean she would talk to him again. She wasn't the naïve person she'd been when she met her ex-husband. She had two children, a business she enjoyed, and friends who loved her like family. A man who changed girlfriends faster than his bed linen wasn't for her.

As Noah looked into Cassie's eyes and repeated his wedding vows, Emma sighed. Even though her own marriage had ended in heartache, she still believed in happily ever after. As unlikely as it was, she hoped that one day she would meet a man who treated her with respect and kindness, and who wanted to be loved as tenderly and sweetly as she knew how.

Beside her, Willow dabbed her eyes. "Their vows are so lovely," she whispered.

Emma nodded. Even though the wedding was a surprise, it was one of the most romantic ceremonies she'd ever seen.

As Noah and Cassie exchanged rings, the late afternoon sunshine fell across the tent. Cassie's beautiful floor-length lace gown shimmered and sparkled, and her veil cascaded behind her in soft folds.

Molly squeezed Emma's hand. "Mommy. I can't see Cassie."

Emma lifted her daughter onto her lap. "Is that better?"

Molly nodded and smiled. "She looks like a princess."

"She does." Unlike her brother, Molly loved fairy tales. If a story included a handsome prince, a forgotten shoe, or a battered and bruised beast, she was happy. At six years old, Molly was willing to forgive any failing or bad decision, as long as the princess wore a sparkly dress and the story ended happily ever after.

Dylan wasn't quite so forgiving. If his stories didn't involve some kind of mystery or adventure, he would change the words, giving the characters exactly what he thought they needed. Even now, sitting amongst the twinkling lights draped inside the tent, he was more interested in looking at the pictures inside the space book he'd brought with him.

Pastor John placed his hands above Cassie and Noah's heads, blessing their marriage and wishing them a long and happy life together.

Emma closed her eyes. She remembered her own wedding vows, her blind faith that Mark would be her rock, her soft place to fall. She took a deep breath. Three years after they'd said I do, Mark had packed his bags and left. And, apart from when he'd given her their divorce papers, she hadn't seen or heard from him again.

The sound of clapping pulled Emma back to the here and now.

At the front of the tent, Noah tenderly kissed his bride, then hugged her tight.

Emma hoped their marriage was strong and true, that Cassie and Noah would work through their differences and continue to see the good in each other.

"You're crying, Mommy," Molly whispered. "Are you sad?"

Emma reached into her pocket and found a tissue. "They're happy tears."

"Are you sure?"

She kissed the top of Molly's head and forced a smile. "I'm sure."

With a worried frown, her daughter turned to the front of the tent.

By the time Cassie and Noah walked down the aisle, Emma was feeling better. Tonight was about celebrating the future, not dwelling on the past.

"Can I talk to Cassie now?" Molly asked.

"We'll see her in a few minutes. Before we say hello, do you need to go to the bathroom?"

Molly shook her head. "Nope. I'm okay. What about you, Dylan?"

Her twin brother frowned. "I'm okay, too."

"In that case," Emma said with a grin. "How about we find a nice cold glass of lemonade for everyone, then see Cassie?"

Molly wiggled off Emma's lap. "Yeah! Come on, Dylan. The lemonade is over here."

With a reluctant sigh, Dylan shoved his book into his backpack and followed his sister.

Emma smiled as she walked behind them. They might be twins, but Molly and Dylan were as different as chalk and cheese. And someday, those differences could make both of their lives so much better.

ON HIS WAY back from getting two cups of coffee, Jack must have spoken to most of the people at the wedding. Each time he visited Sapphire Bay, he was greeted like a long-lost friend. Even people he'd only seen on the street recognized his face and said hello.

After living in New York City, it was a little disconcerting to realize that total strangers were more interested in his life than half the people he usually associated with. But that was part of living in a small town.

He nodded to another person before turning toward his table.

Mabel Terry, the owner of the general store, stood between him and his grandfather. Mabel was the sort of person who knew everything that was happening in Sapphire Bay. As well as keeping her customers informed of the latest events, she regularly updated the community Facebook page. If he looked online now, he was sure he would see photos of Noah and Cassie's wedding.

"It's good to see you, Jack. What did you think of your brother's wedding?"

"It was a wonderful service."

"Did you know Cassie and Noah were getting married today?"

Jack shook his head. "It was as much of a surprise to me as everyone else. How is your husband?"

"Allan's fine. We're as busy as ever in the store. Have you talked to Pastor John since you arrived?"

"Not yet, but Noah told me you've opened another two tiny homes since I was last here."

"We're getting faster. The volunteers are only taking five weeks to build each house now."

"That's great." Jack lifted the coffee cups higher. "I should get back to Granddad before our coffee gets cold."

"Of course," Mabel said reluctantly. "How long are you staying in Sapphire Bay?"

"Ten days. I thought I'd have a vacation while I'm here."

"Well, if you need anything, you know where to come."

"Thanks, Mabel. I'll remember." And before she could ask any more questions, Jack high-tailed it over to his grandfather.

Patrick took one of the coffee cups. "I saw you talking to Mabel. How is she?"

"She seems okay. Why do I always feel as though she'll tell everyone what I say?"

"Probably because she will." Patrick smiled. "She doesn't mean any harm. It's her way of making sure everyone knows what's happening in Sapphire Bay."

Jack's eyebrows rose. "Am I talking to the same man who refused to open a Facebook account because he thought it was a conspiracy against everyone's privacy?"

"I've mellowed since I left Manhattan. Besides, I enjoy reading about what everyone's doing."

"You might not be so forgiving if your name appears on Mabel's social media feed."

Patrick laughed. "My life isn't that exciting. What about you?"

Jack looked warily at his grandfather. "Noah's wedding is as exciting as my life gets at the moment."

"You aren't still thinking about Angela, are you?"

"Her name is Angelique. And no, I'm not." It wasn't until Jack had been dating Angelique for three months that he realized they wanted completely different things. Working fifteen-hour days, socializing with the glitterati of New York, and eating at the finest restaurants wasn't something he wanted anymore.

Sitting on his sofa watching reruns of his favorite TV programs suited him so much better.

When Angelique realized she was dating the wrong man, she walked out of his life and never returned.

"I blame myself for your stubborn independence," Patrick muttered. "I should have listened to your grandma and let you enjoy life instead of pushing you to be better than the next person."

"Being single isn't a disease. Look at Noah. If he hadn't searched for the winner of his company's jewelry award, he wouldn't have met Cassie."

"And I wouldn't be living in Sapphire Bay."

Jack studied his grandfather's face. "Moving here was a huge decision. Are you happy?"

Patrick smiled. "I'm happier than I was in Manhattan. I still miss Starbucks and walking to Sal's Pizza on a Sunday afternoon, but it's good living close to Noah and Cassie. And helping to build the tiny homes has given me a new lease on life."

Jack's granddad used to own one of the largest construction companies in New York City. Seven years ago, he'd sold the company and started an online retail store with Noah. Last year he'd retired completely, leaving the concrete jungle of Manhattan for the wide-open spaces of Montana.

Patrick would have thought his days of building houses was over, but he hadn't counted on meeting Pastor John and the good folk of Sapphire Bay.

Jack worried that his grandfather was doing too much, but no one could slow him down. "Just remember to take some time off once in a while."

He didn't need to hear his grandfather's chuckle to know his comment had fallen on deaf ears.

A flash of purple drew Jack's gaze to the dance floor. The woman he'd spoken to before the wedding was dancing with two small children. She seemed happy and carefree—the complete opposite of the way he felt.

His granddad must have been watching his face.

"That's Emma Lewis and her twins, Molly and Dylan."

Emma's two children laughed as she twirled them in circles.

Patrick smiled. "As well as running her own business, Emma helps at The Welcome Center. While Molly helps her, Dylan is usually in the community garden giving Gordon a hand."

Jack looked around the dance floor. "Is her husband here?"

"Emma's a single mom." Patrick studied Jack's face. "Before you say hello, you need to know one thing. Emma is a good woman. She cares about people and does what she can to help those less fortunate. You'll have to answer to me if you break her heart."

"I don't go out of my way to hurt anyone."

Patrick leaned forward. "I know you don't, but you need to look before you leap. You're thirty-eight years old. What do you want out of life?"

Jack watched Emma lift her son into her arms and spin

him in circles. He knew exactly what he wanted, but he was too scared to lay his heart on the line. "I don't know."

"One day you will. I just hope I'm still here to enjoy being part of it."

Jack didn't need to ask his granddad what he meant. Family meant everything to them, especially after Jack's parents died. But given his track record, his grandfather would be better talking to Noah about happy endings.

At the rate Jack was going, he'd still be single when he turned fifty.

HALF AN HOUR LATER, Emma made sure Molly and Dylan had something to eat before taking them back to their table. Compared with the barbecue she was expecting, the buffet was amazing. Even Molly, the pickiest eater Emma had ever known, managed to find a lot of food she would enjoy.

"I brought everyone a drink," Kylie said. "I hope you like orange juice."

"That's fine." Emma pulled out two chairs for the twins, then sat beside Kylie. "Noah and Cassie's wedding was so beautiful. Did you know your flower arrangements were for the wedding?"

Kylie picked up her cutlery. "Not at first. But when Cassie ordered a bouquet, it was pretty obvious. She made me promise on my grandmother's grave not to say anything."

"I wonder why."

"You know Cassie and Noah. They didn't want everyone to make a fuss. Did you see Noah's brother?"

"I did." Emma didn't trust the gleam in her friend's eyes.

"Megan said he's visited Sapphire Bay four or five times. I wonder why I haven't seen him before."

Emma shrugged. "It's the first time I've seen him, too. He might have spent most of his time with Noah and Cassie."

Kylie sighed. "A mystery man."

Emma didn't think he would remain a mystery for long. Especially if Mabel got hold of him. She had a way of delving into someone's life quicker than they could blink. "Megan said he usually brings his girlfriends with him, but I don't think he's come with anyone."

A mischievous smile lit Kylie's face. "Maybe he doesn't have a girlfriend at the moment. He might be waiting to meet Ms. Right in the middle of rural Montana."

"Or maybe he left his girlfriend in New York City."

"Let me dream for a few more seconds." Kylie gave a dramatic sigh. "Okay. I'm done dreaming. If he has a girlfriend, I'm happy for him. If not, he should spend more time in Sapphire Bay. He's obviously not dating the right kind of women."

"What's dating?" Molly asked.

Emma glanced at Kylie, then back to her daughter. "It's when two people spend time together."

"Like a play date?"

"That's right. A play date for adults." Emma hoped that made sense.

Molly placed her knife and fork beside her plate. "Jessica's mom has lots of dates. Why don't you have lots of dates?"

Emma forced a smile. "Because I'm too busy. Did you like the chicken leg?"

With a blissfully happy grin, Molly nodded her head. "It was de-licious."

"What about you, Dylan? Did you like the chicken legs?"

"I like the potatoes better." And with a big, open mouth, he swallowed a forkful of his favorite vegetable.

"Oh, my goodness," Mabel exclaimed from the other side of the table. "I can't believe it."

Emma had no idea what Mabel was talking about.

With a doubtful frown, Mabel showed her husband her cell phone. "Does that say what I think it does?"

Allan's mouth dropped open. "Are you sure it's accurate?"

"I can't imagine why it wouldn't be." Mabel looked at Emma and pushed back her chair. "You have to see this." She rushed around the table and handed Emma the phone. "We only posted the Christmas video on Facebook yesterday. Look at the number of likes."

Emma's eyes widened. "Ten thousand? That's incredible."

"Read what people have written," Mabel said excitedly. "Everyone is telling us what they want for Christmas."

Scrolling through the post was like looking into the heart of each person who'd seen the ad. They'd not only told everyone what they wanted, but why it was important.

Sprinkled amongst the comments asking for the latest gadgets, the overseas vacations people could only dream about, and the platform shoes that were an absolute must, were touching, heartfelt wishes from folk who had nowhere else to turn.

Kylie looked over Emma's shoulder and frowned. "We only asked people to tell us what sort of Christmas events they wanted."

"We got a whole lot more than that," Emma murmured. She handed Kylie the phone. "What will we do with the comments?"

Mabel returned to her seat while Kylie read more messages. "There isn't a lot you can do."

Emma sighed. "Mabel might be right. We don't have any money to help the people and, even if we did, a lot of the wishes are beyond anything we could provide."

"You can say that again." Kylie flicked through the comments. "Katherine D wants to visit her sister who's in the intensive care unit at Vancouver General Hospital. Her sister was hit by a car and is in an induced coma. Ron P wants to spend Christmas with his son in Australia and Jeff S wants a new set of…"—she grinned—"dentures."

Allan, Mabel's husband, leaned forward. "If you want to help some of the people, you need a plan. Great things don't just happen. They need structure, time frames, people who are responsible for the outcomes."

Mabel patted Allan's arm. "This isn't a corporate takeover. We're talking about people's lives."

"That makes it even more important to do the best you can."

Kylie handed Mabel her phone. "I agree with Allan. We should go through the comments, sort them into ideas for community Christmas events and individual wishes. Once we have the lists, we'll be able to figure out some sort of plan."

"Or even if we want to respond to the one-off wishes." Emma looked around the table at her friends. She hated seeing the disappointment on their faces, but someone had to be realistic. "I know it's upsetting, but we can't help everyone."

Kylie leaned her elbows on the table. "We don't need to help everyone, but we might be able to help a few people."

"And we don't need to do it alone," Mabel added. She glanced across the room and smiled. "I know at least two people who might be able to help."

Emma turned in her seat and frowned at the two brothers standing beside the bride. Noah was the chief executive of an online shopping network. He'd already helped with the tiny home village and lots of other community projects. She didn't know much about Jack, apart from what Megan had said.

"Jack's only here for a vacation," Emma said quickly. "He won't want to get involved in our Christmas program."

Mabel stood and straightened the wrinkles on her skirt. "Jack is a Devlin. If he's anything like his brother and grandfather, he'll be only too happy to help." And without missing a beat, she headed toward Noah and his brother.

"That's my girl," Allan said proudly. "If you want something done, ask Mabel."

Emma glanced at Kylie. She just hoped Mabel didn't put Jack and Noah off from helping them. Because, regardless of how it happened, they had to make a whole lot of Christmas wishes come true.

CHAPTER 3

*J*ack nodded at something Mabel said. For the last five minutes, she had been telling him and his brother about the Christmas events the local church was organizing.

"We'll help with whatever the fundraising team decides to do," Noah said. "But Jack will only be here for a couple of weeks."

Mabel smiled. "I'm sure Emma and Kylie will be thankful for any help they can get. Why don't you come and meet them?"

Jack looked helplessly at his brother.

Noah sent him an amused glance. "I need to rescue Cassie from Granddad. Mabel will look after you."

As if sensing he was ready to run, Mabel placed her hand under Jack's elbow. "Of course, I will. What do you like doing when you're not working, Jack?"

He had no idea why that was important, but maybe Mabel was just being friendly. "I don't get a lot of time away from work, but I enjoy fishing and riding my mountain bike."

"There can't be many biking trails around New York City."

"You'd be surprised." Jack stopped to avoid a collision with another guest.

"Have you seen how far we've come with the tiny home village?"

"I saw the site when I was here for Noah and Cassie's engagement party."

"You won't recognize it now. Our first tenants have moved in and are making the village their home. It's wonderful to see what a difference it's making in people's lives." Mabel stopped beside the table where she'd been sitting. "Jack, I'd like to introduce you to Kylie, the best florist in town. And sitting beside her is Emma. Emma owns her own social media business."

Jack nodded at the two women. They were both blond and pretty but, from the first moment he'd seen her, it was Emma who drew his attention.

If he didn't know better, he'd swear she was slightly embarrassed. Maybe he wasn't the only one who was unsure of Mabel's motives.

He held out his hand. "It's nice to meet you both." When Emma's hand touched his, a spark of awareness shot along his arm. He had no idea where that had come from. Dropping his arm to his side, he tried to act as though nothing had happened.

"And this is Molly and Dylan, Emma's twins," Mabel continued. "After the summer break, they're starting first grade."

Molly looked up at him with eyes that were the same color as her mom's. "You're the man who was standing under the tree."

"That's right."

"We're six. How old are you?"

Emma's cheeks turned pink. "It's not polite to ask someone their age."

"It's okay," Jack assured her. "I'm thirty-eight."

Molly looked as though she was trying to figure out how old that actually was. Dylan whispered something in his sister's ear and she smiled. "That's almost as old as Mommy."

Jack's eyebrows rose. Emma looked a lot younger than thirty-eight.

Emma placed her hand on her daughter's curly red hair. "I'm thirty-two. That's six years younger than Mr. Devlin."

"That's our age," Molly said with a dimpled grin.

Emma cleared her throat and looked at Mabel's husband. "Jack, have you met Allan?"

"We met a few months ago," Allan said with a smile. He stood and shook Jack's hand. "It's good to see you again. Did you know your brother was getting married today?"

"No, he didn't say anything."

"It was a lovely surprise." Mabel beamed at them. "Why don't you join us, Jack. Emma and Kylie can tell you about the Christmas program."

Emma started to say something but stopped when Kylie nudged her arm.

"Only if you're not busy," Emma murmured.

Jack couldn't decide whether she wanted him to stay or if she was giving him a reason to leave.

Mabel pulled out a chair. "You can sit here. Would you like a glass of orange juice or wine?"

"Juice would be great." He looked at Emma and Kylie, watching for any sign that they were uncomfortable with him being here. Emma's earlier hesitation hadn't returned, so he guessed it was okay. "Mabel told me about the Facebook post. You must be feeling a little overwhelmed with the response."

Emma sat back in her seat, making it easier for him to see Kylie. "Something about the post caught people's interest."

"You're being too modest." Mabel handed Jack her phone. "The Christmas image Emma chose was wonderful. And the words she used made people think about the importance of family and community. It's no wonder her social media business is booming."

If Jack could have chosen a career for Emma, he wouldn't have thought of the communications industry. She looked nothing like the people he worked with in Manhattan. "How long have you specialized in social media?"

"That's only one part of what I do. I help people develop their brand and I design websites and find other platforms that can help their business grow."

"And she's good at what she does," Kylie said. "Emma designed a logo for my flower shop and created my e-commerce website. She even showed me how to set up a newsletter and use Instagram and Pinterest. If it weren't for Emma, I wouldn't be selling nearly as many flowers."

"I only showed you the basics," Emma insisted. "It's your hard work that's made your business a success."

Jack studied the Facebook post Emma had designed. The image was of a snow-covered Christmas scene, complete with lights and a small-town village feel. Above the image were the words, "Make Christmas special for the people you love. Tell us about your dream Christmas event."

His eyes widened when he saw the number of likes and comments. A lot of people wanted to share their Christmas ideas. "More than four hundred people have left comments."

"It's incredible," Kylie said. "Who would have thought a little town on the shore of Flathead Lake would attract so much attention?"

Jack knew how difficult it was to make any impression on Facebook. "Is there anything I can do to help while I'm here?"

Kylie looked thoughtfully at him. "The first thing we have to do is sort the comments into some kind of order. You could help us do that."

Emma shook her head. "Jack didn't come to Sapphire Bay to work. He came to spend time with Noah and Cassie."

He wouldn't be spending a lot of time with his brother and sister-in-law for the next few days. "Noah and Cassie aren't going on their honeymoon until October, but I don't want to intrude on the first few days of their marriage. I could help you for the rest of the week, then see what Noah and Cassie are doing after that."

"That sounds awesome," Kylie said. "You could meet Emma and me in my flower shop tomorrow morning. By that stage, we'll probably have more Christmas ideas than we know what to do with."

Given the response so far, Jack could only agree. "Tomorrow sounds great. Is nine o'clock too early?"

"It's perfect." Kylie held out her hand. "Welcome to the Christmas Fundraising Committee."

Jack shook her hand. He wasn't sure whether a few days' work made him part of the committee, but he was happy to help.

By the time Emma arrived at the flower shop the next morning, Kylie and Jack had already started grouping the Facebook ideas together on a spreadsheet.

Half an hour later, they'd sorted a quarter of the comments into categories. From what Emma could see, most people wanted events the whole community could enjoy. And at the top of the list was a Santa Claus parade.

But it wasn't the community events that were making her feel uneasy. It was the personal wishes that were breaking her heart. "I feel bad that we won't be able to help everyone who asked for something special."

"Hopefully, other people see the posts and step forward to help." Kylie wrote down a wish for a new washing machine. "Maybe we could randomly select a few of the personal wishes and try to help those people?"

Jack looked up from scrolling through the comments on his phone. "My company can help with one or two wishes."

Emma frowned. "By donating some appliances?"

"Something like that. We wouldn't be the only business that wants to make a difference. What if you reached out to companies who have already helped the church?"

Emma placed her pen on the table. "Kylie and I thought of that, but we don't want to put the funding for the tiny home village in jeopardy. It doesn't matter how big an organization is, there's only so much money to go around."

"Fair enough." Jack added another three personal wishes to the spreadsheet. "How much time do you spend at the church?"

"Not as much as I'd like. I help in The Welcome Center two afternoons a week. The Christmas event committee is a little more flexible. I can do most of the work from home."

Jack looked across at Molly and Dylan. For now, they were drawing pictures on a small table beside Kylie's work-bench. "It can't be easy juggling two small children with your business and helping the church."

Emma shrugged. "I'm not the only person who has a busy life. Kylie works long hours in her flower shop, but still manages to help at The Welcome Center. Cassie designs jewelry, Mabel and Allan work long hours in the general store, and Willow travels the country taking photographs— and that's only a few of the people who volunteer at the church."

"All of us want to give as much time as we can," Kylie

added. "Most of the people who stay at The Welcome Center have nothing. If it weren't for the church and all the people who volunteer, I don't know what would happen to them."

Emma admired what the volunteers at The Welcome Center were doing. A few weeks after she'd arrived in Sapphire Bay, Pastor John had asked if Molly and Dylan wanted to join the Jumping Jellybeans toddler group. After her twins' first gymnastics class, she'd stumbled across The Welcome Center.

Anyone who needed a warm, safe place to sleep could stay there. Hot meals, clean showers, and good company made what the volunteers were doing priceless. The church even provided wrap-around services. Whether you needed to find work, a good counselor, or budgeting advice—a volunteer was always available to help people through what could be a bureaucratic nightmare.

Emma loved every minute of her work at the center, even if it did make her life a little hectic.

She printed another sheet of comments from the Facebook page and glanced at Jack. His head was bent over the spreadsheet, adding more ticks to the columns as he went through the printouts.

She smiled as a lock of his brown hair fell over his forehead. If anyone had asked her to imagine what Noah's brother looked like, she wouldn't have chosen any of Jack's features. Apart from both having dark hair and gorgeous brown eyes, they were nothing alike.

Jack was a little shorter than his brother and had a much slimmer build. He had a quirky sense of humor and his easy smile and thoughtful words had already impressed her.

Even though she knew next to nothing about him, Emma wanted to know more. "Noah said you live in Manhattan, Jack. Do you work with your brother?"

"I've helped him a few times, but I own my own company. It's called Lost and Found. We look for people who have gone missing."

Her eyebrows rose. "Do you work with the police?"

"Sometimes."

Kylie tapped her pen against her chin. "Are you like the private investigators on the TV?"

Jack smiled. "Probably not. A lot of our work involves searching through databases and electronically tracking a missing person's movements. It's not as glamorous or as exciting as the shows I've seen on TV."

"If I was adopted," Emma asked, "could you help me find my biological family?"

"It would depend on the status of your adoption. If your records are sealed, it would be more difficult. But even with sealed records, there are other ways of searching for birth parents."

Kylie picked up her cup of coffee. "What if I wanted to find a friend I'd lost contact with? Could you help?"

Jack nodded. "You'd be surprised how often that happens."

Emma tilted her head to the side. "What made you want to find lost people?"

Jack's smile disappeared. "When I was nine years old, my parents died. Noah and I went to live with our grandparents. If they hadn't been alive, I don't know where we would have gone. When I was older, I realized a lot of people have never met their extended family. That's why I started my company —to help people reconnect with each other."

"So they wouldn't be alone," Emma murmured.

Jack nodded. His gaze lingered on her face, staring into her eyes as if nothing in the world mattered more than the understanding passing between them.

Emma knew what it felt like to be alone. When she'd arrived in Sapphire Bay, she knew no one. Her parents had told her she was crazy to take two toddlers to a town she'd never seen. But the need to start again, to get away from the life she'd had, was stronger than the stress of starting again.

"What's the strangest thing you've had to do?" Kylie's voice broke through the heavy silence that had fallen across the workroom.

Jack picked up another sheet of paper. "Last year, someone asked us to find their cat. We eventually found him in the apartment below his owner's."

Kylie's mouth dropped open. "Why would anyone ask you to find their cat? It must have cost a fortune."

"The cat belonged to a lady who had died. Her husband couldn't bear to lose his last connection to his wife, so he asked us to find it." Jack's mouth tilted into a lopsided smile. "It ended better than we could have imagined. Not only did we find the cat, but the owner became friends with the person who had been looking after it."

"I like cats," Dylan said.

Emma looked at her son. He'd moved from beside Molly and was standing beside Jack's chair.

Jack smiled. "Do you have a cat?"

Dylan shook his head. "Mom said we could go to the animal shelter and find one."

"That sounds exciting."

"Molly wants a black kitten, but I want a cat that's lots of different colors." Dylan held a piece of paper toward Jack. "I drew a picture for you."

Emma's heart lurched. Dylan didn't usually talk to people he didn't know. Unlike Molly, he was more comfortable standing in the background, watching what was happening.

Whether Jack sensed Dylan's shyness, she didn't know. But the smile on Jack's face was so gentle that it made her wonder what kind of father he would be. As he studied the crayon drawing, Dylan moved closer, explaining everything about the picture.

"I like your cat's long, wiggly tail," Jack said.

"That's so he can tickle me."

The smile Dylan sent Jack was open and trusting, and so unlike her son that she knew she had to be careful.

In a week's time, Jack would be leaving Sapphire Bay. If Dylan was forming an attachment to him, he would miss Jack when he went home. And above everything else, she didn't want her children to be hurt again.

By WEDNESDAY NIGHT, Emma was having a major meltdown. She'd thought asking people what Christmas events they wanted in Sapphire Bay would be easy. And it was, except the response had been overwhelming.

People from as far away as Zurich and Tokyo were telling everyone about their favorite Christmas events. Most of them were so far out of the church's budget that they couldn't be considered. But in between the seventy-foot Christmas trees, over-the-top light displays, and fireworks extravaganzas, were the small community events that could be replicated in Sapphire Bay.

All they needed was twice as much money, ten times the number of volunteers, and thousands of people to visit Sapphire Bay.

A knock on the back door brought her to her feet. With a relieved smile, she waved Kylie into the kitchen. "I'm glad you're here."

"I thought you would be." Kylie handed her a bag of fudge. "I went shopping at Sweet Treats today. Brooke said you were looking a little stressed when she saw you at The

Welcome Center."

Emma sniffed the chocolatey treat. "It's been a busy day. We're up to nine hundred comments on the Facebook post."

Kylie left her tote bag on the counter. "Why don't you delete it? We have more than enough ideas to keep us busy for the next ten Christmases."

"I have, but the original post keeps popping up on people's Facebook pages."

"Look at the bright side. Once we have our Christmas program organized, we could let anyone who clicked on the post know what we're doing. Even if it takes twice as long for the new Facebook post to circulate, the Christmas program will be a huge success."

Emma opened the bag of fudge. "That's a great idea, but we have to organize the events first." She popped a piece of fudge in her mouth and sighed. "I know why I only visit Sweet Treats once a week. This is delicious. Would you like a piece?"

With a grin, Kylie reached into her tote bag. "I'm okay. I ate enough this afternoon to give me a week-long sugar rush." She placed two more bags of fudge on the counter. "These are for Molly and Dylan. I hope they like raspberry delight and strawberry heaven."

"They'll love them. Thank you." Emma turned on the coffeepot and opened a cupboard. "The twins are fast asleep, so we have the kitchen to ourselves."

"It sounds as though we'll need the peace and quiet. What have you been doing?"

"I've updated the spreadsheet and gone through Pastor John's ideas. It looks as though there are four or five events we could organize, but I'd like to hear which ones you prefer."

"What about Jack? He had some great ideas."

Emma took two mugs out of the cupboard. "I haven't seen him since Sunday night. Have you talked to him?"

"No, but Mabel said he came into the general store with his grandfather this afternoon. It must have been hard growing up without his parents."

"It's probably still hard not having them around." Emma couldn't imagine how difficult his life must have been. From what she knew of his grandfather, Patrick would have been a wonderful father figure, but it wouldn't have made up for not having his parents with him. "At least Jack has his brother."

"That's true." Kylie frowned at a basket of letters sitting on the kitchen counter. "Do you have a lot of secret admirers you haven't told me about?"

"That's the other surprise I was given today."

"Letters?"

"Not just any letters. They're from the children at the local school. Their teachers saw the Facebook post and asked their students to write down their ideas."

Kylie's eyes widened. "There must be more than a hundred letters in the basket."

"I know." Emma hoped she didn't sound too over-whelmed, because she wasn't. Not really. What worried her the most was not being able to help everyone—especially the children. "This has become bigger than I thought it would."

"It's just as well Pastor John asked us to help. We'll orga-nize a Christmas program everyone will remember. And if we're lucky, we'll be able to make a few Christmas wishes come true, too."

"I hope so."

Kylie gave her a hug. "I know so. Come on. The sooner we go through these letters, the sooner we can plan what events we'll organize. And don't worry about the amount of work we have to do. Pastor John has a long list of people who are willing to help."

Emma was glad Kylie was feeling so positive. It was one thing putting together a program. It was an entirely different story making people's Christmas wishes come true.

CHAPTER 4

*a*n hour later, Emma was glad she'd asked Kylie to help. Placing the enormous amount of information they'd gathered into a logical order was taking longer than she expected.

While Kylie studied the spreadsheet and Pastor John's notes, Emma went through the children's letters. Using the same categories they'd used for the Facebook comments, she grouped similar events together.

Kylie handed Emma the folder John had put together. "We have to organize a Christmas parade. Most of the people who responded to the Facebook post love the idea."

"I agree. When do you think we should hold it?"

"John wants to have the parade in September. It seems a little early, but we don't have enough volunteers to run more than one event at a time."

Emma opened the calendar on her laptop. "What if we organized one activity per month leading up to Christmas? If we did that, the Christmas parade would be in September. The second Saturday in the month works for me."

"I'd have to check my wedding bookings, but it sounds

39

doable." Kylie picked up the spreadsheet. "There were two other ideas that were really popular. What if we had a Christmas party in October and a Christmas carol competition in November?"

"Sounds good. What about the real-life Santa workshop? We could do that in December."

"I prefer Pastor John's idea of a Christmas train ride. Taking the children around Flathead Lake sounds like fun."

Emma wasn't convinced it would work. By December, everything could be buried under six feet of snow, including the railroad tracks. "What if there's a snowstorm and the event has to be canceled? A lot of families would be disappointed."

"We could organize an alternative event in case that happens."

"Or we could talk to the railroad company. We might be able to postpone the train ride to the following weekend if the weather turns nasty."

Kylie nodded. "Sounds good to me. Maybe the train could take the children to Santa's workshop and bring them home."

"That's a big event to organize."

"We've got plenty of time." Kylie sent Emma a confident smile. "We can do this. All we have to do is work out who will organize each event. Have you spoken to Sam's sister?"

Emma nodded. "I called Bailey this afternoon. Zac offered her a job in his medical clinic."

"That's awesome. When does she start?"

"In four weeks. She's driving home to Bozeman tomorrow, but she's happy to help us organize one of the events when she gets back."

Kylie leaned forward. "What if we asked her to organize the Christmas carol competition? It's not until November. That way, if we plan the Christmas parade and the party, we could help her with the carols. Mabel and Allan will lend a hand, too."

Emma added their names to the spreadsheet. "After I've finished organizing the parade, I'll call the railroad company and see if we can use one of their trains for the December event. In a couple of months, Willow might be able to help, too."

"I hope so. It's going to be a busy time."

"As long as other people are willing to help us, it should be fine." Kylie picked up some of the children's letters. "What will we do about these?"

Emma had been wondering the same thing. "We should send the children a card or something to let them know we've read them."

"We could visit the school. It wouldn't take much time to explain what we're organizing." Kylie handed Emma the letters. "The children put a lot of effort into letting us know what events they'd like."

"Can you call the school and see if they're happy for us to visit?"

"Consider it done. You know..." Kylie didn't finish the sentence. As she studied a sheet of paper she'd unfolded, her gaze darted to Emma.

Not all the children had written letters. Some of the younger students had drawn pictures. Using stick figures or other funny shapes, they'd let their teacher know what events they wanted to see.

Emma didn't know what was on the paper, but it couldn't be good. Kylie had a mile-wide frown plastered across her forehead. "What is it?"

Kylie glanced at the drawing before handing it to Emma. "You'd better take a look at this."

Four crayon figures were standing in front of a Christmas tree. Underneath, in big letters, a child had written, please help us find our daddy. Emma's heart clenched tight when she saw who had sent the letter. It was Molly.

"I didn't know they were so desperate to see Mark," she whispered.

"It might not be anything to worry about. Molly is always talking about her dad. If she knew what he was really like, she wouldn't idolize him so much."

Emma's eyes filled with tears. "She's six years old. I don't want her to think bad things about her father."

"He abandoned them when they were babies. What sort of person does that?"

"The kind who's desperate." Emma had pleaded with Mark not to go. She knew when she'd married him that he had a lot of unresolved issues from his childhood. But she'd thought she could help, that she could make fifteen years of living with an alcoholic father a lot easier to bear.

"Mark needed to come to terms with his past."

Kylie's mouth dropped open. "You're not thinking of searching for him, are you?"

"I've already tried. No one knows where he's gone. And even if I found him, I wouldn't want Mark to have unsupervised visits with Molly and Dylan."

"Maybe you should consider that before you do anything. If you can't trust him with your children, why do you want him in your life?"

Emma looked down at the picture. "He's Molly and Dylan's father. I won't stand in their way if they want to meet him."

"That's very mature of you."

"I've had a lot of time to get over him. When he first left, I was devastated. But the twins and I are happy. We have a great life in Sapphire Bay."

Kylie tapped her pen against her chin. "If you really want

to find him, you could go on one of those television programs where they find long-lost relatives."

"Except they nearly always have a happy ending. I can't see that happening with Mark."

"If you don't think he'll want anything to do with you or the twins, is it worth looking for him?"

Emma didn't have to think too hard about her answer. "It's important to Molly and Dylan. Even if I can't find Mark, at least I can say I tried."

"In that case, I have another idea." Kylie took her cell phone out of her pocket. "I don't have Jack's number, but he's staying in the cottage behind Cassie and Noah's home. Cassie won't mind asking Jack for some advice. If he's half as good at finding people as she said, he might be your only chance of finding Mark."

"Let me keep looking. Jack is already helping with the Christmas program. I don't want to ask him to do anything else."

"Are you sure?"

Emma nodded. Even in the short time she'd known him, Jack had gotten under her skin and made her wish her life could be different. If he helped her find Mark, she would be even more indebted to him. And regardless of how she felt, she could never allow that to happen.

JACK STOPPED his brother's truck in front of a small, wooden home not far from Noah and Cassie's cottage. With its white picket fence, gardens overflowing with colorful flowers, and two bicycles leaning against the front veranda, the house looked warm and inviting. A lot like his parents' cottage on Shelter Island.

As he opened the truck door, he took a deep breath. He

still couldn't believe how different Sapphire Bay was to Manhattan.

For most of the afternoon, he'd been fishing with two friends on Flathead Lake. When he was in New York City, his life involved moving between his apartment and work. Even at the weekends, getting away from the city was impossible. Unlike today's short drive to the lake, he was lucky to get anywhere in under an hour.

Fishing in his friend's boat had become a recurring ritual that Jack looked forward to. Each time he was on the lake it was completely different. Today, the sky was so blue that he'd wondered if his eyes were fooling him. After the drab, gray blanket that permanently covered New York City, he was glad to be here.

Grabbing the cooler off the back seat, he headed toward Emma's home. Three hours after setting out this morning, he'd returned to shore with four brown trout.

Jack had given one to Cassie and Noah, another to his grandfather, and whether it was a good decision or not, he was delivering the third to Emma.

As he opened the gate, Dylan walked around the side of the house. Jack smiled when he saw the bucket and spade clutched in his little hands. "Hi, Dylan."

The six-year-old's eyes lifted to Jack's. He stood silently in the middle of the path, a frown creasing his dirt-smeared face.

"I met you at my brother's wedding on Saturday." Jack held up the cooler. "I brought a fish for your mom."

Dylan's eyes widened. "Can I see?"

"Sure." Jack opened the lid and Dylan looked inside.

"He sure is big. Where did you catch him?"

"On Flathead Lake. My friend owns a boat."

"Mr. Jessop owns a boat, but Mom says I can't go on the lake with him 'cos I don't have a life jacket."

"It's important to be safe on the water."

Dylan took one last look in the cooler before stepping away. "That's what Mr. Jessop says, too. Do you want to see Mom?"

"That would be great."

"She's in the kitchen." Dylan turned around and waited for Jack to follow. "Molly's making ginger cookies, but she always gets stuck on the measuring."

Jack's eyebrows rose. Not because of what Dylan said, but because he was continuing their conversation. When he'd sat at Emma's table on Saturday, Dylan hadn't said a lot. "Moms are good at weighing the ingredients."

The little boy's solemn nod made Jack smile. "What have you been doing?"

"Mr. Jessop gave me some cabbage and broccoli plants for my vegetable garden. See." Dylan held his bucket toward Jack. "We grew them from little seeds in the greenhouse."

"They look great. Do you enjoy gardening?"

"It's fun." Dylan stomped up the wooden veranda steps. "Mr. Jessop says God gave us hands to create something special. That's why I like gardening. It keeps people's tummies full of food. Do you know Mr. Jessop?"

"I do. He works at The Welcome Center." Jack had met Gordon on his last visit to Sapphire Bay. He'd developed the community gardens into something remarkable, providing food for the center and anyone in need.

"Mr. Jessop used to own a ranch with real cows and chickens and goats. One day, I'm going to work on a ranch. But first I gotta grow tall and strong so I can be just like Mr. Jessop." Dylan flicked off his sneakers and opened the back door. "Mom's this way."

The sweet smell of ginger and cinnamon wafted from the house.

Emma appeared in front of them. Her eyes widened when she saw who was with her son. "Jack?"

At least she'd remembered his name. "I've been fishing with a couple of friends. I caught too much trout and wondered if you'd like one for dinner." Emma's gaze dropped to the open cooler he held toward her.

"It's huge. Are you sure you don't want it?"

"I caught more fish than I can eat. It's okay if you don't want it."

"I love trout, thank you." Emma looked around the kitchen. Molly was perched on a chair, licking cookie dough from a spoon. "Why don't you stay for a few minutes? Our first batch of cookies has just come out of the oven."

"And they're real yummy," Molly said with a grin.

Jack looked at Emma. "Thanks, I'd like that." He handed her the cooler. "I know how to fillet a fish, if that helps."

Emma seemed surprised. "That's an unlikely skill for someone who lives in New York City."

"Granddad taught me. My family owns a cottage on an island not far from the city. Apart from riding with Dad on his motorcycle, fishing was the most exciting thing we did."

"Dylan likes fishing," Molly said from her lofty position. "He puts wiggly worms on the hooks, but he doesn't catch fish as big as yours."

Dylan reached for a cookie. "That's 'cos I'm fishing off the jetty. Mr. Jessop said the big fish are in the middle of the lake."

"Maybe you need bigger worms," Molly told her brother. "And you can't have a cookie until you've washed your hands."

Jack smiled as Dylan sighed. He had a feeling he was used to his sister bossing him around.

Emma lifted Molly off the chair. "How about both of you wash your hands before you have anything to eat."

Dylan frowned. "Will Jack still be here?"

Emma took off her son's red baseball cap. "Of course, he will."

With a shy smile, Dylan glanced at Jack before running out of the kitchen.

"Wait for me," Molly shouted.

As the twins raced down the hallway, Jack smiled. It must be a completely different experience being a twin, especially when Molly and Dylan had such different personalities.

Emma lifted the fish onto a cutting board. "It looks as though you've made two new friends."

Jack hoped it was three. Emma intrigued him, and that hadn't happened in a long time. "They're great kids."

"They have their moments." She handed him a knife. "If you fillet the fish, I'll make coffee."

"Sounds good." And somewhere, deep inside, Jack knew it was more than good. The only problem was that he wouldn't be here for long enough to really get to know Emma and her children.

BY THE TIME Emma made two cups of coffee, Molly and Dylan had returned from the bathroom. "That's better," she said as she poured each of her children a drink. "Come and sit at the kitchen table. Mr. Devlin won't be long. He's filleting the trout he caught."

Dylan hesitated before slowly walking across to Jack. "Can I see?"

"Sure." Jack showed him the fish. "It's all finished. And if it's okay with your mom, you can call me Jack."

Dylan looked up at her.

Emma smiled. "It's okay." She stood behind Dylan,

admiring the thick fillets of fish. It wasn't easy removing all the bones, but Jack had done a great job. "That was quick."

Jack shrugged. "I've been doing this for as long as I can remember. Mom was happy to cook whatever we caught, but she didn't like filleting the fish."

"Cassie told me about your parents. I'm sorry you had to grow up without them."

"We had our grandparents," Jack said softly. "That's more than a lot of children have."

Emma looked at Molly and Dylan.

"I didn't mean—"

"It's okay," she said quickly. The last thing she wanted was for Jack to feel sorry for her children. Even though their father wasn't part of their lives, they still had one parent who adored them. "I'll leave your coffee on the table."

Jack rinsed the plate and ran his hands under the faucet. "The cookies smell amazing."

Molly stood on tiptoes, studying the filleted trout. "We made apple and cinnamon cookies. They're our favorite."

Dylan lost interest in the fish. Before Molly moved, he rushed across to the table and bit into a cookie. "Sometimes we make chocolate cake, too. Next time we're baking, you could help us."

"That's a great idea," Jack said. "But I'm not staying in Sapphire Bay for long. I'm going home soon."

Dylan stopped chewing. "When are you leaving?"

"In another week."

"Is that a long time?" Molly whispered to her brother.

Dylan shook his head.

Before everyone became too sad, Emma changed the subject. "I've got good news about this year's Christmas events."

"Are we having a Santa parade?" Molly asked.

Emma smiled. "We are. We're also organizing a Christmas party, a carol competition, and a surprise event."

Dylan's eyes widened. "What kind of surprise?"

"The best kind. But I can't tell you what it is until we've talked to some more people."

"We could draw pictures of the parade," Molly said enthusiastically. Without asking if her brother had finished, she took both their glasses across to the kitchen counter. "Come on, Dylan. We've got work to do."

"But I want to plant my vegetables."

"You can do that later. We need to plan the parade."

Dylan looked at Emma.

She knew Molly could be bossy, but Dylan needed to learn how to tell his sister what he wanted. "Tell Molly what you're thinking."

Dylan's frown deepened. "I want to plant my vegetables first. If you help me, we could use my new crayons to draw the pictures."

"The sparkly ones, too?"

Dylan reluctantly nodded. "But we need to plant *all* the vegetables."

Molly grabbed Dylan's hand and pulled him toward the back door. "I can do it real fast."

With a worried glance at Emma, Dylan disappeared outside.

Jack smiled. "Have they always been like that?"

"It used to be worse. I've tried telling Molly it's important to let Dylan choose what he wants to do, but it's a slow learning curve. Thankfully, Dylan's starting to stand up for himself."

"Noah and I were exactly the same, except I was the one who told him what we should be doing." Jack took a sip of coffee. "I saw Kylie this morning. She's excited about the Christmas program."

"So am I. It's a lot of work, but it will be worth it."

The relaxed expression on Jack's face disappeared. "When I was talking to Kylie, she told me about Molly's Christmas wish."

Emma blushed. "She shouldn't have said anything. Molly has wanted to see her dad for a long time, but it's not going to happen."

"Because you don't want him in their lives?"

She searched Jack's face, wondering how much Kylie had told him. He seemed genuinely interested in her answer and not ready to condemn her for a situation that was out of her control.

"Mark has never wanted to see Dylan and Molly. Until six months ago, I regularly emailed him photos of the twins, but he never replied. If I knew where he was living, I'd invite him to Sapphire Bay, but he's disappeared off the face of the earth."

"Does his family know where he's gone?"

Emma shook her head. "The last time his mom and sister saw him was about the same time he left me."

"What about his father?"

A cold chill ran down Emma's spine. "He died when Mark was seventeen." Her ex-husband's father was a violent alcoholic. Some of the stories Mark had told her were horrific. But it was the tragic circumstances around his father's death that haunted Mark the most.

"My company could search for your ex-husband."

Emma wrapped her hands around her coffee mug. "I thought about hiring a private investigator when the twins first asked to see their dad. It was incredibly expensive."

"We do a few pro bono cases each year. I could add your case to the projects we consider and see what the team thinks."

Emma frowned. "I don't need charity. If Mark wanted to

see Dylan and Molly, he would have contacted me. I still have the same email address and his mom and sister know where we're living."

"It's not charity. Lost and Found work with a number of law enforcement agencies and extremely wealthy people. A percentage of our income goes toward funding cases that otherwise couldn't be investigated." When Emma didn't reply, Jack sighed. "What's the worst that could happen?"

A lump formed in Emma's throat. "Mark could be dead." It made her sad to think about her ex-husband's life, the choices he'd made to protect himself, and the possibility that he might never see the wonderful children they'd created.

Her parents thought she was crazy to want Molly and Dylan to meet their father. But she wanted them to know where they had come from, what Mark liked and didn't like. But most of all, she wanted them to know they were loved.

Jack studied her face. "At least you'd know what happened to him."

Emma sighed. After all the time she'd spent trying to find her ex-husband, how could she say no? Without Jack's help, Dylan and Molly might never meet their dad. "Okay, I'll accept your generous offer. But I can't let you do it for free. If someone in your team could let me know how much it will cost, I'll work out a way of paying you."

"It isn't necessary."

Instead of disagreeing, she picked up her coffee mug and walked across to the counter. "I'd better see what Molly and Dylan are doing. Would you like to see the vegetable garden?"

"I'd love to. Do you think Dylan would let me help?"

"Absolutely, but I'd better warn you that he takes his gardening very seriously."

Jack smiled. "I'll do my best to follow his instructions."

Emma smiled as she opened the back door. She could see

why Dylan enjoyed talking to Jack. He was calm, relaxed, and slotted into their family as if he'd always been here.

All she had to do was remember he was leaving soon.

JACK SAT on the veranda of Acorn Cottage and opened his laptop. Before he'd left Emma's home, she'd given him as much information as she could about her ex-husband.

After dinner, he'd searched some of the databases his company used to locate missing people. Although it wasn't easy to vanish off the face of the planet, Mark Lewis had done a good job of covering his tracks—which made Jack wonder whether his disappearance was as unplanned as Emma thought.

"You're deep in thought." Noah stood on the edge of the veranda with two mugs in his hands.

"I'm trying to find Emma's ex-husband."

"While you're contemplating where he could have gone, here's a coffee."

Jack took the cup from his brother. "Thanks. Isn't it a little late to be over here?"

"I couldn't sleep. When I saw your lights were still on, I thought I'd come and annoy you."

"You can annoy me anytime if you bring coffee. Why couldn't you sleep?"

Noah pulled a chair closer. "We've had a few delays with the launch of a new product. We might have made a mistake when we contracted the company who is making the furniture."

Most people would assume that managing an online retail store would be less time-consuming than a bricks and mortar store. But Jack had seen the long hours his brother worked. The success the company enjoyed hadn't come easy and no one, including Noah, was taking the future of the company for granted.

"When will the furniture be ready?"

"If we're lucky, in two weeks. I'm flying to Louisiana on Tuesday to make sure the first shipments are on track."

"It's just as well you decided to postpone your honeymoon until October."

Noah ran his hand through his hair, a sure sign he was as tired as he looked. "Part of me can't wait to travel to Europe with Cassie. But I'm worried about what will happen while I'm away. All Stacey needs is another hold-up like this and our winter catalog will be in trouble."

"Don't worry about Stacey. She keeps everyone on their toes as much as you do."

"Maybe, but it doesn't make going away for four weeks any easier." Noah shifted his gaze to Jack's laptop. "Why can't you find Emma's ex-husband?"

"Either he's living off the grid and doesn't want to be found or he knows more than the average person about hiding his electronic footprint."

"What do you think?"

Jack stared across the backyard toward Flathead Lake. "Mark had a rough childhood. He learned from an early age how to keep a low profile and stay away from his father. His military career would have taught him how to survive in the toughest of conditions. My guess is that he's living off the grid."

"Does Emma have any idea about where he's gone?"

"She gave me a list of the places she's already checked. Mark didn't have a lot of friends but, after he was discharged from the Army, he worked for the same construction company for a few years. Someone there might know where he's living."

"You know what's going to happen, don't you?"

"I'll find Mark and everyone will live happily ever after?"

Noah shook his head. "You'll find Mark and open a can of worms. Family relationships are complicated at the best of times, let alone when someone doesn't want to see their children."

Molly and Dylan were great kids. How anyone could turn their back on them was as foreign to Jack as walking on the moon.

"What will Emma do if Mark wants to be part of their children's lives?"

Jack frowned. "I don't know."

"You'd better find out. If she isn't prepared for the possibility of shared custody, she might want to reconsider looking for her ex-husband."

"Dylan and Molly want to see their dad."

Noah sighed. "When I was ten, I wanted to sail around the world but it never happened."

"This isn't the same."

"No, it isn't. It's worse. How many times does Lost and Found deal with young children looking for their parents?"

Jack knew what his brother was about to say. "I know this case is unusual, but it's important to Emma."

"What if you find him and he doesn't want to see Dylan and Molly?"

"I can't answer that question. Emma needs to work out what will happen if I locate Mark."

Noah wrapped his hands around his cup. "Do you remember what Granddad said when you started Lost and Found?"

How could Jack forget? When his grandfather told him to think with his head and not his heart, he'd thought he was being cold and callous. But as the years had gone by, Jack and his team had learned to distance themselves from their clients. Becoming emotionally involved in any search for a

54

missing person not only left you vulnerable, it took away your biggest advantage—a logical perspective on what had happened.

"I'm not emotionally involved in the case."

Noah's eyebrows rose. "Really? If any of your team was on vacation, what would you tell them if they started looking for a missing person?"

"It would depend on the situation," Jack muttered.

"I don't think so. You'd tell them to wait until they returned to work or send the information through to the office."

His brother was right, but it was too late. Jack had promised Emma he'd help find Mark. And until he ran out of leads, he would do everything he could to make that happen.

Jack glanced at his brother, not liking the I-told-you-so expression on his face. "Not that long ago, you told me rules were meant to be broken."

"That was before I married Cassie."

"What difference does being married make?"

"I'll let you figure that out. Just be careful. Dylan and Molly are great kids, but they're not *your* kids."

No, they weren't. But when Jack looked into their eyes, he could see shadows of himself at the same age. Their lives were full of hope and wonder. They made the most of each day and let their mom look after everything else.

But when your friends had two parents at home, it was tough.

It was even worse when both your parents were gone.

Jack gazed at the full moon. If he could find Mark, Dylan and Molly deserved the chance to meet him. If that meant working through his vacation, he wouldn't complain.

Because one day, the twins' dad wouldn't be alive. And all the questions they wanted to ask him would go unanswered.

CHAPTER 5

*E*mma tapped her pen against her chin. "Mabel and Allan Terry are happy to distribute the Christmas decorations. If we can decide what we want in the next couple of weeks, they'll be here in plenty of time."

Kylie ran her finger down the list of business owners who wanted to decorate their stores for the Christmas parade. "Everyone we've spoken to has said they want to help. Once we've chosen the decorations, I don't think we'll have a problem finding the money to pay for them."

Neither did Emma. Noah Devlin had offered to provide the decorations at a heavily discounted price. When she'd shown Kylie the catalog of options, they'd become even more excited. The decorations they chose would last for years and make the town look incredible.

"Talking about money," Emma leaned sideways and picked up her bag. "Pastor John was talking to a friend who lives in Bozeman. They read our Christmas Facebook posts and wanted to donate some money toward one of the wishes."

Kylie's eyes widened when she saw the check Emma was

holding. "That would make a lot of people's wishes come true."

"It would if they didn't need braces on their teeth. This money is for Suzie Miller. Her mom and dad can't afford to pay for her orthodontic treatment. This will cover all her expenses."

"Have you told Suzie and her family?"

Emma shook her head. "I wanted to wait until I saw you. I thought we could both tell them."

"I'd like that. Do you think they'll accept the money?"

"I hope so, although they won't be getting the full amount all at once. The person who donated the money asked John to deposit the money into the church's trust fund. Whenever a bill needs to be paid, it will come from there."

"That sounds like a good idea. At least that way the person who donated the money knows it's being spent on the braces."

"Exactly. I'll call Suzie's parents soon. If they can see us tonight, would that work for you?"

"It would be perfect. How is Molly and Dylan's Christmas wish coming along?"

"I'm not sure." Emma bit her bottom lip. Even after talking to Jack and giving him all the information she had about Mark, she didn't know if she was doing the right thing. "I took your advice. Jack is helping me find Mark."

Kylie smiled. "That's fantastic. Has he discovered anything you didn't know about your ex-husband?"

"Not that I'm aware of. Jack told me it could take a long time to find him."

"At least someone is helping. Will you tell Dylan and Molly you're looking for their dad?"

"Definitely not. I don't want them to get their hopes up, especially if we can't find Mark."

"You won't regret asking Jack for help. He seems like a really nice person."

Emma opened a document on her laptop. "I'm sure he is, but that won't make ordering the Christmas decorations any easier." She turned the screen toward her friend. Choosing the decorations was more productive than thinking about Jack. "Which style do you like?"

Kylie sighed. "It's just as well I know how your mind works. It's okay to admit that you like him."

"There's no point liking Jack. He isn't staying in Sapphire Bay."

"Not at the moment, but that could change. His granddad, brother, and sister-in-law have made their home here. Even if he doesn't permanently move to Montana, he'll come back to visit his family."

Emma knew Kylie meant well, but she didn't want to jump headfirst into a long-distance relationship. Apart from looking after Dylan and Molly, she owned a business that needed her undivided attention.

And talking about her business...they really needed to choose a theme for the decorations. Otherwise, she wouldn't be able to design a website for the Christmas program.

She pointed to the screen. "There are a lot of options. But if you don't like any of the decorations, let me know."

Kylie sighed. "You're stubborn."

"I know. Now look at the decorations."

With her hand on the touchpad, Kylie scrolled through the photos. "They're all so pretty."

Emma was just as impressed. Noah's company had all sorts of decorations, from traditional pine wreaths with red bows to glittery white garlands filled with pink and blue ornaments. His company catered to the uber-rich and, no matter how hard Emma tried, she couldn't find a single item under one hundred dollars.

"I like these ones."

Emma looked at the collection Kylie was studying and smiled. "I like those, too." The decorations were part of the traditional range. In one photo, a heavy pine wreath with gold ribbon was wrapped majestically around a wrought-iron balustrade. In another, a tree taller than anything Emma could fit in her home was filled with cream and gold sparkly decorations. It was so lifelike that she could have sworn she was looking at a real pine tree.

"Look at the miniature Christmas trees," Kylie said excitedly. "With their red ribbons, they'd be perfect for outside each store. We could give each owner some fairy lights and have a prize for the best window display."

"And snow," Emma murmured. "I can see the sidewalk covered in fluffy flakes of snow with bells jingling as people walk into each store."

"It would be incredible." Kylie sighed. "But look at the prices. We'll need at least fifty small trees, plus decorations."

"Noah knows we don't have a lot of money."

"We should look at something else. Even with a big discount, I don't think we'll be able to decorate the whole street."

"Noah wouldn't have told me to choose from his online collections if he thought they were too expensive. I'll show him a list of what we'd like and see what he says."

Kylie frowned. "We could find other sponsors for anything that's beyond Noah's donation. But it won't be easy asking businesses for money, especially for a Christmas program that starts in September."

"Don't worry. If anyone can make this happen, we can."

"You're right." Kylie picked up the list they'd made of local businesses. "When everyone sees what we're doing, they'll want to help. We're going to organize the best Christmas events anyone has ever seen."

Emma smiled. They had a lot of work ahead of them but, with some careful planning and more than a good dose of luck, no one would forget this year's Christmas in Sapphire Bay.

JACK OPENED the door to The Welcome Center. When he'd first visited Sapphire Bay, his brother had introduced him to Pastor John and showed him around the tiny home village.

Not long afterward, John had given him a tour of The Welcome Center and, after meeting the volunteers, Jack realized it wasn't a shelter or a drop-in center. It was a home away from home, a soft place to fall when no one else seemed to care.

Pastor John had created a place where people could eat a home-cooked meal, find a warm, safe bed for the night, and enjoy some great company. The center gave people a sense of hope and a way forward.

Now that he'd been here a few times, he couldn't imagine Sapphire Bay without this incredible service.

John walked out of the dining room and smiled. "I wondered when you'd make it back. It's good to see you." He shook Jack's hand. "Have you been to the tiny home village yet?"

"That's on tomorrow's list of things to do. Granddad needs a hand with some drywall."

John's smile widened. "That sounds like Patrick. Make sure he gives you a lunch break. When he starts drywalling, there's no stopping him."

"He said another two houses are almost finished."

"The tenants are looking forward to moving in. If you've come to see Cassie or Noah, they aren't working tonight."

"I came to see Emma. I wanted to talk to her before I head back to Acorn Cottage."

"In that case, I'll leave you to it. She's in the office designing a new website for the Christmas program."

"I won't take too much of her time."

"I'm sure she won't mind seeing you." John glanced at his cell phone. "I have to go. A family of six needs somewhere to stay and I'm not sure if we have that many spare beds. If I don't see you again tonight, I might see you tomorrow."

"Has Granddad volunteered your services again?"

John laughed. "How did you guess?"

"He might have mentioned something about your painting skills."

"They're better than they were. Take care."

As John made his way down the corridor, Jack headed toward the administration area. Knocking on the office door, he poked his head around the doorframe. Emma sat behind a large wooden desk, her blond hair falling around her shoulders.

"I hope it's okay to interrupt what you're doing."

Emma's surprised smile made Jack's heart skip a beat.

"I was just thinking about you," she said with a grin.

"I hope they were good thoughts."

"Very good. I've been talking to Noah. We've finalized the Christmas decorations for Main Street."

"Congratulations."

"Thanks. Your brother thinks you'd make a great Santa for our parade."

Jack's eyes widened. "He does?"

Emma nodded. "He's found a costume for you and he knows where he can hire an authentic sleigh."

There was something about the mischievous gleam in Emma's eyes that made Jack wonder if she was joking. He hoped so. Pretending to be the big man in red wasn't something he'd considered. Noah, on the other hand, would make an awesome Santa.

"I wouldn't want to spoil Noah's fun. My brother would enjoy sitting on the sleigh more than I would, especially if Cassie was Mrs. Claus."

Emma typed something on her keyboard, then turned the screen toward him. "He said he would be too busy judging the window display competition. What do you think?"

Oh, man. She wasn't joking.

He peered at the computer, hoping the red velvet costume was only available in extra, extra, large sizes.

As if reading his mind, Emma pointed to the images. "Don't worry. We can add some pillows to puff out your chest."

Jack felt mildly insulted. "Santa doesn't need a bulging chest or stomach. Maybe he's more health conscious and is looking after his weight."

"Does that mean you'll do it?"

"No, definitely not. I really don't want to be Santa."

Instead of looking disappointed, Emma grinned.

Jack groaned. "You have a warped sense of humor."

"I saw the costume this afternoon. Noah flat-out refused to wear it, but he thought your granddad might be willing to step out of his comfort zone."

Jack breathed a sigh of relief. "Granddad will enjoy riding on the sleigh, especially if there's a Mrs. Claus."

"That's a great idea. And I know just the person." Emma scribbled someone's name on a sheet of paper and added it to a folder. "I'm guessing you didn't come here to talk about the Christmas sleigh. How can I help?"

Jack sat in the chair opposite Emma's desk. "I want to ask you some questions about Mark."

"I've told you everything."

The last thing Jack wanted was to give her false hope, but he needed to know if Mark had mentioned anything about his camping trips. "I was speaking to someone who worked with your ex-husband. Mark used to talk about a resort in Colorado. Did he ever mention a place called Evergreen Lodge?"

Emma frowned. "His uncle used to take him fishing, but he never mentioned where they went. I assumed it was somewhere near Boulder. Do you think he's living in one of the cabins?"

Telling Emma what he thought wouldn't be helpful, especially when he couldn't verify what Mark's co-worker had said. The only way he would know whether her ex-husband was using the cabins was to visit them. "The information could lead me on a wild goose chase. But I won't know until I see the cabins."

"You're going to Colorado?"

"It isn't that far away. I'll fly out of Polson and be there in a few hours."

Emma's cheeks turned red. "I thought you had to ask your team about looking for Mark."

"If I start now, it will give everyone a head start when I return to the office."

"But you're on vacation."

"This is more important than hiking and fishing."

Emma frowned. "Why are you doing this?"

Jack looked down at his hands. It was never easy talking about his mom and dad. Their death had affected him in ways he never thought possible. "I would give everything I own to spend more time with my parents. Dylan and Molly want to know where their dad has gone. The least I can do is answer their question."

For a few seconds, Emma sat silently in her chair. "You're a good man, but do you need to fly to Colorado? Someone must look after the campground. You could call them and ask if they've seen Mark."

Jack had already discounted that idea. "If your ex-husband is living in one of the cabins, there's a chance he isn't using his real name. If someone starts asking questions, he might leave. It's better if I look for him."

Emma sighed. "Is there anything I can do for you while you're away?"

"Convincing Granddad he would make a great Santa is all the help I need."

"I'll do my best."

Jack looked into her big blue eyes and smiled. "I know you will."

THE FOLLOWING AFTERNOON, Mabel knocked on Emma's front door. "I hope I'm not intruding, but I had to come and see you."

Emma looked up from the card game she was playing with Dylan and Molly. "Don't be silly. You're welcome here anytime. Would you like a glass of cold lemonade?"

"That sounds delicious." Mabel smiled at the twins. "How are my two favorite children?"

Molly grinned. "We're good. Did Mr. Terry come with you?"

"Not today. He's looking after the store while I'm here."

"Do you want to play snap?"

"I'd love to, but I need to speak to your mom first."

"Come with me," Emma said to their friend. "You can tell me your news while I make everyone a drink."

"I'm pleased it's okay to talk to you," Mabel said as they walked into the kitchen. "Kylie said you were here, but I thought you might be working."

Emma opened the refrigerator. "I usually get up early and do most of my work before Molly and Dylan are out of bed. It makes the days long, but it's better than being grouchy when I can't finish my work."

"I used to do the same thing when my boys were little." Mabel pulled a piece of paper out of her pocket. "I wanted to show you something important. Pastor John forwarded this email to me. It looks as though we have a good Samaritan in Sapphire Bay."

As she read the message, Emma's heart pounded. "Are you sure?"

Mabel's face glowed with excitement. "Positive. We ordered the washing machines and refrigerators an hour ago. Five families will be very happy."

Emma couldn't believe someone had made so many Christmas wishes come true. "How did the donor know the people live in Sapphire Bay?"

"Those Christmas wishes weren't left on the Facebook page. They were part of the messages collected by the church. Kylie added them to the page later."

"Did John tell you who donated the appliances?"

"He promised he would keep their identity a secret." Mabel took the glass of lemonade Emma handed her. "Isn't it exciting! We have a real-life Santa Claus in Sapphire Bay."

"They might live somewhere else."

Mabel waved away Emma's logic. "They must live close to Sapphire Bay. Otherwise, they wouldn't have seen the messages displayed at the church."

"It could be more than one person," Emma mumbled. "Or an organization could have donated the appliances." She reread the email. "Do you know the people who are getting the washing machines and refrigerators?"

Mabel sat on a kitchen stool and smiled. "I do. They're super nice folk who don't have an unkind word to say about anyone. My heart is fit to burst with pride. Helping a family in need is such a wonderful thing to do."

"I hope the person who made the donation knows how much their gifts will be appreciated."

"Don't worry. John has let them know. Do you want me to take some photos when the appliances are delivered? It would make a great article in the local paper. We could even add the images to our community Facebook page."

Although she wanted to share the good news, Emma was worried the extra publicity would inspire more people to write to them. They already had enough wishes for ten Christmases.

"I think it's better to wait until the New Year. That way, there's less chance someone will find the person who donated the appliances."

Mabel gave a resigned sigh. She loved keeping the community Facebook page up to date and this would have made a great story. "If you think that's for the best, we'll leave it until after Christmas. I saw Suzie's mom yesterday. They have an appointment with an orthodontist in two weeks. Suzie can't wait to get braces."

"I'm happy for them." Emma sipped her glass of lemonade. When they told Suzie someone was paying for her braces, she burst into tears. It was one of the most humbling moments Emma had experienced. "Have you seen our Christmas program?"

"John showed me what you've planned. Just let me know what you need. Allan and I will be happy to help."

"That's really sweet. I'll definitely come and see you." Emma placed half a dozen cookies on a plate for Mabel's husband, then filled another plate for Molly and Dylan. "Let's go into the living room and have some cookies with the twins. They love it when you visit."

Mabel grinned. "It's the stories I tell them. They love a good mystery."

"You should write a book."

Mabel's cheeks filled with color. "I wouldn't know where to start."

Emma took a pen and notebook off the kitchen counter. "It starts with a great story and you've got plenty of those. I'll write down what you say, then give you the notebook to take home. When you're happy with the story, come back and see me. We can add illustrations and format it into a book."

"But you're so busy. Do you have time to help me?"

"A little birdie told me you've always wanted to write a children's book. We might be able to make your wish come true, too." Emma gave Mabel a hug. "You help a lot of people. This will be something special for you."

Mabel dabbed the tears from her eyes. "I'll be a real author."

"I've got a feeling you'll live happily ever after, too."

"I already am," Mabel whispered as they walked into the hallway.

JACK HAD LEARNED a long time ago not to assume anything. But, for some reason, he'd expected the cabins at Evergreen Lodge to be rustic, budget-friendly hideaways for fishermen and tourists. He couldn't have been more wrong.

In the mid-afternoon sunshine, the log cabins looked warm and inviting. The path to each cabin was lined with flowers. A wide porch, complete with tables and deck chairs, gave each vacation home an uninterrupted view of the lake.

When he saw half a dozen fishermen sitting on the boardwalk, he stopped to see what they were catching. Large bass, catfish, and bluegill ran freely in the clear water. By anyone's standards, the fishing here was great.

But that wasn't why he'd come to Colorado.

As he walked to his truck, Jack checked his phone. A picture of Emma's ex-husband stared back at him. With his red hair, blue eyes, and dimpled cheek, he could have been looking at a photo of Dylan in another thirty years.

Yesterday, one of his staff had looked through a database Jack didn't have access to in Sapphire Bay. What he'd learned made him even more determined to find Emma's ex-husband.

Behind Mark's carefree smile was a man who lived a complicated life. From the moment he was born, his life had led him down a path of self-destruction.

"Are you lookin' for someone?"

Jack turned around. The weathered face of a man who must have been close to eighty stared back at him. "Hi. A friend told me about these cabins. I thought I'd drive out here while I'm in the area."

"You a fisherman?"

"A long time ago. Mark Lewis told me this is the place to come if you want to catch the biggest bass this side of The Rockies."

Some of the weariness in the man's gaze disappeared. "You know Mark?"

"We went to school together. I'm Jack." He held out his hand, hoping the gesture made the conversation easier. "I haven't heard from Mark for a few months. I was hoping he was still here."

"Comes and goes. What did you say your last name was?"

"Devlin. Jack Devlin."

The man shuffled sideways, pointing down the dirt track. "You want to head that way. Last cabin on the left. Mark was there this morning, but he could be anywhere by now."

Jack peered into the distance. There must be at least a dozen cabins between Jack's truck and the end of the road. "Do you live here permanently?"

The man spat on the ground. "Most people round here come and go as they please. Don't need no one telling them when it's time to move on. You might want to keep that in mind when you're speaking to Mark."

Jack had no idea what he meant, but at least Emma's ex-husband was here. "Thanks for your help."

The man grunted, threw his backpack over his shoulder, and ambled toward the lake.

Jack returned to his truck. Parking his vehicle outside Mark's cabin seemed like a good idea. Especially when he didn't know what Mark would do when he saw him.

As he slowly drove by the other homes, Jack's gaze sharpened. The resort reminded him of the houses around his parents' cottage on Shelter Island. There was an understated elegance to the cabins. It was a place you went to relax and unwind. Or hide from your past.

Jack stopped his truck outside the last cabin. Apart from the wooden sculptures sitting either side of the front door, this cabin looked exactly like the other houses.

Picking up a folder, Jack opened his door and let his gaze travel around the property.

Tall pine trees rose from behind the cabin. An empty clothesline swung in the breeze. It would take only a few minutes to escape onto the lake; even less time to disappear into the forest.

He walked up to the front door, knocked, and waited.

When no one answered, he peered through the front window. Two overstuffed chairs sat in front of a stone fireplace. A few magazines and books had been left on top of a wooden coffee table. The only piece of technology Jack could see was a laptop sitting on a desk on the far side of the room.

Mark Lewis was tidy, methodical, and valued his privacy. But not enough to completely let go of the twenty-first century.

"I never went to school with anyone called Jack Devlin."

Jack slowly turned around. Mark stood halfway between Jack's truck and the front door.

"Do you want to tell me why you're here or do I need to call the sheriff?"

CHAPTER 6

*J*ack kept his hands where Mark could see them. Emma's ex-husband wasn't holding a gun, but the tone in his voice was all the warning Jack needed to be careful.

Mark was more intimidating in real life than in the photos Jack had seen. Emma hadn't mentioned that her ex-husband was at least six foot three and built like a quarterback.

"Do I need to repeat myself?"

Jack stared him in the eyes. "Emma asked me to find you."

A flicker of emotion skimmed across Mark's face. "Are Dylan and Molly all right?"

At least he was worried about the twins. A lot of the fathers Jack and his team tracked down couldn't care less about their family. "They're okay. They asked Emma if they could see you."

The scowl on Mark's face deepened. "I can't see them."

"Can't or won't?"

Mark's eyes narrowed. "It's none of your business. Who are you?"

"I own a company called Lost and Found. We look for people who have gone missing."

Before Mark could reply, Jack stepped forward. "I've got something for you."

He opened the folder and took out the drawing Molly and Dylan had made. As he walked toward Mark, he tried to keep an open mind. People left relationships for far less than what Mark had gone through. The scars of an abusive childhood could cripple a person for the rest of their life. Some people learned how to cope with the trauma. For others it was a constant struggle that often ended in another abusive situation.

Then there was Afghanistan. Whatever strategies Mark used in his civilian life would have been blown to shreds in the army. Piling one stressful situation on top of another would have led to disaster.

He handed Mark the drawing. "Emma is organizing a Christmas fundraising program for The Connect Church. The teachers at the local school asked their students to write letters or draw pictures about the type of events they wanted in Sapphire Bay. Instead of focusing on events, some of the students made pictures of what they wanted for Christmas. Molly drew that picture."

Mark's hand tightened on the sheet of paper. "How long have they been asking to see me?"

"A while."

He looked up.

In that moment, Jack saw more than Mark would have wanted. The loneliness and fear in his eyes gave Jack a reality check. The man standing in front of him wasn't a deadbeat dad. He was a man who had done what he thought was best for his family.

Jack handed Mark a photo of the twins. "They're great kids."

He silently stared at the photo.

"Do you want to see your children?"

Mark's jaw clenched. "It wouldn't be in anyone's best interest if I saw them."

"Why not?"

"I haven't been part of their lives since they were babies. They're better off without me."

Jack wasn't pushing his luck. He'd arrived unannounced and had given Mark enough to think about for one day. "If you don't want to see your family, that's your decision. But Emma would appreciate an email to let her know you're still alive." He handed Mark a business card. "If you decide you want to see Dylan and Molly, give me a call."

Without saying a word, Mark nodded and walked toward his cabin.

It wasn't until Jack was driving along the highway that he realized Mark still had the photo of his children and the poster Molly had drawn.

Perhaps the flight to Colorado hadn't been a waste of time, after all.

When Emma saw Jack walking toward her house, her heart sank. She knew the chance of finding Mark was remote but, even so, she thought they would have more luck.

"You didn't find him, did you?"

Jack met her halfway along the garden path. "I wish it was that simple." He looked over her shoulder.

"Molly and Dylan are spending a couple of hours with Kylie. Are you telling me you found Mark?"

"He's living in a cabin beside Evergreen Lake, but he doesn't want to see the twins. I thought he might have emailed you."

Emma wished he had. At least then she might have been able to hide her disappointment. "Did he say how he's doing?"

"We didn't speak for long."

She shouldn't have expected anything less. "At least he isn't dead." Jack's sympathetic expression made her feel even worse.

"You don't have to be brave. I know you were hoping Mark would change his mind and come to Sapphire Bay, but he's not ready."

"Do you think he'll ever want to see the twins?"

"I don't know. The only thing I can tell you is that he held onto Molly and Dylan's photo and drawing." Jack searched her face. "He thinks you're better off without him."

She took a deep breath. "That's what he told me when he left. Everyone needs someone they can depend on, but Mark never had that. Thank you for finding him."

"I'd feel better if he'd emailed or called you."

"So would I." She looked at Jack and forced a smile. "Would you like a glass of lemonade?"

For a moment, she thought he was going to say no. But for some reason, he changed his mind. "That sounds great."

Emma led the way, determined not to let Mark's decision ruin a beautiful day. "Now that you don't have to worry about my ex-husband, what are your plans for the rest of your vacation?"

Jack held open the front door. "My brother's taking me fishing in a couple of days. But, before I go anywhere near the lake, Granddad wants me to help him paint another tiny home."

"You haven't had much of a rest."

"It doesn't matter. I'd probably be driving Noah and Cassie insane about now if I didn't have other things to keep me busy."

She didn't need to ask what things he'd been doing. Even though Jack had found Mark in record time, it was still at least two days out of his vacation. "I feel bad about taking so much of your time. How would you feel if I invited you to dinner tomorrow night? You could bring Noah and Cassie and your granddad. Dylan and Molly would enjoy the company and so would I."

Jack sipped the drink she'd given him. "Sounds good. I'll ask everyone if they can come."

"Don't bring anything."

"I can't guarantee my family will listen, but I'll tell them. How are you finding the summer break? It can't be easy juggling work with everything else."

"I do my best, but sometimes it doesn't quite work out. That's why Kylie is looking after the twins. I got behind on one of my contracts and she offered to babysit for a couple of hours."

"I shouldn't be taking any more of your time—"

"It's okay," Emma told him. "You can stay. I finished the job a few minutes before you arrived."

Jack sat back down on the kitchen stool. "Have you always worked in the IT industry?"

Emma smiled. "I used to be a teacher, but I've helped people build websites and advertise on the Internet since I was at college. When I moved to Sapphire Bay, I couldn't afford to start my own business, so I worked at the local elementary school for two years. In the evenings, I worked on IT projects. Eventually, I was able to resign from the school and focus on my business."

"I'm impressed."

The heat of a blush hit Emma's cheeks. "Mom and Dad thought moving here was the craziest thing I've ever done. But I couldn't afford to start my business in New York City.

Sapphire Bay is a lot quieter and less expensive. We have a great life and even better friends."

Jack's eyebrows rose. "I didn't realize you're from New York."

"I lived in Park Slope for twenty-two years before I met Mark. I love eating pastrami on rye, bagels and lox, and Mom's lemon cheesecake." She grinned at Jack. "And until I moved to Sapphire Bay, I'd never missed a Yankees' home game."

"You can't get any more patriotic than that."

Emma clicked her glass against Jack's. "Exactly."

"Do you miss anything about New York City?"

"I liked spending time at Prospect Park. I miss the ballet and going to concerts. But most of all I miss my parents." She looked at her glass of lemonade. "I always thought that one day I'd go back, but Sapphire Bay has become my home."

"Do you visit your parents very often?"

Emma sighed. "I stay with them a few times a year and they come here when they can. It isn't nearly enough, but it's better than nothing. Once the school year starts, it will be even harder to get away."

She looked around the kitchen. Talking about her mom and dad made her feel sad. "Would you like some cake?"

"Have Molly and Dylan been baking?"

"Not this time. I popped into Sweet Treats yesterday and bought one of Megan's chocolate cakes. She was raising money for the tiny home village."

Jack seemed surprised. "Does everyone raise money for the village?"

Emma thought about the events that had been organized over the past few months. "The easy answer is yes. The tiny homes mean a lot to the community. The village won't get built without our support, so we all do our best to make the project a success."

"Pastor John is lucky. There aren't many communities who would work this hard to help other people."

"You've been living in a city for too long." Taking two plates out of the cupboard, she handed one to Jack. "Nothing worthwhile ever gets accomplished on your own. It's important to feel part of something so big and exciting that it gives you goose bumps just thinking about it."

"And the tiny home village gives you goose bumps?"

Jack was laughing at her, but she didn't care. "It does and I'm proud of every one of them."

The smile Jack sent her made an entirely different set of goose bumps skitter along her skin. Grabbing the cake, she quickly cut two slices and placed each of them on a plate. "When are you going back to Manhattan?"

"I've been thinking about that."

Whatever Jack was about to say, sounded serious. "About going home?"

"I thought I'd stay in Sapphire Bay for a couple more weeks."

"Why?" The word was out of her mouth before she could stop it. "I didn't mean…you don't have to tell me why you're staying. It's none of my business."

Jack cleared his throat. "I want to spend more time with Noah and Granddad."

"What about your company?"

"Apart from going home for a couple of meetings, I can run it from here."

Emma ignored the butterflies in her tummy. It wasn't as if Jack wanted to spend more time with her and the twins. And even if he did, a few weeks would never be enough.

Instead of making a fool of herself and telling Jack how much she liked him, Emma smiled. "That's the best news I've heard all day."

"It is?"

She leaned closer and patted his arm. "From one worka-holic to another, I'm proud of you. Taking life at a slower pace is difficult, but you won't regret staying here a little longer."

Jack brushed a stray lock of hair off her face. "I don't think I will, either."

Emma's breath caught. "Are you...? Do you...?" She cleared the frog out of her throat.

Jack's hand cupped her jaw. "Yes."

"Yes?"

She looked into his serious brown eyes and sighed. "Do you want to spend more time with Molly and Dylan and me?"

"I do."

She let go of the breath she'd been holding. "I'd like that, too."

Jack's gaze dropped to her mouth.

Emma's heart raced. "I need to tell you something. It's been a long time since I dated anyone. I might be a little—"

Jack's lips gently nudged her mouth. His kiss was as soft as a summer's breeze and left her wanting more.

She lifted her hands to Jack's shoulders and held on tight. For once in her life she was tired of being careful. Even if she totally messed this up, she was ready to take a giant leap of faith. In Jack. In each other. And in the promise of what could be.

CHAPTER 7

*E*mma pressed 'Enter' on her keyboard and gave a satisfied sigh. After two hours, she'd finally finished the last updates on a client's website.

As she stretched her arms above her head, she looked through the kitchen window. It was hard to believe that Jack had returned from Evergreen Lake ten days ago. In that time, they'd gone fishing, had lots of family meals together, and laughed so much that her ribs hurt.

Thankfully, Molly and Dylan enjoyed spending time with him. Whether Jack was hooking fresh worms onto Dylan's fishing rod, helping them in the vegetable garden, or playing basketball with them, they were happy and content.

Jack was calm and patient. He knew how to make people laugh and when to simply be there for support.

Even though he was the most amazing man she'd ever met, they were taking things slowly. One day, in the not too distant future, he would head back to Manhattan. Neither of them wanted a long-distance relationship but, right now, it was the only choice they had.

She shook away the depressing thought of Jack not being here and opened her email account.

"Knock, knock."

Emma turned and smiled. "Come in, Kylie. I was wondering if you'd be able to make it."

"I nearly didn't. Allan came in just before I closed and wanted an enormous bouquet of flowers for Mabel. It took longer than I thought to make. Where are the twins?"

"Dylan is playing with his trains and Molly is designing a house."

Kylie turned on the coffeepot. "I bet she'll be an architect when she's older."

"Either that or an artist. She loves drawing more than anything else."

"I know what I'm buying her for Christmas. When I was in town the other day, I saw an incredible paint set. She could spend hours creating her own masterpieces."

Emma closed the lid of her laptop. "She'd love that. Natalie is organizing a series of children's art classes at The Welcome Center. Molly has already enrolled."

"It sounds exciting. And talking about exciting, a little birdy told me you've been a naughty girl."

"I have?"

"When were you going to tell me about you and Jack?"

"There isn't much to say. We've been on a couple of dates, that's all."

Kylie took two mugs out of a cupboard. "That's a couple more than you've been on in the last three years. He must be special."

"He is." Emma tried not to be gushy or make their relationship into something it wasn't, but she'd never felt this way about anyone. "Molly and Dylan like him. He even spoke to Mom and Dad on the phone the other day. When he goes back to Manhattan, he's promised to visit them."

Kylie's eyebrows rose. "That's awfully brave of him. None of my boyfriends would have visited my parents without me."

Emma smiled. "That's because they're not Jack. How are the plans going for the Christmas party?"

"Don't tell Pastor John, but I haven't started. I've promised myself that by the end of next week I'll have a venue organized and the tables and chairs booked."

"Once you have a short-list of venues, let me know. I heard back from Noah's company. They expect the Christmas decorations to arrive at the end of next week."

"Are they shipping them straight to the church?"

Emma took a carton of milk out of the refrigerator. "They are. I can't wait to see them."

"Neither can I." Kylie's hand froze over the coffeepot. "I almost forgot," she said excitedly. "A friend of mine lives in New Zealand. I told her about the Christmas train ride we want to organize around Flathead Lake. They do something similar in her town." She pulled out her cell phone and started typing. "I'll show you their website."

"Use my laptop," Emma said as she lifted the lid. "The photos will be bigger."

"Good idea." After a quick search, Kylie found the site.

"Oh, my goodness," Emma said. "It's fantastic."

The organizing committee called the train the North Pole Express. When everyone was on board, volunteers dressed as elves and fairies, handed out candy and small gifts to each of the passengers. Halfway through the journey, the train stopped at Santa's secret workshop. The families could meet Santa, sing Christmas carols, enjoy a drink and something to eat, then catch the train home.

Kylie showed Emma the photos of last year's event. "Jenny is happy to send us their project plan and a list of the things they've tried but haven't worked."

"That would be incredible. I've organized a lot of events, but nothing like the train ride." Emma closed the website. Her email account appeared on the screen. "Sometimes it's not what you know, but all the things you don't that make—"

She stared at the screen. Sitting beneath a message from one of her clients was an email from her ex-husband.

"Are you okay?" Kylie asked.

"Mark has sent me a message."

Kylie frowned. "Your ex-husband?"

Emma nodded.

"What does he want?"

"I don't know. I haven't opened it." Emma bit her bottom lip. After more than five years of not hearing anything from him, she was terrified of what he'd say.

Kylie rubbed her shoulder. "If you'd like to read the email without any interruptions, I can say hello to Dylan and Molly."

Being alone was the last thing Emma wanted. "I'd like you to stay. In the next few minutes you might be the most rational person in the room."

"It won't be that bad. Jack has already spoken to Mark. He would have told you to be careful if your ex-husband was a weirdo."

"Mark isn't weird."

"Perhaps I'm being too harsh," Kylie muttered. She looked at the laptop, then at Emma. "I thought you wanted him to contact you."

"I did. But there's a big difference between wanting to know if he's okay and finally hearing from him." Emma's heart was racing out of control. She felt as though she was sitting at the start of a giant roller coaster, waiting for the first terrifying drop to the ground. "Mark probably wants to thank me for the photo Jack gave him."

"Or he might want to see the twins."

Emma chose to remain silent. If Mark wanted to come to Sapphire Bay, he would have done it a long time ago.

"You'll bite your nails to the quick if you keep nibbling on them." Kylie sighed. "You won't know what he has to say until you read his email."

She was right, but it didn't make it any easier to open the message.

Before Emma had a nervous breakdown, she pulled back her shoulders and sat taller in her seat. With a trembling hand she clicked on the message, praying that whatever Mark wanted wouldn't change their lives for the worse.

She focused on the screen, reading each word carefully. When she was finished, she rubbed her eyes, then reread the message.

"What did he say?" Kylie asked.

Emma couldn't believe it. "Mark has changed his mind. He wants to visit Molly and Dylan."

Kylie's sharp, in-drawn breath reflected the way Emma felt. Ten days ago, Mark wanted nothing to do with his children. The complete U-turn was hard to believe.

"What do you think he wants?"

Emma frowned. "What do you mean?"

"If I say what's on my mind, you'll think I'm being mean. But I'm worried about you and the twins."

"Tell me what you're thinking."

Kylie leaned her elbows on the table. "You've never had a shared custody arrangement with Mark. What if he wants to take the twins back to Evergreen?"

"He hasn't taken any interest in their lives before now. The Family Court would take that into consideration if he wants Molly and Dylan to live with him."

"Maybe. When does Mark want to come here?"

The headache that had been building behind Emma's eyes was getting worse. "His flight arrives on Friday afternoon."

"That's two days away. He hasn't given you much time to get everything ready."

"Apart from telling Dylan and Molly, there isn't a lot to do." Emma sent a copy of the email to the printer. After Kylie went home, she'd read it again to make sure she hadn't missed anything. "Mark's reserved a room at a bed-and-breakfast in town."

A knock on the back door made Emma jump.

"Jack's here!" Molly shrieked as she thumped down the stairs.

Emma dropped her chin to her chest. If she'd thought today couldn't get any worse, she was wrong. Now all she had to do was explain to Jack why she had tears in her eyes, tell her children their dad was on his way to see them, and hope Kylie stayed out of Mark's way.

As soon as Jack saw Emma, he knew something was wrong. Her eyes were filled with tears and Kylie was frowning. Molly was the only person in the room who was smiling.

"Is Dylan all right?" he asked.

"I'm here." Dylan ran through the doorway. His smile was just as wide as his sister's. "Did you bring the book?"

Jack held a bag in front of him. "It's in here. How about you go into the living room with Molly and start looking at it. I'll be there in a few minutes."

They didn't need any extra encouragement. Within seconds, Dylan was leading the way, taking his sister away from whatever was happening in the kitchen.

"I haven't seen the twins move so fast in a long time," Emma said. "You'll have to tell me your secret."

Jack sat on the chair beside her. "The other day I told the twins about a book I borrowed from the library. It has some amazing photos of the Egyptian pyramids. Molly was fascinated by the pharaohs and the hieroglyphics. Dylan loved the mystery surrounding the design of the pyramids. I told them I'd bring the book with me so they could look at the pictures. What's happened?"

Emma handed him a sheet of paper. "Mark emailed me. He's coming to Sapphire Bay on Friday afternoon."

Jack read the brief message. He was surprised, but not as shocked as Emma seemed to be. "That's what you wanted, isn't it?"

Emma nodded. "I guess I'm a little stunned. I'd resigned myself to the fact that we wouldn't see him again. And now..."

"You don't know what he wants?"

She nodded.

Jack wrapped his arm around her shoulders. "I'd feel the same way if I was in your place." He read the email again, searching for anything that might hold a deeper meaning. But from his perspective, there was nothing that would worry him. "Do you want me to meet Mark at the airport?"

"It's probably better if I pick him up. Kylie has offered to look after the twins while I'm gone."

That made sense to Jack. What didn't make sense was Emma's reaction to her ex-husband's unexpected arrival. "Will you be all right?"

Emma's big blue eyes stared at him. "I have to be. This is important for Dylan and Molly. It could be the beginning of a relationship with their father."

Or it could end in disaster, Jack thought. He hoped Mark's arrival wouldn't fall under the heading of being careful what you wished for.

He kissed the side of Emma's face. Regardless of what he'd told her, Jack wanted to stay in Sapphire Bay for a lot longer than a few weeks.

He was falling in love with Emma and the twins and, with Mark's arrival, he didn't know what to do about it.

THE NEXT MORNING, Emma sat at the kitchen table, cradling a cup of hot chocolate. She didn't know what was worse; telling her children their father was coming to see them or hiding the reason he'd left in the first place.

When she looked at Dylan and Molly, she was proud of who they were. Sometimes they were so much like their father that it hurt a piece of her heart she'd locked away.

Molly picked up a knife and spread thick raspberry jam across her toast. "Can I visit Nora today? William made her a playhouse and it's got pink walls and a big fluffy rug inside."

"I'll call Megan and see if it's okay. What would you like to do, Dylan?"

"Can we go to the library? I really liked Jack's book about the pyramids."

"We can do that. After we've been to the library, I need to buy some groceries." Emma watched her children eat their breakfast. "I've got something important to tell you."

Molly stopped chewing. "Are we getting a kitten?"

"No, but someone is coming to visit."

Dylan's eyes widened with excitement. "Is it Grandpa and Grandma?"

Emma's heart sank. "Your dad is coming to visit us. He'll be here tomorrow afternoon."

The frown on Molly and Dylan's faces was identical.

"Our real dad?" Molly asked.

Emma nodded. "How do you feel about seeing him?"

"Does he like fishing?" Dylan wiped the jam off his mouth with the back of his hand.

"He lives in a cabin beside a lake, so I imagine he likes fishing."

"How come you don't know?" Molly asked.

"I haven't seen your dad in a long time. When we were living in New York City, we didn't go fishing. But people change." Hopefully for the best, she thought.

"We asked Santa if we could see him." Molly's eyes were as round as saucers.

"He saw your Christmas wish. That's why he's coming to visit."

Molly's excited gaze darted to her brother. "I told you Santa isn't make-believe. He found our dad and he's bringing him home."

Dylan didn't share his sister's enthusiasm. "What if we don't like him?"

Emma moved to the other side of the table and hugged her children. "You don't have to like everyone, but it would be nice if you spent some time with your dad. He's coming a long way to see you."

"Why didn't he want to see us before?"

"'Cos we didn't ask Santa," Molly told her brother. "Santa knows everything."

"Does not. I bet you Jack knows more than Santa and more than our dad, too."

Molly tilted her chin at a determined angle. "No one knows more than Santa."

Emma jumped into the conversation before it became too heated. "You can ask your dad that question, Dylan."

"You could show him your trains," Molly said. "I bet he'd like them."

Dylan didn't say anything.

"It will be all right." Emma hugged her children. "I'll be with you the whole time. If you don't want to spend a lot of time with your dad, that's fine."

"Will he come back another time?" Molly asked.

Emma sighed. "I don't know, but we can make the most of this visit. Do you want to have a special dinner with him?"

"Yes, please." Molly grinned. "Can we buy an ice cream cake from Megan? The ones with sprinkles and cotton candy on top are amazing."

"That's a great idea." Emma forced a good dose of excitement into her voice. In all honesty, she felt a lot like Dylan. Mark had let everyone down and it would take time to rebuild that trust. "Let's finish our breakfast and then go into town. We can go to the library first, then buy our groceries and order a cake. When we get back, I'll call Megan and ask if Molly can spend time with Nora."

"Yeah!" Molly squealed. "Let's go, Dylan. We've got shopping to do."

Reluctantly, Dylan picked up his plate and took it across to the dishwasher. It didn't surprise Emma that he wasn't the least bit enthusiastic about going shopping.

It was the last thing she felt like doing, too.

CHAPTER 8

*B*y Friday afternoon, Emma was feeling more than a little stressed.

Twenty minutes ago, she'd left Molly and Dylan with Kylie and driven to Polson Airport. Apart from the weekends, there was never a lot of traffic, and today there was even less. Which was just as well. Concentrating on the road was difficult when there were so many thoughts racing through her mind.

What if she didn't recognize Mark? What if more than one man had red hair and deep blue eyes? She hadn't thought to ask Jack if he had a recent photo of her ex-husband.

Mark had always kept in shape. Running helped him deal with what was happening in his life. But five years had gone by and Emma didn't know what he was doing to help him through the tough times. Or even if there were tough times. He might have a great life with no financial issues or emotional baggage weighing him down.

He could have remarried, have children of his own.

A part of her hoped he'd found happiness. The other part was as lost and frightened as the day Mark had left.

As she drove into the airport, she looked for a parking space close to the terminal. If Mark had changed his mind and decided not to come, she wouldn't have to walk for miles to go back to the truck. No one would wonder why she was leaving without a suitcase. Or why no one was with her.

In the end, she had no choice but to take the first parking space she saw. Unlike the roads, the airport was busy.

Before she got out of her truck, she sniffed the small bouquet of lavender Kylie had given her. Emma couldn't tell if it was helping her to relax but, at this stage, she was willing to try anything.

She looked through the windshield and watched a man load his family's luggage onto a cart. Everyone seemed happy, as if they were going somewhere exciting for a vacation.

Emma envied them. She would give anything not to be sitting here, putting off the moment when she saw her ex-husband.

If she was this nervous, she could only imagine how Mark was feeling. Coming to Sapphire Bay was a big decision. He knew how upset she'd been when he left and how hard it would have been for her to raise their children on her own.

From the first time they'd met, Mark had wanted to take care of her. But after he left, he never called to make sure she was okay or sent money to help pay for some of their expenses. Through all the times when she felt like giving up, Mark's complete disconnection from their family was the only thing that kept her going. She was Molly and Dylan's mom. Apart from her parents, she was the only family they had. And no matter what, she wouldn't let them down.

Her hand gripped the door handle. At the last minute, she remembered to check her cell phone.

Mark's flight was still on time.

Taking a deep breath, she stepped out of the truck and straightened her skirt.

It was time to meet her ex-husband.

"YOU'LL WEAR a hole in my floor if you don't stop pacing," Noah said to Jack. "Emma will be all right."

"I still don't know why she wouldn't let me go to the airport with her."

"You aren't her bodyguard. Mark isn't violent and he's never been arrested. No one you spoke to had a bad thing to say about him."

"That doesn't mean he should have flown to Sapphire Bay so suddenly. Dylan didn't sleep last night and Molly is beside herself. Emma is putting a brave face on how she's feeling but she's worried, too."

"I can't blame her. The guy ran out on their family when the twins were babies. That's not something you forget in a hurry."

It was bad enough that Mark had abandoned Emma. But to leave when his children were so young was unforgivable. If Jack had been in Emma's position, he wouldn't let his ex-partner anywhere near their children.

Noah handed him a folder. "If you want something to do, you can look through this report. I need to do a cost-benefit analysis on a new product line."

"I don't know if I'm the right person to help."

"You're the only person who can help. Stacey is busy working through some issues with another contract and my PA is shortlisting candidates for a new position. It will take your mind off what's happening at the airport."

At the mention of the airport, Jack checked his watch. Mark's flight would have landed by now. He just hoped

Emma stayed safe and didn't let her emotions get the better of her. She wanted to be strong for her children. Jack wanted her to be strong for herself and for the life they could have together.

But from where he was standing, there wasn't an easy solution to anything that was happening. Perhaps Noah was right. Finding Mark could have opened a can of worms that would upset a lot of people. And he didn't know how Emma or her children would react to being let down for a second time.

EMMA STUDIED the passengers walking into the Arrivals area. So far, no one looking remotely like Mark emerged from behind the glass doors. But with two flights arriving at the same time, there was a good chance he would still be waiting for his luggage.

"Emma?"

She could have sworn her heart skipped a beat. Regardless of what Mark looked like now, she would know his voice anywhere. Slowly, she turned around, preparing herself for the moment she'd been dreading.

"My flight was diverted, but it was supposed to arrive at the same time..." Mark took a deep breath. "You haven't changed."

Neither had Mark. He still had an unruly mop of red hair that refused to sit in one direction. His shoulders were broader than she remembered. He'd filled out, lost the lankiness that he'd tried to camouflage.

When she looked into his eyes, her heart pounded. He was older, more wary than when they were together.

She'd met Mark when she was twenty-two years old. He'd swept her off her feet, told her she was the best thing that had ever happened to him. His damaged soul had called to her, made her believe she could make his life better. A year later, their fairytale wedding only reinforced how perfect they were for each other.

It wasn't until Emma was pregnant with Molly and Dylan that she began to see the cracks in their relationship.

And now, here they were. Two people who had promised to love each other for the rest of their lives, staring at each other like wounded strangers.

Mark's eyes filled with tears. "I'm sorry. For everything. I let you down and I've never known how to apologize."

Emma tried to harden her heart. She'd spent the last five years imagining this moment. She would hold her head high and be strong and proud. But grief clogged her throat—for the years they weren't together, for the twins' childhood he'd chosen to miss. For the empty promises they'd made to each other.

Instead of speaking or doing any of the things she thought she would, she held out her arms.

Mark stepped forward, hugging her tight.

When her tears stopped falling, Emma moved away and blew her nose. "I wasn't supposed to cry."

Mark started to say something, then stopped. "It's okay. I feel the same way."

She studied the heartache that showed on his face. This was as hard for him as it was for her. "Would you like to get a coffee before we head home? A friend is looking after Dylan and Molly. I could show you some photos of them and answer any questions you might have."

"That would be great. Thank you."

Emma wiped her eyes. "There's a café on the other side of the room. Most people won't stay in the terminal for long, so it shouldn't be too busy."

"I'll follow you." Mark held the handle of his suitcase, pulling the bag behind him.

As they dodged families arriving home from vacations, and sports teams checking they had all their luggage, Emma did her best to steady her pounding heart. She didn't know what would happen next, but at least Mark was here.

It was a start.

AIRPORTS WEREN'T Emma's favorite place. For the most part, they were soulless, noisy buildings built to transfer people from one location to another.

Whenever she went to an airport, she was either worried she'd miss her flight or anxious about meeting family or friends. Today, her stress levels were off the chart, and it wouldn't get better anytime soon.

Mark walked around a sports team. "I thought Polson was a small town."

"Compared to a city, it is." Thankfully, the café wasn't far away. "How was your flight?" Mark hated flying. Even on their honeymoon, he'd taken a sleeping tablet to get through the five-hour flight.

"It was better than I thought. There wasn't too much turbulence and the food was okay."

"That's good." Emma stood at the edge of the café and pointed to a table that looked as though it was in a quieter area than the others. "Do you want to sit there?"

Mark nodded and pulled his suitcase close to one of the chairs. "Can I get you a coffee or a cup of hot chocolate?"

"I'll have an iced tea, if they have any. Otherwise, a bottle of water will be fine."

"I'll be back in a minute."

While Mark was getting their drinks, Emma sent a quick

text to Kylie and Jack. They were both worried about how this visit would go, and she couldn't blame them. Even though Molly wanted to see her dad, his presence in Sapphire Bay would stir up a whole lot of feelings that everyone had buried.

"Here you go." Mark placed a glass of iced tea in front of her. "I didn't know whether you wanted anything to eat, so I bought two muffins, anyway." Mark pulled out a chair and maneuvered his wide frame behind the table.

"Jack said you live beside Evergreen Lake in Colorado. How did you end up living there?"

"After I left New York, I moved around a lot. One summer I decided to visit Evergreen Lake. I'd been there a few times when I was younger. I guess the memories of fishing and being away from my dad made the place a bit of a sanctuary. While I was there, the owner of the lodge was looking for someone to manage the resort. The pay wasn't great, but the salary package included a house and all the utility bills. When the owner decided to sell the cabins, I bought them from the money I inherited after Mom died."

Emma's mouth dropped open. "When did your mom die? I spoke to her last year and she said everything was fine."

Mark looked down at his cup of coffee. "She died ten months ago from a heart attack."

"I'm sorry. It must have been a difficult time." Emma didn't know why Mark's sister hadn't called her. She would have gone to his mom's funeral, paid her respects to a woman who had lived through a terrible marriage, but had always worked hard to help other people.

"Mom didn't want a funeral," Mark said softly, as if reading her mind. "She used to say that, apart from her parents, the good Lord welcomed her into the world alone, and that's the way she wanted to leave."

Emma could imagine Martha saying that. "I'm glad you and your sister gave her what she wanted."

"So am I. Thanks for emailing Mom and me the photos of Molly and Dylan as they were growing up. I know she enjoyed seeing them, and so did I."

"I wasn't sure if you got them or not. Why didn't you keep in contact with us?"

Mark sighed. "Some days it was hard enough getting out of bed. My depression returned and I had trouble coping with everyday life." He pulled out his cell phone and showed Emma a picture of a black and white dog. "I found Buster eating out of some trash cans on the side of the road. He's been living with me for four years. Between managing the cabins and looking after Buster, I pulled myself out of the hole I was heading into."

"He's a lovely dog. Were you able to get any counseling in Evergreen?"

"It's a small town. It doesn't have the services that other cities take for granted."

Emma had never been more thankful for Pastor John and the work the community was doing to provide food, shelter, and counseling to anyone who needed it. "While you're in Sapphire Bay, I'll take you to The Welcome Center and the tiny home village. I think you'll be impressed with what we're doing."

"I'd like that. Why did you move to Montana?"

If Mark wanted the truth, she'd tell him. "After you left, I couldn't stay in our apartment. With all the bills that needed to be paid, my savings wouldn't have lasted more than a year. Even if I went back to work, the cost of childcare would have taken all my salary. Mom and Dad wanted me to come home, so I did. The twins were happy and my parents enjoyed having us there. By the time Dylan and Molly were eighteen months old I was teaching part-time at a local elementary school. A year later, a friend invited us to Sapphire Bay for a vacation. I loved it and decided to stay."

"Apart from being more affordable, why did you stay? There can't be that many teaching jobs available."

Emma had never told Mark about her business. "I'm not teaching. I started a communications business. I build websites, run online advertising programs, and manage my clients' social media accounts. I couldn't have done any of that in New York."

"You used to hate change."

Her fingers tightened around her drink. "I got used to it."

A blush hit Mark's face. "I deserve that. What about Dylan and Molly? What do they enjoy doing?"

"They're like any normal six-year-olds." Taking out her cell phone, Emma showed Mark some photos of the twins. "The photo Jack gave you was taken a couple of weekends ago. These are some pictures I took last week when we were fishing."

Mark stared at her. "You've been fishing? Whenever we went near the water you got bored."

"I still don't like sitting still for hours, but in small doses I'm fine. Dylan loves fishing, but Molly would sooner be drawing or playing with her Legos."

Mark studied the next photo. "Does Jack live in Sapphire Bay?"

Emma looked at the picture. Jack had his arms around Dylan and Molly as they each held up a fish they'd caught. "Jack comes here to visit his family. The rest of the time he lives in Manhattan."

"That's a big commute. It must be difficult having a long-distance relationship."

"We don't... I mean... Jack and I have only started dating. I don't know what will happen when he goes home. What about you? Do you have a girlfriend or have you remarried?"

Mark rubbed his hands across his eyes. He looked exhausted. "I've already failed once at being a husband. I'm not in a hurry to repeat the same mistakes."

"You left because you thought you'd run out of options."

"I left because I was worried I'd hurt you or the twins."

Emma didn't want to state the obvious, but he'd hurt them anyway. If there was one thing she'd learned, it was that walking away from a situation never solved anything. All it did was make everything ten times worse.

"Would you like to see Dylan and Molly now?"

For a split second, Mark looked terrified. "I'd like that very much. How do they feel about meeting me?"

"Molly is excited but wary. Dylan is more worried."

"What can I do to make them more comfortable around me?"

"Just be yourself," Emma murmured. "It's all we've ever wanted."

CHAPTER 9

*D*uring the twenty-minute drive back to Sapphire Bay, Mark told Emma about managing the cabins, about the characters who came to Evergreen, and the people who never left.

Anyone listening to them would think they were long-lost friends who were getting to know each other again. Maybe they were, but it didn't make the knots in Emma's stomach go away.

When they reached her house, she parked inside the garage and turned to Mark. "How are you feeling?"

"Nervous."

"It will be all right. I've made dinner for all of us, but if you want to go back to your accommodation before then, just let me know."

Mark rubbed his hands along his jeans. "I will." He took off his seatbelt and picked up two gift-wrapped boxes from beside his feet. "I hope this goes well."

So did Emma. When she'd brought the twins to Sapphire Bay, she'd wondered what they would think about their father when they were older. Now it was time to find out.

The door into the garage opened. Molly was staring at the truck, waiting to see her father.

"She looks so much like you," Mark whispered.

"Except for the red hair." Emma opened her door and forced a smile. "Hi, Molly. Come and meet your dad."

Mark stepped out of the truck and walked across to his daughter. He must have realized how intimidating his six-foot plus frame could be to a child, because he knelt a short distance away from her.

"It's nice to meet you, Molly. I'm sorry I haven't spent any time with you since you were a baby."

Molly's big blue eyes were fixed on Mark's face. "You've got red hair like me and Dylan."

"My mom had red hair, too. I've got a present for you." Mark handed her one of the boxes. "I made it from the wood behind my cabin."

Molly sat on the garage floor and ripped the wrapping paper off the box. When she opened the lid, any worry about meeting Mark for the first time, disappeared. "She's beautiful."

Emma's eyes widened. Molly was holding a sculpture of a ballerina. Standing en pointe, with her arms extended above her head, it was the most exquisite carving Emma had ever seen.

Mark smiled. "Your mom always wanted to be a ballerina."

Molly looked up at Emma. "You did?"

Emma nodded. She was surprised Mark remembered. "When I was a little older than you, Grandma took me to ballet classes. I loved wearing my tutu and slippers, and dancing with my friends."

"Can I do ballet classes?"

"We don't have any in Sapphire Bay, but I could show you some of the steps."

Molly hugged her sculpture to her chest. "Could you show me today?"

"We'll see." Emma ruffled Molly's curls. "I might be able to find one of my leotards for you."

Kylie and Dylan joined them in the garage.

If Mark saw the distrust in Kylie's eyes, he didn't show it. Instead, he said hello and shook her hand.

Dylan stood to the side of Kylie's legs, looking unsure and worried.

Once again, Mark knelt on the floor. "Hi, Dylan. It's good to see you." When Dylan didn't reply, Mark held the last gift-wrapped box toward him. "I made this for you. I hope you like it."

Slowly, cautiously, Dylan took the box. "Thank you."

"You're welcome."

Molly stood beside her brother. "Are you going to open it?"

Dylan looked down at the gift-wrapped box, then at the ballerina in Molly's hands.

"I could help you," Molly offered.

He shook his head. "I can do it." Slowly, he peeled back each piece of tape and handed Kylie the bright orange paper. When the lid was open, he took a beautiful star-shaped sculpture out of the box.

"When you were a baby, I used to sing, 'Twinkle, Twinkle, Little Star' to you. I thought you might like having a star in your room."

Dylan held up the sculpture, watching the three-dimensional sides slowly spin from beneath a red ribbon. "Did you make it all by yourself?" he asked shyly.

"I did. A man who lived close to my cabin at Evergreen Lodge was a master sculptor. He taught me everything I know."

Molly's fingertips brushed the edge of the wood. "It's pretty."

Tears stung Emma's eyes. Now that the twins were older, they were even more like their dad. Seeing them talking with Mark, getting to know the man who had given them life, was something she never thought would happen.

And now that they were together, she was determined to do everything she could to make sure they never lost contact again.

As she prepared dinner, Emma watched Mark play basketball with the twins.

"At least he's good with children," Kylie said.

"He was always good with Molly and Dylan." Emma turned from the kitchen window. "He isn't a bad person."

"Is he different from when you were married?"

"I don't know. He seems more settled, but I'm the last person who should be judging his behavior. Before he left, I knew our relationship had a few problems, but I didn't think he would leave."

Kylie chopped a tomato into quarters and added it to the salad. "Dylan is more relaxed now that he's met Mark."

"Dylan has missed having his dad around. I think that's why he likes Mr. Jessop's company so much."

"And Jack's."

Emma glanced at her friend. "This morning, Dylan asked when Jack is going home. He wants him to stay in Sapphire Bay."

"I'm not surprised. They get along really well."

A loud cheer rang out from the backyard. Molly had scored another goal.

Emma enjoyed spending time with Jack and she knew the

twins did, too. After being on her own for so long, she never thought she'd meet another person who made her feel so alive.

She'd fallen in love with Jack, but finding Mark had changed everything.

Jack had said he was here for them all and that, no matter what, he would make sure they were okay. But she didn't want him looking after them. She'd worked hard to provide for Dylan and Molly. Allowing someone to take care of them was as alien to her as meeting her ex-husband at the airport.

"I know finding Mark is a big deal," Kylie said. "But you're still the same person you were before he came here. You're strong, brave, and courageous. You're raising two beautiful children who know what it's like to be loved. You don't need to feel overwhelmed by what's happening."

Emma took a deep breath. If she weren't careful, she'd start crying all over again. "I'm happy Dylan and Molly have met their dad, but I'm worried about what will happen next."

"Have you talked to Mark about the future?"

"Not yet. Mom and Dad want me to contact my lawyer, but I don't want to scare Mark away."

Kylie wrapped her arm around Emma's shoulders. "Don't worry about him. He made the decision to stay out of your life. Your parents only want to protect the twins and make sure whatever happens is in everyone's best interest."

"You think I should call my lawyer?"

"I think you should do what's best for you and your children. If that means talking to lawyers, counselors, or anyone else who has been in the same situation, then do it."

Emma looked through the kitchen window.

Dylan high-fived Mark before throwing the basketball through the hoop.

Her worst fear was that Mark would become part of their children's lives, then leave. If that happened, she'd need all the help she could get to make sure Molly and Dylan didn't feel abandoned.

Kylie took an oven mitt off the counter. "Why don't you play basketball with Mark and the twins? I can make sure everything's ready for dinner."

"Are you sure?"

Kylie grinned. "That's what friends are for. Besides, you won't know if Mark has changed unless you get to know him."

Emma squeezed Kylie's hand. "Thank you. I don't know what I would do without you."

"Don't speak too soon. I might burn the garlic bread."

"I have complete faith in you."

Kylie smiled. "I could say the same about you. Now go and enjoy some fresh air."

Emma wiped her hands on a dishtowel and headed outside. Today was the first day of a new relationship with her ex-husband. And, for everyone's sake, she hoped it wasn't the last.

JACK SCREWED another sheet of drywall onto the frame of a tiny home. After working alongside his brother for most of yesterday, he needed a change of scenery. And the workshop was the perfect distraction.

An hour ago, he'd joined his grandfather in the old steamboat museum, helping to finish the walls of two houses before the painters arrived.

"When we're ready to plaster the walls, don't be surprised if it looks as though we don't have enough compound," Patrick Devlin said from the front doorway. "Bob has ordered more from the suppliers but it hasn't arrived."

"Does that mean I can finish work early?"

Jack's grandfather laughed. "You'll be lucky. We've got a lot more work to do on the houses before Monday."

Working in the old steamboat museum wasn't as calming as Jack thought it would be. Screwing the drywall into place kept his hands busy, but it hadn't stopped his brain from thinking about Emma and the twins. Even after speaking to her last night, he was still uneasy about her ex-husband.

"You're not usually this quiet," Patrick said. "What's on your mind?"

Jack grabbed a handful of screws out of the bucket. "Emma is showing Mark around Sapphire Bay today."

"And that worries you?"

It worried him more than he wanted to admit. "I care about Emma and the twins. I don't want them to get hurt."

Patrick looked around the tiny home. "We all get hurt. I can guarantee the person who lives here will have had their fair share of knocks and bruises. But, somehow, they found their way to Sapphire Bay and the beginning of a new life. Emma is no different. She rebuilt her life once. If inviting Mark back into her life doesn't work out, it won't be the end of the world."

Jack thought about what his granddad had said. When he was growing up, his grandma had told him not to worry about the things he couldn't change. He guessed this was one of those times.

"Before you give yourself ulcers," Patrick said with a smile. "You can help me drywall the second story of this home before lunch."

"Has anyone told you you're bossy?"

Patrick laughed. "Your grandmother told me that all the time. But, even at my best, I wasn't a match for her. Did I tell you about the time we flew to Vancouver for a friend's wedding?"

Jack had heard the story many times, but he never got

tired of it. His grandma was a sweet and kind woman. But if anyone upset her grandsons, she turned into a ferocious lion. "Go ahead. I'm listening."

As Patrick retold the story of how an airline staff member thought he was abducting his grandsons, Jack smiled. Everyone needed someone to love them, and Jack and his brother had struck gold with their grandparents.

All he had to do was let Emma know that he was there for her, no matter what she decided to do. Or what Mark did.

CHAPTER 10

*H*alf an hour later, Jack was fastening the last sheet of drywall into place when a little girl giggled behind him.

He looked over his shoulder and smiled. "What's my favorite girl doing here?"

"I'm looking for Mom. Pastor John was showing us around and they got lost."

Considering this was a construction site, Molly was lucky she hadn't hurt herself. Jack stood and held out his hand. "We'd better find your mom, then. She might not like being lost."

Molly slipped her small hand into his. "Did you know my dad is visiting us? He's really big and he's got red hair, just like Dylan and me. And guess what."

"What?"

"He makes things out of wood. He made me a pretty ballerina and Dylan got a star. I like the star 'cos it turns around in circles, just like me."

Before Jack could stop her, Molly held her arms either side of her and turned around like a spinning top. He waited a couple of seconds, then caught her hand gently in his. "We'd better find your mom before you spin away."

"Like a tornado," Molly said dramatically. "Dylan told me all about tornadoes. Did you know Mr. Jessop had lots of tornadoes on his ranch? I got scared when he told me his cows blew away."

Jack's eyebrows rose. "That would scare me, too." And probably, if he were six years old, it would give him nightmares for the rest of his life.

"He doesn't know where they went, but Dylan said they probably went to Oz. Do you know about Oz, Jack? It's where Dorothy went with her little dog. I like dogs. Do you like dogs?"

"I do. When Noah and I lived with our grandparents, we had a Golden Labrador called Carrot."

Molly giggled. "That's a funny name for a dog."

Jack smiled. "He liked to eat lots and lots of carrots. Sometimes, he would dig them out of my granddad's garden and run through the house with them."

He looked around the building for any sign of Pastor John and Emma. "Is Dylan with your mom?"

"Yep. He's lost, too."

If John was showing Emma around, he would probably take her outside to the two homes that were ready to leave the yard.

As they passed the other volunteers, Jack told them where they were going in case Emma came in another entrance.

When they stepped outside, Molly hesitated. "It's real bright out here."

Jack held his hand above his eyes. "If you squint it makes it easier to see."

Molly looked up at him, then squeezed her eyes tight until they were almost closed.

His mouth tilted into a smile. "Better?"

"Yep. How do you know about squints?"

"Granddad showed me." He glanced across the yard and saw John stepping out of a tiny home. "I can see Pastor John. Hopefully, your mom and Dylan are with him."

As they walked across the yard, Molly's arm swung between them. "I like you, Jack."

His heart squeezed tight. "I like you, too."

"Is it okay to have two daddies?"

He almost tripped over his feet. "Umm...what made you ask that question?"

"Dylan said we can't have two daddies, but I want you and my real daddy. Why can't I have two daddies?"

Jack thought carefully before he said anything. "Some people have more than one father. But becoming a dad is a big deal."

"Bigger than getting a kitten?"

"Much bigger."

Molly looked up at him and frowned. "I still want two daddies."

Jack squeezed her hand. "I know you do."

They'd only taken a few steps when Molly pointed at the tiny home. "There's Mom."

And, if Jack's eyes weren't playing tricks on him, Mark and Dylan were right behind her.

EMMA RUSHED ACROSS TO MOLLY. "Why are you with Jack? You were supposed to stay with Mr. Devlin in the cafeteria."

"Jack's granddad had to answer the phone. I looked for you, but you'd gone. Did you get lost?"

"No, we weren't lost. It's good you found us, though. Thanks for looking after her, Jack."

He searched Emma's face, wanting to know if she was all

right. When she smiled, his shoulders relaxed. "I don't think Molly was wandering around the workshop for too long." He held out his hand to Mark. "Welcome to Sapphire Bay."

"Thanks. Emma and the twins have been giving me a guided tour. Sapphire Bay is a lot like Evergreen."

"Except we have better ice cream," Emma said half-jokingly.

Mark smiled and Jack's stomach clenched.

"Emma wanted me to see the tiny homes before I left. John has been showing us around. I'm impressed with what everyone has achieved."

"They're important community projects," Jack said. "Have you visited The Welcome Center?"

Mark nodded. "I wish we had something similar back home. It would make a big difference to a lot of people."

Pastor John took his cell phone out of his pocket. "We're working on ways we can share our service model with other communities. If you'll excuse me, I need to answer this call."

Emma held Molly's hand. "We've also taken Mark to the general store, Kylie's flower shop, and bought him some of Brooke's fudge."

"You've had a busy day."

"What have you been doing?" Dylan asked Jack.

"I'm helping Granddad drywall the two tiny homes inside the workshop."

Emma held her hand above her eyes, shielding her face from the bright sunshine. "We were about to go to the cafeteria for something to drink. Would you like to join us?"

"Say yes," Molly begged. "You can have some of the fudge we bought from Brooke's store. It's your favorite."

"Caramel deluxe?"

Molly giggled. "No, silly. It's chocolate with little nuts in it. You told us it's your most favorite fudge in the world."

"In that case," Jack said with a smile. "How can I say no?

But before I go to the cafeteria, I have to tell the site foreman where I've gone."

Dylan's hand wrapped around Jack's fingers. "Can I come with you?"

"Me, too," Molly said. "I'll be real good."

Everyone looked at Emma. "Okay, but stay with Jack."

Molly nodded vigorously. "We will, won't we Dylan?"

Her brother frowned.

Jack gave Dylan's fingers a gentle squeeze. "Let's go, then. We'll meet your mom and dad in the cafeteria in a few minutes."

As they walked across the yard, Jack thought about the question Molly had asked him. It was hard enough referring to Mark as her dad. It was worse realizing he might never be her other daddy.

LATER THAT NIGHT, Jack sat on a chair on the veranda of Acorn Cottage, staring across Flathead Lake. For someone who'd started the day wanting to take his mind off Emma and her ex-husband, he hadn't done a good job.

Meeting them at the old steamboat museum was fate's way of telling him he needed to get his priorities straight. He'd seen firsthand how Mark interacted with his children, the genuine interest he had in their lives and, more importantly, the love that had never gone away.

It would have been easier to dislike Mark if he had issues that went against everything Jack knew to be right. But he didn't. Mark was as sane and rational as Jack. He wanted what was best for the twins and for Emma. He'd also found a career that gave him a deep sense of satisfaction as well as financial security.

The sculptures he'd made for Molly and Dylan were only

the beginning of his talent. Mark regularly exhibited his work at some of Colorado's finest galleries. He'd told them that learning his craft from one of the most respected sculptors in America had not only improved his skills, it had opened the door to networking opportunities that didn't come along every day.

When Jack arrived home, he found Mark's website and looked at the other sculptures he'd created. What impressed him the most was the way Mark imagined each piece in its setting. Whether the sculpture was five feet tall and made of bronze, or a small, hand-sized ornament, each piece was perfect.

He hoped Mark used the same skill to grow his relationship with his children. It was obvious to anyone seeing Molly and Dylan that they were curious about their dad. Only time would tell if that curiosity turned into anything else.

"Do you want company or are you happy on your own?" Noah stood on the edge of the veranda holding two cans of beer. "It's a warm evening. I thought you might like something cold to drink."

"You must have read my mind. Did you have a good day with Cassie?"

Noah handed Jack one of the cans and sat down. "The regatta at Bigfork was bigger than anything we've had here. We enjoyed it, but it took more than two hours to drive home. How was your day?"

"Interesting. I spent nearly an hour with Mark, Emma, and the twins."

"By choice?"

"What do you mean?"

"You told me you were staying away from Emma and her children so they could spend time with Mark. What happened?"

"Granddad happened. He asked me to help drywall the

tiny homes. While I was there, John was showing them around the houses. One thing led to another and I ended up in the cafeteria with them."

Noah leaned back in his chair. "And?"

"And nothing. Mark is all right. I still think what he did was wrong, but it doesn't change the fact that he wants to get to know Dylan and Molly."

"How do the twins feel about him?"

"I'm not sure. Molly will talk to anyone. Dylan is still considering his options."

"At six years old?"

Despite being worried, Jack smiled. "Dylan isn't like any boy I've ever met. His mind is as sharp as a pin. He knows things I hadn't heard of until I was twice his age."

Noah grinned. "I don't mean to state the obvious, but you weren't exactly Einstein."

"I did better than you at school."

"Only because you sweet-talked your way through each class." Noah's smile disappeared. "Where does all this leave Emma?"

"I don't know. I didn't get a chance to speak to her on her own." He waited a heartbeat before telling his brother what worried him the most. "Molly asked me if she can have two daddies."

Noah choked on his beer. "What did you say?"

"That being a father is a big deal."

"You need to be careful."

Jack took a deep breath. "From the first time I met Emma, I knew her children would be an important part of any relationship with her. I don't want anyone getting hurt."

"If your relationship with Emma doesn't work out, everyone will get hurt. When does Mark leave?"

"Tomorrow afternoon. On Monday, I'm flying to

Manhattan for a few days. When I get back, I'll see how Emma feels about everything."

"Sounds sensible."

Jack left his beer on the table. "I don't want to be sensible. Emma has never held a grudge against Mark. For some reason, she forgives him for what he did. What if she wants them to be a family again?"

Noah frowned as a flock of birds flew overhead. "Do you want me to answer your question or leave you to ponder the meaning of life?"

"It isn't funny."

"I didn't say it was."

In frustration, Jack ran his hands through his hair. "I know what you'll say. Emma loved Mark. She can forgive him because she knows him better than anyone else. Then you'll tell me that a love like that never goes away. It might change but, fundamentally, it will always be there."

And, in a best-case scenario, any relationship with Emma and her children would include Mark. Whether Jack liked it or not.

At thirty-eight years of age, he was finally willing to admit that sometimes, life sucked. Big time.

CHAPTER 11

*B*y Sunday afternoon, Emma was a little less confused about what Mark wanted. They'd talked last night, caught up on all the things they couldn't say in front of their children.

This morning, Emma's lawyer replied to her email. While Dylan and Molly were playing outside, Mark and Emma had discussed some custody options and set boundaries for any future contact Mark would have with them. They'd tried to make the transition from not having their dad in their lives to Mark suddenly being there easier for Molly and Dylan.

At this stage, moving to Sapphire Bay wasn't an option he wanted to consider. And for that, Emma was extremely grateful.

If she could have imagined the best outcome for this weekend, this would be it. Mark had slotted into their lives as if he'd always been there. They'd enjoyed each other's company, even shared a few jokes. But she couldn't help feeling that something wasn't quite right. That, if she took one step out of place, the whole weekend would end in disaster.

In ninety minutes, her ex-husband would be sitting on a plane, flying back to Colorado. But, before he left, they had one last place to visit.

Molly had convinced them they needed to take Mark to the animal shelter. She said she wanted to show her dad her favorite place to go, but Emma knew she had an ulterior motive.

Emma had promised Molly that one day they would adopt a kitten. In her daughter's mind, the more kittens they saw, the sooner one would arrive.

As soon as they were in the shelter, Molly wrapped her arms around a pure white kitten. "She's so cute," she whispered. "Can we take her home?"

Emma rubbed its paw. "She's lovely, but we've only come to look at the animals."

"But she needs a home. If we come back another day, she might be gone."

Dylan stroked the little kitten between her ears. "I thought you wanted a black cat."

"I changed my mind. I want this kitten because she's soft and cuddly."

As if sensing that her fate depended on what happened in the next few seconds, the kitten rubbed her face against Molly's. She purred so loudly that Emma would have been able to hear her from the other side of the room.

"Aww, look." Molly sighed. "She loves me."

Dylan wandered across the room. Getting down on his hands and knees, he peered inside a round tube. "Look at this kitten. He's just like the quilt Grandma has on her bed."

Molly held the white kitten close to her chest and walked across to her brother. "He won't be as cute as my kitten."

With infinite patience, Dylan coaxed the shy kitten close to the edge of his hideaway. His black, white, and ginger coat was gorgeous. "Look. He wants to come home with us."

116

Emma glanced at Mark and sighed. This was the worst part of coming to the shelter. If Emma could, she would give a home to all the stray animals. But looking after a houseful of animals wouldn't stop the constant arrival of more stray cats and dogs.

The only thing that gave her comfort was knowing the shelter did their best to find loving forever homes for each of the animals.

Mark knelt beside Dylan. "They're both great kittens. How about we look at the dogs? We might see one that looks like Buster."

The photos of Mark's dog had been a huge hit. And when Molly and Dylan heard how Mark had found Buster, they'd wanted to give him lots of cuddles.

Molly kissed the top of the white kitten's head. "I'll be back soon." Carefully, she placed her back in her bed and waited for Dylan. "We should ask the lady at the desk to make sure no one takes our kittens."

"We aren't taking them home," Emma said gently. "The shelter will find wonderful families for them."

"What if they don't?"

"They will. Come on," Emma held out her hand. "What do we do before we go into the kennels?"

"Wash our hands," Dylan said from the doorway.

"That's right." Emma closed the door behind them. "And when we've finished in the kennels?"

"Wash our hands and take dad to the airport?" Molly asked.

Emma kissed the top of her head. "That's right. Let's go and see the dogs."

With a reluctant sigh, Molly held her dad's hand as they walked outside.

Emma hoped with all her heart that someone did adopt

the kittens. Because Molly and Dylan were right. They were adorable.

KYLIE OPENED the lid of a large box and smiled. "It feels like Christmas."

Emma glanced up from the packing slip she was studying. "It *looks* like Christmas. I've never seen such a big delivery of decorations. I hope Noah's company didn't send more than we ordered."

"I don't think they would have. What surprised me the most is how quickly they arrived."

Noah had promised the decorations would be here well before they needed them, and he'd been right. Pastor John and the store owners would be thrilled. Not only were they here in plenty of time, the quality of the decorations was amazing. Each wreath, tree, and string of fairy lights looked better than they had in the catalog.

"Main Street will look incredible."

"I agree. If this doesn't bring more tourists into town, nothing will." Kylie pulled out her phone. A few seconds later, the sound of Christmas carols filled the church's storage area. "Now it really feels like Christmas."

Emma hummed to the music as she ticked another two trees off the packing slip. "Bailey called me last night. She's found somewhere to stay and will catch up with us next week."

"I'm looking forward to meeting her." Kylie placed three gorgeous Christmas wreaths on an empty shelf. "Do you think we'll have enough space for all the decorations?"

"I hope so. John said if we run out of room, we can take the rest of the decorations to the old steamboat museum. There are a couple of rooms that aren't being used."

"Wherever they go, they won't be there for long. The store owners will want the decorations in the next three weeks."

Emma couldn't believe how quickly the weeks were flying by. It only seemed like yesterday that they were planning what they would do. "I thought I'd set up a small Christmas scene with the decorations and photograph them for the website. That way, anyone booking tickets for our events will get a taste of what Sapphire Bay will look like."

"That's a great idea."

The door to the storage room burst open and Molly and Dylan rushed inside.

"Hi, Kylie!" Molly yelled from behind a dinosaur mask. "We're big, mean, dinosaurs. Grrr."

"And there's a bigger one behind you," Mr. Jessop said as he lumbered through the door. "And this dinosaur likes eating little dinosaurs for dinner."

Molly and Dylan shrieked before sprinting around Mr. Jessop and heading into the foyer of the church.

"Don't worry," Mr. Jessop said. "By the time dinner is ready, all the children would have calmed down."

"How many arrived for story and craft time?" Emma asked.

"Sixteen. Word is spreading about the storytelling dinosaur in Sapphire Bay." With a proud grin, Gordon Jessop straightened his dinosaur costume and stomped out of the room.

Kylie laughed. "You won't need to worry about Molly and Dylan waking up during the night. They'll be so tired they'll sleep through anything."

Emma placed the packing slip with the ones she'd already checked. "That would be bliss. By the time Jack arrives, they could be sound asleep."

"I didn't know he was back from Manhattan."

"He flew into Polson this afternoon. Some days, I feel like I'm stuck between a rock and a hard place. After Mark left, I've focused on making sure Dylan and Molly are happy. I don't know if I can be part of Jack's life, too."

"Do you want to be part of his life?"

"I do, but it isn't that easy."

"When have our lives ever been easy? If you don't follow your heart, you might regret it."

"You should have been a counselor instead of a florist."

Kylie grimaced. "It's easy to give people advice, but not so easy to see what's happening in your own life. If I ever meet the man of my dreams, you might have to give me a reality check."

"Whoever you decide to love will be the luckiest man in the world."

"What if he's allergic to flowers?"

Emma smiled. "As long as he isn't allergic to love, you'll be fine."

JACK STOOD outside Emma's home. He could hear Molly and Dylan playing in the backyard, laughing at something they were doing. He had only been gone four days, but he'd missed seeing them, listening to their funny stories, and being part of their lives.

He looked down at the flowers he'd bought from Kylie's flower shop. The pale pink roses were fragile and delicate. A lot like the way he felt. He hoped Emma had thought about where she saw their relationship heading because, right now, he didn't have a clue.

"Jack!" Dylan raced toward him with a big grin on his face. "Come and see what we've made." His small hand wrapped around Jack's, pulling him around the corner of the house. "Mr. Jessop pretended he was a dinosaur at The Welcome Center. Molly's helping me make a dinosaur house. We haven't put it by the vegetable garden because dinosaurs like their greens. Do you want to help?"

Jack didn't know how he could possibly say no. Not only was Dylan looking up at him with big blue eyes, but Molly had joined her brother.

"The flowers are pretty," she said wistfully. "Mom grows roses but they don't look as nice as those ones."

Very carefully, Jack pulled one of the stems out of the bouquet and handed it to Molly. "This is for you. It matches the color of your T-shirt."

When she grinned, his mouth dropped open. "You've lost your front tooth."

"It fell out yesterday. The tooth fairy took it home with her last night."

"She got two dollars and the other tooth is wiggly," Dylan said with barely contained excitement. "If Molly gets two dollars for the other tooth, that will be four dollars."

"I'll be rich," Molly said proudly. "Thank you for the flower."

"You're welcome. What can I do to help you build your dinosaur house?"

Dylan picked up an old broom and pulled it across the backyard. "We need to put this against the wheelbarrow. Then we can use a blanket to make a roof."

"'cos dinosaurs need a roof on their houses in case it rains," Molly said matter-of-factly.

Jack hoped Emma knew what the twins were doing.

So far, their dinosaur house consisted of four deck chairs and a wheelbarrow placed in a circle. It reminded Jack of the indoor forts he used to make with Noah. His mom's furniture would be turned around, the back of the sofa or chairs used as walls in their imaginary playground.

Dylan tugged a blanket across the grass. "Here it is," he huffed. "We tried lifting it over the chairs, but it was too heavy."

"Does your mom know you've got one of her blankets?"

"She doesn't mind." Molly grabbed a corner of the blanket and pulled. "But we have to take it into the garage before we go to sleep."

With some dubious teamwork and a lot of luck, the blanket landed on the roof of the dinosaur house.

Molly dropped to her hands and knees and crawled through the makeshift door. "This is awesome. Come and have a look, Dylan."

Dylan and Jack looked through the legs of the chairs at the same time. Even if he said so himself, Jack thought they'd done a good job of creating an imaginary house.

A pair of jean-clad legs appeared beside him. "Are you looking for the dinosaurs?"

Jack and Dylan poked their heads out of the tent.

Emma stood beside them holding a green plastic container.

"You found them," Dylan said as he reached for the box.

"You left them in the living room. Hi, Jack."

He could have gazed at Emma all night. With her hair caught in a ponytail and a cap shading her eyes, she looked as though she was going to a baseball game. "Do you want to look inside the dinosaur house?"

Emma crouched beside him. "I've been hearing a lot about it." She crawled into the center of the tent. "This is wonderful."

Molly took a pink dinosaur out of the container. "This is the mommy. She's the same color as your flowers, Jack."

Emma looked around the dinosaur house.

Jack had left the roses beneath the barbecue table. He cleared his throat and started backing out of the tent. "I'll be back in a minute." He was nearly clear of the chairs when his foot caught the edge of the broom. With the weight of the blanket pressing against its brushes, it didn't take much to send the broom crashing to the ground.

One side of the blanket collapsed, taking the next chair with it. Like a pack of cards, the whole tent started to wobble.

"The dinosaurs will get squashed!" Molly shrieked.

Emma jumped to her feet, holding up the center of the blanket with her head and arms. "They'll be okay. Pick up the chairs, Dylan, and set them back on their legs."

Jack stood and grabbed the edge of the blanket.

Dylan picked up the chairs before looking inside his dinosaur container. "They're okay."

"Mommy saved us from a disaster." Molly rushed into the tent and wrapped her arms around Emma's legs.

Emma's voice was heavy with laughter. "It's all in a day's work for supermom. Can I let go of the blanket now?"

Jack made sure the edges were over the back of the chairs. "It should be fine." While Emma was backing out of the tent, he collected the roses he'd bought for her.

Her eyes widened when she saw the large bouquet.

"These are for you," he said nervously. "I thought you might like them."

"Jack gave me a flower, too," Molly said. "It's pretty and pink, just like my T-shirt."

The blush on Emma's face was as soft as the rose petals. She took the flowers and lifted them to her nose. "They smell amazing. Like cotton candy and gummy bears."

"Can I smell them?" Molly asked. As she inhaled the sweet scent, she smiled. "They're yummy."

Dylan picked up his container. "Come on, Molly. Let's play with our dinosaurs inside."

Jack smiled as they tore across the yard. "I guess that leaves us to put everything away."

"Not quite." Emma held onto his shirt and pulled him close. "I'm glad you're here."

And with the kind of kiss he'd been dreaming of, she welcomed him back to the only place that felt like home.

CHAPTER 12

*B*y the time Dylan and Molly were in bed, Jack was less nervous about talking to Emma. But that didn't mean he was completely relaxed.

Her family was going through some big changes and he didn't know what would happen.

"Thank you for listening to the twins' stories." Emma placed a cup of coffee on the table beside him.

"I enjoyed hearing them, especially when Molly roared like a dinosaur."

Emma smiled. "It was louder at The Welcome Center. There were sixteen children, plus Mr. Jessop, trying to see who could be the biggest, loudest dinosaur."

Jack cradled the cup of coffee in his hands. "How was Mark's visit?"

"It was better than I expected. It took Dylan a little while to get used to him but, in the end, it all worked out. Molly and Dylan emailed him last night and they got a reply straight away. I guess that's a step in the right direction."

"Does he want shared custody of the twins?"

"Not at the moment. My lawyer is sending through a

parenting agreement that we'll look at next week. Mark has invited us to Evergreen Lodge. It will have to wait until the next school break, but it will be nice for Molly and Dylan to see where their dad lives."

Jack was glad the twins had enjoyed Mark's visit. It couldn't have been easy meeting a father who was a stranger to them.

He studied Emma's face. Jack wasn't sure her experience of the weekend was as positive as her children's. "Are you okay?"

"It was a little surreal seeing Mark again. I thought he might have changed, and he has, but it just confused me even more. He has a lot of regrets, and the twins and I are at the top of his list." Emma looked down at her coffee. "It took him a long time to come to terms with his childhood and work out what's important to him. When he saw you at the cabin, he panicked."

Last night, Jack had reread the profile his company had made of Mark. Apart from some sealed juvenile records, his life read like a textbook case of a child who had lived with a highly abusive parent in a toxic environment. "What happened when Mark was seventeen?"

For a few seconds, Emma was silent. "If I tell you, you have to promise not to say anything to anyone else. It's a part of Mark's life that still haunts him."

"I promise."

Emma closed her eyes and took a deep breath.

When she looked at Jack, the pain of what her ex-husband had lived through was etched on her face. "You know from Mark's file that his dad was a violent alcoholic. When he wasn't in prison, he used his family as punching bags. When Mark turned fifteen, things got really bad."

Emma bit her bottom lip. "Mark had been in and out of the juvenile courts for a long time. On his seventeenth birthday, his dad took a cocktail of drugs and alcohol. He attacked Mark's mom and starting punching Briana, Mark's sister. When Mark came home and saw what was happening, he tried to stop his father. They were outside his parents' apartment when his dad's head hit the concrete curb. He died an hour later. If it weren't for a good defense lawyer, Mark would be in prison."

Jack held Emma's hand. Her eyes were bright with unshed tears. "What happened after Mark's father died?"

"You'd think their lives would have been better but, for a long time, they were worse. Mark started using drugs and his sister became suicidal. It wasn't until he nearly killed himself, that Mark's life changed for the better. When I met him, he had a full-time job, an apartment, and big dreams. He wanted to make a better life for himself. And, for a while, he did."

"What changed?"

Emma glanced toward the staircase. "Becoming a parent brought back a lot of the feelings he'd tried to bury. He was worried he'd turn into his father; that he wouldn't be able to provide for our new family."

"So he left?"

Emma nodded. "Coming to Sapphire Bay was one of the hardest things he's ever done." She looked directly into Jack's eyes. "You probably think I'm crazy to want Molly and Dylan to have a relationship with Mark, but he's their father."

"He's also your ex-husband."

"I don't understand."

Jack swallowed deeply. As much as he didn't want to ask, he needed to know if Emma wanted Mark to be part of her life. "Is there a chance you'll get back together?"

"With Mark?" Emma frowned. "I don't know why you would ask me that question. Mark has come a long way and I'm really pleased he's met Molly and Dylan. But I don't want any kind of romantic relationship with him."

Jack breathed a sigh of relief. "I'm pleased you said that. You seemed to get on so well that I thought—"

"You thought I'd want Mark in my life permanently."

"Something like that," Jack muttered.

Emma squeezed his fingers. "Kylie asked me the same thing. I've forgiven Mark for leaving me with two babies, a mortgage, and no income. But that doesn't mean I want to rekindle our relationship. We're trying to make this new relationship work for Dylan and Molly's sake."

"I don't know if I could do that."

"If we don't, it will be the twins who suffer."

Jack kissed her cheek, then reached for his jacket. "I bought you this while I was in New York City. I hope you like it."

Emma stared at the rectangular jewelry box in horror. "You shouldn't have bought me anything. I really don't wear a lot of—"

Jack opened the box.

"Oh, my," Emma whispered. "It's beautiful."

Nestled against a silky length of satin was a glowing pearl necklace. "When I met you at Noah and Cassie's wedding, I heard you say you'd borrowed the pearl necklace you were wearing from a friend. As soon as I saw this one, I knew it was made for you."

"I can't—"

"You can." Jack took the necklace out of the box. "If it makes you feel any better, it wasn't expensive."

"It wasn't?"

The hope on Emma's face made his small, white lie a little easier to digest. "I'll still be able to pay my rent. Would you like me to help you put it on?"

"Yes, please." Emma carefully lifted the necklace out of the box and turned sideways.

Jack clicked the clasp into place. "It looks amazing. You're even more beautiful than the day we met."

A blush warmed her cheeks. "I'm wearing my old jeans and a T-shirt."

"It doesn't matter. It's what's inside your heart that's important."

Emma sighed. "I'm beginning to realize, Jack Devlin, that you can very easily sweep a girl off her feet."

He held Emma's face between his hands. "As long as it's you I'm sweeping off her feet, I'm happy."

Emma leaned forward. "So am I."

As their lips touched, Jack knew he'd found the woman he wanted to spend the rest of his life with. All he had to do was tell her how much he loved her.

And for someone who had trouble telling his brother how much he meant to him, that wouldn't be easy.

EMMA LEFT her backpack on the grassy bank and breathed deeply. Earlier this morning, Jack had picked her and the twins up and driven to one of the hiking trails around Flathead Lake.

With only a few days left until Molly and Dylan started first grade, it was wonderful to be out of the house enjoying the fresh air and each other's company. The fact that Jack could share it with them was an added bonus.

Jack stood beside her. "I'm glad we didn't turn back. The view is spectacular."

He wasn't wrong. Sunlight glistened off the deep blue lake. A gentle breeze took away the sting of the heat, but it was still incredibly warm. In the distance, mountains rose high into the sky, giving the landscape a rugged beauty.

"Can we have something to drink?" Dylan asked.

Emma smiled at her son. "Of course, we can. If you don't have enough water left in your drink bottles, I've got more water in my backpack."

Dylan and Molly had done so well today. It had taken two hours to get to the top of the trail. Even though they'd left early, the sun had still made the climb tiring.

Molly dropped to the ground and sighed. "Are we at the top yet?"

"We are," Jack said. "We've made it to the top of Grouse Mountain."

"Yeah! Does that mean we can have our candy?"

Jack smiled and opened his backpack. Four small bags of fudge appeared in his hand. "There's one for each of us. Brooke made the fudge this morning."

Emma could taste the sweetness already. "Brooke collected her decorations for the Christmas on Main Street event yesterday. She can't wait for the opening night Santa parade."

Jack handed Dylan a bag of fudge. "Isn't it a little early for her to be decorating her store?"

"I'm photographing Sweet Treats for the website. Brooke probably has the largest newsletter list of any of the businesses in Sapphire Bay. Between her customers and the social media advertising we'll do, news should spread quickly about the Christmas program."

"How many visitors do you need to break even with your costs?"

"It depends on the event, but we don't have many overhead expenses. The entire program is being run by volunteers and Noah's company has donated the Christmas decorations for the Main Street event. We'll need at least one hundred guests to make the Christmas party pay for itself, but not as many for the carol competition."

Jack bit into a piece of fudge and smiled. "Yum. What about the train ride? Are you still doing that?"

"I'm waiting to hear back from the company that owns the railroad tracks and the trust that owns the steam train. I have no idea how many tickets we'll need to sell, but it will need to be more than for the other events."

"If you want any help, let me know."

Emma kissed his cheek. "I will."

"Jack, can you come with us when we start first grade?" Molly asked. "We'll be in Ms. Oliver's class. She's really nice."

"Are you sure it's okay?"

Dylan wiggled closer to Jack. "Mom will be there, too."

When Jack looked at Emma, she smiled. "It's fine. They start school a week from Monday. We have to be there by eight-thirty and the parents and friends leave at nine."

"We've already met our teacher. She has a pet spider. You could look at it while you're there," Dylan said helpfully. "Molly thinks it's creepy, but I think it's awesome."

A shiver ran through Molly's small body. "I don't like spiders."

"That's 'cos you're a girl."

Emma's eyebrows rose. Since they were babies, she'd tried hard to make sure the twins didn't slip into old stereotypes. "Who told you that?"

Dylan frowned. "Mr. Jessop said girls don't like worms or spiders or anything slippery."

"That's not true," Molly said with a growl. "Girls can do anything."

Jack nudged Dylan. "Molly's right. Girls and boys can do anything they set their minds to."

"But I won't set my mind to spiders," Molly said quickly. "Or worms. Want to look for something slippery?"

Dylan swallowed his last piece of fudge. "Sure."

Jack stood and held out his hand to Emma. "This could be

an adventure for everyone. Finding slippery things won't be easy on top of a mountain."

Grinning, she scrambled to her feet. "Or it could be easier than you think. Girls and boys can do anything."

BY TUESDAY AFTERNOON, Emma was sitting in the church office putting the finishing touches on the Christmas program's website. So far, everything was coming together nicely. The railroad company had agreed to let them use the tracks and the steam train trust was happy to donate the train for the fundraiser. All the church had to do was pay the driver and provide all the gifts and food for the passengers.

Getting final approval from Pastor John, organizing a meeting with the fundraising committee, and making sure all the tasks for the other projects were on schedule were next on her list.

"Hi, Emma. I heard you were in the office." John walked into the admin area holding two large files. "How was your weekend?"

"It was great. We went on a long hike, washed a mountain of dirty washing, and made enough cookies to sink a ship. What about you?"

"It wasn't as exciting as yours."

Emma sighed. "You spent all weekend working, didn't you?"

"Maybe."

It didn't matter what anyone said, John worked 24/7. He was always there for everyone, ready to lend a hand with whatever needed fixing. Having The Welcome Center right beside the church didn't help, either. It was too easy for him to pop in and see what was happening.

"The world won't fall apart if you turn off your phone and do something for yourself."

"That's easier said than done."

"I know, but it's important."

John smiled. "If it makes you feel better, I won't be here on Wednesday and Thursday."

She'd heard that before but, nine times out of ten, an emergency brought John back to the church. "Are you staying in Sapphire Bay?"

"I'm driving to Lakeside and spending two days fishing with a friend."

"Thank goodness for that. I hope you have a great time."

"So do I. Is there anything you need me to do before then?"

Emma looked down at the laptop. "It would be good to schedule a time to review the Christmas program's website."

John sat in the seat opposite the desk. "We can do it now, if you like? Willow has given me a pile of invoices to sort through, but they can wait."

"Are you sure? You know what she said the last time she was in the office."

John was a wonderful person, but finances weren't his strong point. To keep the IRS happy, they'd organized a roster of people who spent two hours each week keeping everything up to date. Willow was one of those volunteers.

"I know," John muttered. "These invoices are part of her plan to make me financially independent."

"You can't keep everything in your head. If something happened to you, no one would know what to do."

John pulled himself to his feet. "All right. I'll code these invoices and sort them into date order before we meet. How does twenty minutes sound?"

"Perfect. If I'm not here, I won't be far away. Dylan and

Molly are helping Mr. Jessop in the garden. I want to make sure they're okay."

"Sounds good to me. I'll see you soon." He started to move away, then stopped. "I saw Mabel over the weekend. She's excited about the book you're helping her publish."

"I'm glad. She's spent a lot of time polishing the manuscript. Did she tell you Natalie is creating the illustrations?"

"She did. It will be a great book."

Emma glanced at the files.

"Okay. I get the hint." With a reluctant sigh, John walked into his office.

Emma smiled. With John busy with the church's finances, and Molly and Dylan working in the garden, she had more than enough time to finish the last page on the website. And if she were lucky, she might be able to phone Kylie and arrange their next meeting.

JACK STUDIED a realtor's website on his laptop. He couldn't believe he'd been living in Sapphire Bay for five weeks. Apart from a few nights when Cassie and Noah had other bookings for Acorn Cottage, he'd been able to stay in the small house overlooking Flathead Lake.

But he couldn't live here forever. Most of September and October were booked solid with tourists wanting to enjoy the fall colors of Montana. From then on, skiers would be filling the small cottage to capacity. With the Blacktail Mountain ski area only an hour away, Sapphire Bay was a great location for a winter getaway.

He clicked on a link to a four-bedroom home for sale at Finley Point. The property wasn't far from Sapphire Bay and had an incredible view of Flathead Lake. The photos showed a 1960s house in need of some remodeling, but it had all the space and street appeal Jack was looking for.

He added it to his wish list and kept scrolling. After another ten minutes of viewing properties, he was baffled by the limited supply of houses. Even in his price range, no one wanted to sell their homes. His only other option was to purchase a plot of land and build a new home. But land with a view was even more scarce than an existing home.

How anyone on a limited income could afford to buy or rent in and around Sapphire Bay was a mystery. Emma had told him it was hard to find any accommodation, but he'd thought she was exaggerating. Thank goodness for Pastor John and the tiny home village. Without the houses they were building, even more people would be living on the streets.

"Are you in the middle of something or can I interrupt?"

Jack looked up at his grandfather. "Come in. I was just hunting through a few realtors' websites looking for a house. There's hardly anything available."

"It's like that year-round. I was lucky to find my home as quickly as I did. Why are you looking at properties?"

"I'm thinking about moving here."

Patrick Devlin didn't bother to hide his delight. "I've got the name of the realtor who found my house. I'll send you her contact details when I get home. Do you want me to talk to Mabel? She has her finger on the pulse of what's happening in town. If anyone knows of properties that are coming on the market, she will."

"That would be great." He didn't want his granddad getting too excited. A lot needed to happen before he moved anywhere.

"How are the two houses coming along that we drywalled?"

"The plastering is finished and the first coat of paint is

drying. Bathrooms go in on Thursday. By Saturday, they'll both be finished."

Jack was impressed with how quickly the tiny homes were being built. "If I could find an empty plot of land, I'd ask the volunteers to build me a modular home."

"It's funny you should say that. After the tiny home village is complete, the young people doing Pastor John's building apprenticeship won't have much work. We're looking at starting a construction company that specializes in building modular homes and transporting them on site, ready-made."

"You're eighty-one years old, Granddad. You're supposed to be enjoying your retirement, not starting a new company."

"I will have an advisory role, that's all."

Jack's eyebrows rose. "Are you sure?"

"As sure as I can be about anything," his granddad replied evasively. "But I didn't come here to talk about modular homes. Emma asked if I wanted to be Santa in the Main Street Christmas Parade. You didn't put her up to it, did you?"

"You'll have to talk to Noah. Will you do it?"

"Absolutely not. Sitting on a bright red sleigh in the middle of the street isn't my idea of fun."

Jack shrugged. "It's for a good cause. Besides, you'd make a great Santa. All you need is a little more padding around the middle."

Patrick looked down at his flat stomach.

"Before you make up your mind, think about the children who will be watching the parade. They won't care if you feel uncomfortable on the sleigh. All they want is to see Santa."

Patrick crossed his arms in front of his chest. "I'll think about it."

"When do you need to tell Emma if you'll do it?"

"She's ordering the costume on Thursday."

Jack didn't take any notice of his granddad's grumpy

voice. He could be stubborn when he needed to be but, this time, Jack was sure Patrick would help Emma. He had a soft spot for Molly and Dylan and wouldn't want to let any children down.

"While you're here, can I ask you a question?"

"Sure." Patrick sat on a kitchen chair. "I'm listening."

"Emma and I talked after her ex-husband went home. I know she likes me, but I don't know if she thinks of me as a friend or something more. How did you tell grandma how much she meant to you?"

Patrick smiled. "I gave her daisies."

Jack's eyes widened. "I hope you bought them and didn't pick them out of someone's garden."

"I might have borrowed them from a neighbor's house," Patrick admitted. "But they were on vacation and the flowers were going to waste."

"And that makes it all right?"

His granddad's smile softened. "It made it so right that we hardly left each other's side after that. You don't need grand gestures to impress the right woman. What you need are small gestures that mean the world."

Jack wished a bouquet of daisies would have the same effect on Emma. "When I came back from Manhattan, I gave Emma a pearl necklace."

"And what did she say?"

"That it was beautiful."

"Well, there you go. Next time, buy her daisies and see what happens."

Judging by the twinkle in his grandfather's eyes, Patrick assumed a lot would happen. Jack wasn't so sure.

CHAPTER 13

The following day, Jack was working from Acorn Cottage when his phone rang. He smiled when he saw who was calling. "Hi, Emma."

"Hi. I just saw your granddad. How did you do it?"

For a moment, Jack had no idea what she was talking about. Then he remembered the conversation about Santa. "Are you talking about the Christmas Parade?"

"I am. Patrick came to see me. He's happy to be Santa. I didn't think he wanted to sit on the sleigh."

"Neither did I." Jack saved the document he was working on and closed the file. "It must have been the thought of disappointing all the children that did it."

"Well, whatever you said, it worked. Thank you."

"You're welcome. I only have one question—how will a sleigh carry Granddad down Main Street? Unless it suddenly starts snowing in September, the sleigh won't move."

"A company in Bigfork is lending us their Christmas parade sleigh. Hidden in the bottom of the frame are wheels. As long as we replace Santa's reindeer with motorcycles, it will be perfect."

Jack could imagine the reaction of the crowd when a whole lot of bikers, dressed in their black leathers, pulled Santa down Main Street. "Do you know a motorcycle club that can help?"

"I spoke to a friend in Bozeman. The Mothers' Motorcycle Club does a lot of charity rides. The bikers will be in Missoula for another event and are happy to drive a little farther north for our parade."

"You've been busy."

Emma sighed. "It's been chaotic, but I'm getting there. I still need final approval from John and the rest of the committee before I confirm everything."

"How are you managing to do all your other work?"

"Kylie and Willow have been great. So have Mr. Jessop and Pastor John. Between all of us, I've been able to keep up to date with my own work and still have time to volunteer at The Welcome Center. Hang on a minute. Someone has just come into the office."

While Emma was helping whoever had arrived, Jack thought about what his granddad had said. If a bunch of daisies was the turning point in his relationship, Jack was willing to try the same thing.

"Sorry about that," Emma said quickly. "John has gone to the steamboat museum and no one else is in the office. Are you getting lots of work done?"

"More than I thought. I need to go back to Manhattan at the end of next week, but working from Sapphire Bay has been easier than I imagined. Would you and the twins like to come to Acorn Cottage for dinner?"

"We'd love to, but we can't. I've organized a fundraising committee meeting at my place. If you don't mind eating a little earlier than usual, you could have dinner with us."

Jack didn't mind what time he ate, as long as it was with

Emma and the twins. "I'll bring dessert. What time do you want me there?"

"Any time after four-thirty. We'll have dinner at five."

"Sounds good. I'll see you later."

"Bye."

Jack checked his watch. He had two hours before he needed to leave. That would give him enough time to finish the reports he was working on, have a shower, and find some daisies.

On impulse, he walked across to the window overlooking Noah and Cassie's cottage. Sure enough, sitting under one of the large windows were two daisy bushes.

If raiding someone's garden was good enough for his granddad, it was good enough to for him. Especially when the flowers belonged to his brother and sister-in-law.

"Are you stealing our flowers?"

Jack jumped and almost speared his toes with the scissors. "Give me a warning next time you sneak up on me."

"It wouldn't be as much fun if you heard me. Why are you decapitating the daisy bushes?"

Jack snipped another handful of flowers off one of the plants. "It's for a good cause." He looked in the bucket he'd brought with him. It was overflowing with white daisies, but was it enough to impress Emma?

"You might want to define 'a good cause'. If Cassie sees the hatchet job you've made of her plants, she won't be impressed."

"They aren't that bad."

Noah made a scoffing sound. "There's a big hole in the side of one plant, and the other looks like it's had the worst haircut of its life. Why do you need so many flowers?"

"I want to make a good impression."

"On who?"

"Emma."

Noah's eyebrows rose. "You've been talking to Granddad."

"How did you know?" Jack used his hand to fluff the worst daisy bush. It didn't make any difference. Unfortunately, it still looked like a wild animal had devoured it.

Noah took the scissors off Jack and tried to make everything look a little less mauled. "The daisy story will go down in history as the beginning of life as we know it. When I was dating Cassie, he told me the story about giving Grandma some daisies." Noah gestured at the bushes. "You could have taken the flowers from one bush. At least that way we could have pretended you were pruning the plants."

Jack frowned. Nothing Noah did was making any difference to the forlorn bushes. "Do you think Cassie will notice?"

"Is the sky blue?" Noah handed him the scissors. "I'll leave you to tell her what you've done. Knowing Cassie, she'll think it's romantic, then send me outside to clean up your mess."

Noah checked his watch. "I'm running short of time, but I can tidy up the bushes tomorrow."

"Thanks for the offer but, if I let you lose with a pair of hand pruners, we might not have any daisies left."

Jack picked up the bucket. "I could have a hidden talent."

"Not that I can tell." Noah studied Jack's face. "Good luck with Emma. I hope whatever you're planning goes well."

"So do I. When did you know you loved Cassie?"

Noah's smiled was instant. "She was standing a few feet from here, teaching herself how to waltz. As soon as I saw her dancing barefoot on the grass, I knew I was in love. I'm not sure she felt the same way but, in the end, it didn't matter. Is it that serious between you and Emma?"

"I feel whole when I'm with her, as if I've been waiting my entire life to meet her and the twins."

Noah's deep frown made Jack's heart pound.

"Be careful," his brother warned. "Emma's dealing with a lot at the moment."

"I know. That's why I'm giving her the daisies."

Noah gave a rueful grin. "I hope she realizes what we've sacrificed."

"I'll tell her after she realizes she loves me. See you tomorrow."

"Don't bring your scissors," Noah yelled after him.

"I won't need them," he yelled back. At least he really hoped he didn't need to raid his brother's garden again. Apart from running the risk of annoying Cassie, Jack didn't want Emma to think he couldn't afford to buy her flowers. Because he could, many times over.

But, as his grandfather had told him, this wasn't about a grand gesture. It was about a message coming straight from his heart—and his brother's daisy bushes.

THE FIRST THING Emma heard after Jack arrived was Molly's excited voice. She waited for them to come into the kitchen but, no one appeared, not even Dylan.

As soon as she'd finished preparing the chicken for dinner, she washed her hands and made her way through to the living room. "Hi, Jack. I hope you..." Emma stared at the huge bouquet of daisies he was holding.

"Aren't they amazing?" Molly was jumping up and down. "They're for you!"

Jack held the bouquet toward her. "Thanks for inviting me to dinner."

Emma looked into his eyes. A warm rush of emotion slipped along her spine, cartwheeled inside her tummy, and headed straight to her heart. "They're lovely. Thank you."

"You're welcome. I also brought ice cream and chocolate cake for dessert."

Molly rushed across to a box on the coffee table. "They're in here. Jack said we need to put the ice cream in the freezer in case it melts."

Before she could answer Molly, Dylan appeared beside her holding a large glass vase.

She quickly took it out of his hands before it dropped onto his bare feet. "That was good thinking."

"We still need to put water inside. Otherwise, the flowers will die."

"We could add some water to the vase now if you like?"

"Could I carry the flowers?" Dylan asked.

"Of course, you can. Here you go." Emma smiled. The bouquet was as wide as his chest and rose above his eyes.

Molly leaned over the box. "I'll put the ice cream in the freezer. You can follow me." She looked at the floor, then at the bouquet in Dylan's arms. "Don't step on the Lego."

Jack scooped up the spaceship they'd made earlier. "You've got a clear run to the kitchen now."

Cautiously, Dylan followed Molly.

She held open the door, giving her brother instructions about what was ahead of him.

Emma and Jack followed.

"I feel spoiled," Emma said. "These will look so pretty in the kitchen." She felt Jack's hand rest lightly on her waist. The gentle pressure made her turn around.

"I've missed you."

Emma smiled. "We spoke on the phone yesterday."

"It's not the same."

She knew what Jack meant. It was nice spending time together, doing normal things that most people took for granted, especially when they were in a relationship.

Emma hugged the vase close to her chest. "It will be hard when you go back to Manhattan."

The smile on Jack's face disappeared. "How would you feel if I stayed here?"

"Has something happened to Noah or your granddad?"

Jack's eyes widened. "No, they're okay. I meant—"

"Mom, I'm ready for the vase."

While Emma was speaking with Jack, Dylan had pulled a chair across to the counter and was waiting beside the sink.

"I'll be there in a minute." She looked at Jack and frowned.

"It's okay," he said. "It can wait until after dinner."

"Are you sure?"

"Positive."

"Are you sure your family is okay?"

"They're fine. Dylan's perched on the edge of the chair, waiting for you."

Emma was sure he could wait another few minutes, but if Jack wasn't in a hurry to explain why he wanted to stay in Sapphire Bay, then after dinner it would have to be.

"I'll get the cake," Molly said as she ran past them.

Jack smiled at Emma. "I'll go with Molly. I'm not convinced the chocolate cake will make it to the kitchen in one piece."

With Jack helping Molly, Emma filled the vase with water and held it steady while Dylan arranged the flowers.

With all the chatter and laughter filling the kitchen, they sounded like a regular family. Except they weren't. But maybe, if Jack was thinking about staying in Sapphire Bay, they would have time to see if they could be.

Emma kissed the top of Dylan's head. Two months ago,

they hadn't met Jack and she didn't know where Mark had gone. Now, everything had changed.

Hopefully, for the better.

CHAPTER 14

*A*fter they'd finished dinner, Jack was getting dessert ready when someone knocked on the front door.

Molly leaped off her chair. "I'll get it."

Emma checked her watch. "It could be Pastor John or Bailey and Kylie."

"Would you like me to go home?" Jack asked.

"Definitely not, unless you need to be somewhere else? Our meeting shouldn't go for very long. I only want to make sure everyone's happy with the Christmas program before I confirm the bookings."

Jack took another three plates out of the cupboard. "In that case, I'd love to stay."

Emma smiled. "Consider yourself an honorary member of the Christmas fundraising committee."

When she kissed his cheek, Jack smiled. It still amazed him how quickly he'd become part of Emma and the twins' lives. He hated to use the word settled, but that's how he felt. After years of feeling as though something was missing from his life, he'd finally found somewhere that felt like home.

Molly rushed into the kitchen. "It's Kylie and the lady we met yesterday."

Dylan took a handful of spoons out of the cutlery drawer. "Her name is Bailey. I remember that 'cos it's the name of my friend."

Kylie walked into the kitchen first. "I hope it's okay to come a few minutes early." She grinned when she saw Jack. "Hi. I thought you might have gone back to Manhattan."

"Not for a while. How's your flower shop?"

"It's so busy." Kylie left her bag beside the kitchen counter. "Usually, by this time of the year, the wedding season is slowing down. But, for some reason, I've been inundated with couples tying the knot. Putting all the flower arrangements together, along with the bouquets and table decorations, makes life a little stressful. Jack, have you met Bailey?"

He smiled at the young woman standing beside Kylie. "No, I haven't. It's nice to meet you."

"Same here. Have you moved to Sapphire Bay, as well?"

Jack hadn't talked to Emma about moving here and, until that happened, he wasn't saying anything. "I'm temporarily staying in my brother and sister-in-law's vacation home."

"You're lucky. It was almost impossible to find a house I could rent for a few months."

"Did you get something?"

"I did, but only because my sister knows the owner."

Emma touched Jack's arm. "Bailey's sister moved here about eighteen months ago. She married Caleb Andrews."

Jack looked more closely at Bailey. "Is Sam your sister?" Although Bailey had darker hair than Sam, the smile on her face was so much like her sister's that they could have been twins.

"I'm Sam's younger sister. How do you know Caleb and Sam?"

"I met Caleb through another friend who lives in Sapphire Bay. It's a small world."

"It definitely is."

Another knock on the door had Dylan moving fast. "Stay there, Molly. It's my turn."

Jack held back a smile as Molly veered right, rushing across to the windows overlooking the front yard. "It's Pastor John."

Emma turned on the coffeepot. "I'll go."

"Stay here with Bailey and Kylie," Jack said. "I can bring John through to the kitchen."

"Okay. I'll make coffee."

By the time Jack walked through to the living room, Dylan was halfway across the room with John.

Jack had no idea what John had been doing, but he looked terrible.

"Do you think Pastor John would like to see the star Dad made me?" Dylan asked.

"That sounds like a great idea." After Dylan left the room, Jack pointed to the sofa. "If you want to relax for a few minutes, we can wait here. Emma's making Kylie and Bailey coffee. They're not in a rush to start the meeting."

John sat on the sofa. "Thanks. It's been a long day."

"You look like death warmed over. Is everything all right?"

"I'm tired, that's all."

Jack had met John too many times not to know it was more than that. "Is there anything I can do?"

John shook his head. "A young couple from the church were involved in an accident this morning. They're in the hospital in Polson. When they're more stable, they'll be flown to the Intensive Care Unit in Kalispell.'"

"Will they be okay?"

"The doctors don't know." John rubbed his eyes. "Their

families are devastated. It's days like this that make me realize how fragile our lives are."

Jack had never considered the stress John must be under. Not only was he providing services and programs to the community's most vulnerable, he was also a shoulder to cry on, someone who listened to a person's deepest, darkest fears, and a sounding board for things to come. John was everything to everyone and that kind of commitment could take its toll.

Jack studied the dark circles under John's eyes. Everyone needed to unwind, recharge their batteries, and be happy. He suspected that, taking time away from his congregation, from the people who turned to him for help, was something John didn't do often.

"Noah, William, and I are going fishing tomorrow morning. You should come with us."

"I can't. I've got a busy day ahead of me."

Jack wasn't giving up that easily. "It will only be for a couple of hours. William wants to be on the lake by six o'clock. We'll be back before some people are getting out of bed."

John leaned back in his chair. "Two hours?"

"That's all. No one will ask you to bless the fish we catch, if that's what's worrying you."

For the first time since he arrived, John smiled. "That's a relief. Okay. I can do two hours."

"Do you want me to pick you up on my way into town? I'll be driving past the church at about five-fifty."

"Thanks. I'd appreciate a ride." John took a deep breath. "I think I'm getting into fishing mode now. I feel better than I did when I arrived."

"Wait until you taste the chocolate cake I brought. The sugar rush will give you a permanent smile." Jack turned as Dylan walked into the living room.

"I found the star. Molly had it in her room." Dylan stood in front of John, holding his gift in the palm of his hands. "My dad made this from a piece of wood he found around Evergreen Lake."

John admired the intricately carved decoration. "It's incredible. Your dad is a very talented person."

"He made Molly a sculpture of a ballerina. Do you want to hold the star?"

"I'd love to."

Dylan carefully placed the star in John's hands. "Stars are special. They make pictures in the sky called constellations. Did you know you can follow the stars so you don't get lost?"

John's gaze connected with Dylan's. "I did, but every now and then I need to be reminded. Thank you for sharing your star with me."

"That's okay. Do you want some dessert?"

"I'd love some." Carefully, John gave Dylan's star back to him.

With Emma's son leading the way, they walked into the kitchen.

Jack believed that, sometimes, the strangest coincidences created the most impactful moments of your life. And tonight, he'd seen another.

Dylan's six-year-old logic had single-handedly reminded both Jack and John that, even when life threw you a curve ball, there was always a way through the turmoil. All you had to do was follow the stars to find your way home.

EMMA DIDN'T KNOW where Jack and Dylan had gone. It shouldn't have taken more than a few minutes to bring John into the kitchen.

Bailey must have seen her glance at the kitchen door. "Is Jack your husband?"

"No, he's my friend."

Kylie took three more cups out of the cupboard. "Special friend, boyfriend, soon to be so much more."

Emma's cheeks flamed under Bailey's amused grin. "Don't listen to Kylie. Her eyes see things that aren't there."

"I'm a family therapist," Bailey said. "I'm trained to see things that aren't there, too. How long have you known each other?"

"Five or six weeks." But, in a good way, it felt a lot longer. She poured everyone a cup of coffee. "There's sugar and cream on the counter."

"And lots and lots of chocolate cake," Molly said from the other side of the kitchen. "Can we have cake now, Mom?"

Emma counted the dessert bowls. "It looks as though Jack's got everything ready. I can't see why not."

Dylan walked into the kitchen, holding his star. John and Jack followed closely behind. She didn't know what John had been doing, but he looked exhausted.

"Hi, John," she said. "Would you like a cup of coffee?"

"I'd love one. Hi, Kylie. Hi, Bailey."

Both women said hello and smiled.

"Have you had dinner?" Emma asked John.

"Not yet. I came straight here from Polson."

"You're in luck. I made chicken salad and we've got plenty of leftovers. Would you like some?"

"It tastes yummy," Molly said as she pulled herself onto the stool beside John.

"In that case, how can I refuse?"

"Do you know what we're having for dessert?" Molly asked.

John's lips twitched. "No, but I'm sure you'll tell me."

"It's chocolate cake," she whispered. "I don't think Jack made it. It looks like one of Megan's cakes."

"That was nice of Jack to bring a cake."

"He likes Mommy."

If Emma's cheeks were red before, they were burning now.

Jack laughed. "I do like your mommy, Molly, but, even if I didn't, I still would have brought a cake with me."

Emma opened the refrigerator, grateful for the cool air hitting her hot face. She pulled out the large bowl of leftovers and made John something to eat. If she fussed around a little too much, no one said anything.

Thankfully, Kylie picked up the Christmas project plan and started talking about the events they were organizing. Even Molly and Dylan seemed to enjoy the easy conversation flowing around the kitchen counter.

By the time they had discussed each step of the projects, John had finished his salad and they'd all moved to the kitchen table.

As the first bite of chocolate cake melted in Emma's mouth, she smiled. If she could choose the best moment of the day, this would be it.

The man she'd fallen in love with was sitting beside her. Molly and Dylan were licking their fingers clean after devouring their cake, and Kylie and Bailey were laughing at something John had said.

Love, laughter, and happiness. You would have to go a long way to beat those three things.

"Have I told you how amazing you are?"

Emma swatted Jack with the dishtowel. "You have, but it won't get you out of washing the dishes."

Jack grinned. "It's a genuine compliment. And, just for the record, I like washing the dishes. It reminds me of staying at the cabin on Shelter Island."

"I knew there must be a silver lining to the dishwasher pump not working."

"We can spend quality time over the soapsuds."

"And dirty dishes." Emma glanced at the plates and bowls stacked on the counter. "Where did all the dishes come from?"

"Seven hungry mouths. Talking about food, I saw Mr. Jessop yesterday. He wanted me to remind you that he'll be planting another crop of vegetables tomorrow. If the twins want to help, he'll be in the garden by nine o'clock."

"He has a soft spot for Dylan and Molly. He'll miss them when they start school next week." Emma handed Jack a pair of bright pink gloves. "These will stop your hands from getting wrinkly."

Jack grinned. "I like the color."

"Molly chose them." She picked up the dishcloth and rinsed it in the soapy water. It had been a wonderful evening. They'd worked through each project plan, approved all the tentative bookings, and added a few more tasks onto their to-do list.

Bailey felt more confident about organizing the Christmas carol competition, and Kylie was looking forward to putting the finishing touches on October's Christmas party.

The train ride around Flathead Lake, however, was still in jeopardy.

"What are you worried about?"

Emma wiped down the counter. "Do you think I'm crazy creating a Santa cave in the middle of nowhere?"

"Only if you don't believe in the magic of Christmas. We could organize it together."

"It will take a lot of time."

Jack shrugged. "It's only for a few months."

At the meeting, they'd gone through the project plan for the train ride. Even to Emma, it seemed like a daunting task. If Jack was serious about staying in Sapphire Bay, having him here would be a huge help. But if he suddenly went back to Manhattan, the whole project could be in trouble.

She finished wiping down the counter and handed Jack the dishcloth. "Of all the events, the train ride will take the most amount of time to organize. Are you sure you can commit to such a big project?"

"I'm positive. Have I told you about the Santa cave beneath one of the large stores in New York City?"

Emma shook her head.

The smile on Jack's face softened. "When I was little, Mom and Dad used to take Noah and me to a store called, B. Altman & Company. The building was like a palace, with towering cream walls and hundreds of windows looking onto Fifth Avenue and 34th Street. At Christmas, huge pine garlands covered the walls and carolers sang on the street corner."

Emma picked up the dishtowel. She knew what he was going to say, but she didn't want to spoil his story.

"The store had the most amazing Santa cave in its basement. There was a carousel and a huge display showing Santa and the elves making gifts for children around the world. You could have your photo taken with Santa and everyone got a free piece of candy. Even when it wasn't Christmas, I used to dream about visiting the cave."

"Did you leave your Christmas wish in the North Pole mailbox?"

Jack's eyes widened. "You went there?"

"It was one of the best things about Christmas. I cried the year Mom told me they weren't having a Santa cave."

Jack sighed. "I was disappointed, too. That's why I'll help you with the train ride. We can create our own cave for the children of Sapphire Bay."

Emma's smiled disappeared. If he really wanted to help, Jack would have to stay in Sapphire Bay for at least four months. If she didn't ask him about what he'd said earlier, she never would. "Everyone has gone home and the twins are in bed. Apart from helping with the train ride, why do you want to stay in Sapphire Bay?"

Jack's hands stilled in the hot, soapy water. "I thought you might already know."

Emma's heart pounded. "I hope I do, but I'd like to hear it from you."

Slowly, Jack peeled off the kitchen gloves and turned to face her. "I love you, Emma. If I go back to Manhattan, I'll miss you and the twins too much. If you'd like to be part of my life, I'd move heaven and earth to make that happen."

She held Jack's hands. He meant the world to her, but telling him how she felt was more difficult than she'd imagined. "I'm happy when we're together. I look forward to seeing you and miss you when I don't." Taking a deep breath, she stepped closer. "Molly and Dylan think you're wonderful, and Kylie told me our souls are destined to be together."

"It sounds as though we've got everyone's seal of approval." Jack wrapped his arms around her shoulders. "What do you think?"

"I want to be a special part of your life. I love you." His relieved smile made her sigh. "I must be bad at showing you how I feel if you were worried about my answer."

"I was terrified you'd tell me you only wanted to be friends."

"Being friends is important."

"So is this," Jack whispered as he nudged her lips with his mouth.

Emma melted into his embrace. She'd only told one other man she loved him, and that relationship had ended in disaster. She hoped and prayed that, this time, everything would be all right.

EMMA OPENED the truck's passenger door. "Hold my hand, Molly. It's busy this morning."

Molly jumped out of the cab, gripping Emma's hand tightly. "Do you think the kittens are still here?"

"I'm not sure." Emma glanced across the truck at Jack. She'd called the animal shelter yesterday, hoping no one had adopted the kittens the twins had seen almost two weeks ago. From the description the staff gave her, Emma was ninety-nine percent positive they were still here. But, until she saw them, she wasn't making any promises to Molly or Dylan.

"Mr. Jessop found his cat here." Dylan didn't need to be reminded about holding someone's hand. He was already standing beside Jack, his small hand wrapped around Jack's fingers. "He called it Oscar."

"That's a good name," Molly said as they waited for a truck to reverse out of a parking space. "I'm going to call my kitten Snowflake, 'cos she's white, just like snow."

"Our kittens might have gone home with someone else."

Molly's bottom lip quivered. "They'll be there, won't they, Jack?"

"I hope so. Let's go and see."

Normally, Molly would be excited. But not today. As they walked into the main reception area, she stayed close to Emma, not saying a word.

Jack spoke to the lady behind the desk and, within a few minutes, they were walking toward the kitten room.

Dylan let go of Jack's hand and stood beside his sister. Silently, he held her hand.

Emma's heart clenched tight. She had a strong suspicion that it wouldn't matter how old Dylan and Molly were, they would always share a special bond. And right now, they were both unsure of what they'd find.

When they reached the door, Dylan held his hand under the sanitizer and squirted the clear gel on his fingers.

Taking a deep breath, Molly copied him and waited for Jack and Emma.

Standing on tiptoes, Dylan peered through the glass panel of the door. "I think I see Snowflake," he said. "Does she have a pink nose?"

Molly's gaze darted around the large room. "I think so. Where did you see her?"

"Over by the sofa. She's sitting beside the red cushion."

With her hands clean, Emma opened the door. "Remember to walk, not run. It keeps the kittens nice and calm."

With a level of patience that surprised Emma, Molly cautiously approached the white kitten. The smile on her face told everyone she'd found Snowflake.

"That's my kitten," Molly whispered. "She's a lot bigger than the last time we saw her." Holding out her hand, she slowly moved toward the white bundle of fur.

Snowflake blinked twice, then ran to Molly, purring as her back was stroked.

Molly smiled. "Snowflake remembers me." When she looked at her brother, her smile disappeared. "Can you see your kitten?"

Dylan looked inside the tube where the kitten he liked had been hiding. He got down on his hands and knees and searched under the sofa and all the other hideaways. "He's not here."

"Maybe he's asleep on the veranda?" Emma walked outside and checked the boxes and furniture. She hoped like crazy they could find Dylan's kitten.

Jack looked behind a climbing frame. "The lady at the front desk said there was a tortoiseshell kitten in here. I'll ask her if he's been moved."

Dylan stood in the doorway, his eyes shining with unshed tears. "What if he's gone home with someone else?"

"Let's double-check first before we decide what we'll do." Jack knelt in front of Dylan. "It will be all right, buddy. I'll come right back after I've asked about the kitten."

"Okay," Dylan said softly. "I hope he's still here."

"So do I." Jack sent Emma a concerned glance before he left the room.

Choosing another kitten wouldn't make Dylan feel any better. He'd been so excited when she told the twins they were visiting the animal shelter. And now they were here, Emma wished she'd come on her own to make sure the kittens were still available.

Molly left her kitten on the sofa and walked across to her brother. "We could share Snowflake. She likes you, too." With her hand resting in Dylan's, Molly pulled him across to the white kitten. "If you pat her, she purrs."

As soon as the kitten saw Dylan, she rubbed her head against him, tugging a smile from a very disappointed little boy.

"See," Molly said with delight. "She really does like you."

A soft tap on the door had everyone turning around.

As Jack opened the door, Emma breathed a sigh of relief. Curled in his arms was a very sleepy tortoiseshell kitten.

"One of the volunteers moved him into another room," Jack said quietly. He knelt on the ground, bringing the kitten closer to Dylan.

Dylan's eyes shone with happiness. Gently, he stroked the

kitten between his ears. "Hello. Do you want to come home with us?"

The little kitten yawned, and Dylan smiled.

"What are you going to call him?" Molly asked.

"Patch. His name is Patch Lewis."

"That's a nice name. Patch and Snowflake can be friends."

Jack held the kitten toward Dylan. "Would you like to hold him?"

Dylan bit his bottom lip as Jack gently lay the kitten in his arms. "He's so soft."

The kitten purred and the look on Dylan's face was priceless. He was utterly, hopelessly, in love with his new friend.

"Can we take Snowflake and Patch home with us?" Molly asked.

Emma nodded. "We have to fill out some forms before we can leave. Would you like to do that now?"

Dylan cuddled Patch close. "Yes, please."

As they made their way to the front desk, Emma held Jack's hand. Molly and Dylan were happier than they'd been in a long time, and Jack was here to enjoy the moment with them.

Life didn't get much better than this.

CHAPTER 15

On Sunday evening, Emma opened an email from Pastor John and smiled.

Kylie and Bailey had arrived half an hour ago to work on the Christmas carol competition. But as soon as they walked through the front door, Molly and Dylan had shown them the kittens. While Emma's friends enjoyed lots of cuddles with Snowflake and Patch, she'd updated the Christmas event website and checked her emails.

All the stores on Main Street had collected their decorations and were ready for the opening night of the Main Street Parade. The last and, for Emma, the most important item still waiting to be delivered was the artificial snow that would line the sidewalk.

Pastor John had been receiving emails from across Montana about the events. Ticket sales were beyond anything they'd expected, and that was before any of the press releases hit the newspapers and local radio stations.

"That was wonderful," Kylie said as she sat at the dining table beside Emma. "I haven't cuddled a kitten in ages. I'd forgotten how soft and warm they are."

"They're very cute. Molly and Dylan haven't let them out of their sight all weekend."

"I don't blame them. It almost makes me wish I had a kitten at home."

"They take a lot more work than I thought, but they're adorable." Emma turned her laptop around. "John sent through the latest ticket sales spreadsheet. The opening event for Christmas on Main Street is almost sold out."

Kylie's eyes widened. "That's incredible. The tickets have only been available for a week."

"What's incredible?" Bailey asked from the doorway.

"The night market is almost sold out," Kylie said to their friend. "I'm glad we decided to do something special to start the Christmas events. The money we raise will go a long way toward paying for another tiny home."

"Make that three tiny homes," Emma said. "John received an anonymous donation of twelve thousand dollars this afternoon. That will more than cover the cost of one house."

Bailey dropped into the seat opposite Emma and Kylie. "Are you sure the money was for the tiny homes?"

Emma nodded. "Someone read a Christmas wish that was left on the Facebook page. The person who posted the message was desperate for somewhere to live. Our donor made their Christmas wish come true."

"I don't mean to seem ungrateful, but can someone skip ahead of the line like that?" Kylie asked. "Some people have been on the waiting list for a tiny home for more than a year."

"John had the same concern until he saw the name of the person who will be going into the tiny home. She volunteers at The Welcome Center and was one of the first people to add her name to the list for a house."

Bailey sighed. "So her Christmas wish really has come true."

"That's what I thought, too." Emma glanced at the kitchen doorway. "It's awfully quiet in the living room. I'd better check what Molly and Dylan are doing."

"You don't need to," Bailey said. "The twins went to bed a few minutes ago."

"On their own?" Most nights, Emma had to read them a long bedtime story before they closed their eyes.

Bailey smiled. "They weren't exactly on their own. The kittens were with them."

"I was the same when my family adopted a kitten," Kylie said. "Once the novelty wears off, life will go back to normal."

"I don't mind," said Emma. "Looking after the kittens is teaching them to be patient and kind." She checked her watch. In another few minutes, she would make sure they were okay. "I can't believe the twins are starting first grade tomorrow."

"Before you know it, they'll be at college." Kylie grinned. "And we'll still be meeting to talk about fundraising ideas for the church."

"Talking about fundraising ideas..." Bailey opened the project plan for the Christmas carol competition. "I made a list of the local choirs. Did you know Sapphire Bay has eight singing groups?"

"There are a lot more in Polson," Kylie added. "It could be a big event."

Emma opened another document on her laptop. "I've made a folder of the emails John has received from singing groups in Montana. They've all been asking about the competition."

Bailey's eyes widened. "I thought there would only be six or seven choirs."

"There'll be a few more than that," Kylie said. "But don't

worry. By the time the competition starts, Emma, John, and I will be able to give you a hand."

"And possibly Mabel, Willow, and Jack," Emma added.

"How is Jack?" Kylie asked. "I haven't seen him for a while."

Emma couldn't hide her smile. "He's busy working on a complicated case, but he's still in Sapphire Bay. We're taking the twins to school tomorrow."

Kylie sighed. "When a man goes to the first day of school with your children, it's serious."

Emma leaned her elbows on the table, wanting to share how she was feeling with her friends. "After Mark left, I was determined to stand on my own two feet. I didn't want to rely on anyone again. But sharing our lives with Jack feels so right."

Bailey grinned. "It sounds like Cupid has struck again."

With a sigh, Emma studied her laptop. "You're right, but thinking about Cupid won't help us with the carol competition. Do you want to talk about what's happening on the day of the event?"

Bailey pulled out a folder. "I've been working on a timetable. I can alter it to fit the number of entries we have."

Emma and Kylie moved around the table to look at the spreadsheet.

"This is great," Emma murmured. "You've thought of everything."

"I don't know about everything, but it's a start."

As Bailey went through the event, line by line, a deep sense of pride filled Emma. After spending a lot of time putting together the Christmas program, everything was finally coming together.

After they were finished, the tiny home village would get a much-needed injection of cash and a lot of people would be happy. And that, more than anything, was why Emma was volunteering so much of her time.

JACK PARKED his truck in Emma's driveway and checked the time. It was only seven-thirty in the morning, but Molly and Dylan needed to be at school in an hour. At least this way they'd know he hadn't forgotten about them.

He could still remember when he started first grade. He'd filled his backpack with a new Spiderman lunch box and drink bottle. When he arrived in the classroom, everything had seemed so big and intimidating. If it weren't for Noah being at the same school, he didn't know how he would have survived the day.

As he stepped out of the truck, the front door of Emma's house swung open.

Molly rushed onto the veranda. "Jack!"

A white blur of fur ran after her.

Molly stopped suddenly, gathered Snowflake into her arms and grinned at Jack.

"You've lost another tooth!"

"It fell out when I was eating breakfast. Dylan said I'm going to be rich."

Jack didn't know about rich, but she was definitely cute. "It was good that it fell out this morning and not while you were at school."

"That's what Mommy said. Do kittens lose their teeth?"

"I don't know. We'll have to look on the Internet."

"If they do have wobbly teeth, there might be a tooth fairy just for kittens."

Jack smiled and stroked the top of Snowflake's head. "Did the kittens keep you awake last night?"

Molly shook her head. "They were real quiet until

Mommy woke up. Then they pounced all over us until we got out of bed."

Dylan met them on the garden path. "Hi, Jack. Did Molly show you the hole where her tooth used to be?"

"She did. Have you got any wobbly teeth?"

"No," he said sadly. "But Molly said she'll buy me something special with her tooth fairy money."

"We're going to Sweet Treats after school. I'm buying lots and lots of candy."

Jack followed the twins into their home. "It sounds as though you've got an exciting day ahead of you." When they were in the living room, he took two small gifts out of the bag he was carrying. "If you've got one of these for school, you could keep this gift at home."

Molly looked to see if the front door was closed before placing her kitten on the floor. "I like the wrapping paper."

Jack had hunted through the supply of paper at the general store. Right at the back of the shelf was a sheet of purple gift-wrapping paper with pictures of cats across it.

Dylan carefully pulled the last piece of tape off his present. Lying between sheets of tissue paper was a purple pencil case with stars and planets printed on the fabric.

Molly's pencil case had a pink and purple cat design. "You got us colored pencils, too," she said excitedly. "They're just like the ones we saw in town."

Dylan wrapped his arms around Jack's waist. "Thank you."

"That's okay, buddy. You and Molly will have a great day at school."

"I want to stay here with Patch."

"He'll still be here when you get home," Emma said from the doorway.

Jack turned and smiled. It didn't matter what time of the

day or night he saw her, Emma took his breath away. "Good morning. I hope I'm not too early."

"Your timing couldn't be better. Would you like a cup of coffee before we drive into town?"

"I'd love one."

"Look what Jack bought us," Molly said. "Can we take these pencil cases to school instead of our other ones?"

Emma nodded. "While you're changing over the pencil cases, you can put your lunch boxes in your bags, too."

While the twins raced around the house getting everything ready, Jack walked into the kitchen with Emma. He smelled the sweet scent of cinnamon and sighed. "Your kitchen always reminds me of my grandparents' house. Grandma always seemed to have a tray of cookies baking in the oven."

"I baked something nice for Dylan and Molly to put in their lunch boxes. But I had to be careful what I made."

"Because of allergies?"

Emma nodded. "And also because the school has a healthy eating policy. The cranberry and apricot bars have almost no added sugar, no chocolate, and they're gluten and dairy free." She took a container out of the pantry. "You can try a piece, if you like."

"I'd love some. I'll make the coffee."

Emma took two plates out of the cupboard. "Did your staff find the missing person you told me about?"

"Not yet, but we have a few more leads than we did last week." A fifty-two-year-old businessman had disappeared without a trace. Jack still wasn't sure if he'd deliberately left his family and career behind or if something more sinister had happened. "The police are investigating a couple of sightings of him but, more often than not, they don't lead to anything."

"It's not easy finding someone when they don't want to be found."

Jack poured two cups of coffee and sat at the kitchen counter. "Have you heard from Mark?"

"He called the twins last night to wish them all the best for today." Emma cradled her cup of coffee in her hands. "I wish he hadn't stayed out of Molly and Dylan's lives for so long."

"At least he wants to get to know them now."

"I suppose so."

Jack frowned. "Are you worried about him contacting the twins?"

"I worry about everything to do with my children." She sighed. "Mark isn't the same person I married. I guess I'm a little uneasy about what the future holds."

"I imagine that's normal. Are your parents happy he's back?"

Emma looked over her shoulder at the kitchen door. She was probably making sure the twins weren't around. "Mom and Dad have never forgiven him for leaving so suddenly. They're the reason I contacted my lawyer so quickly after Mark visited us. Otherwise, I'd be even more worried about him wanting custody of the twins."

"Has he signed the parenting agreement?"

Emma nodded.

"Then you're safer than you were five weeks ago."

"You're right." Emma looked at the clock on the oven. "We'll need to leave soon and I still need to get my laptop ready. Will you be okay while I—"

"Dad's here," Molly yelled from the living room. "Dylan! Dad's here."

Emma's mouth dropped open. "It can't be Mark. He told me he was too busy at the lake to go anywhere." She walked into the living room and, even from where Jack stood, he could see her shoulders stiffen.

"What are you doing here?"

Emma sounded more surprised than annoyed. Jack wasn't sure he would have been quite so forgiving.

Mark untangled Molly and Dylan's arms from around his neck. "I hope you don't mind. I've missed a lot in the twin's lives and I didn't want to…"

Jack moved farther into the room.

Mark's eyes widened. "Jack?"

"Hi. You must have left before sunrise to be in Sapphire Bay at this time of the morning."

"I caught an early United flight. I didn't realize you'd be here."

That much was obvious. "Molly and Dylan asked if I'd come to school with them."

Mark didn't look impressed.

"And we're ready," Molly said excitedly. "What about Snowflake and Patch? Where will they go?"

Emma looked at the kittens. "We'll leave them in the laundry room with their blanket, some toys, and a bowl of water. They'll be okay until I come home."

"We changed their litter box this morning," Dylan said. "So that's nice and clean."

"Well done." Emma picked up the two wriggling kittens. "I'll put these two away and then it's time to leave."

Jack wondered if Emma's hurried exit had more to do with Mark being here than with taking the kittens to the laundry room. Fortunately, Dylan and Molly were too busy talking to their dad to feel the uncomfortable undercurrents in the air.

For Emma's sake, he hoped the parenting agreement covered unexpected visits. Otherwise, the rest of her life could be filled with a whole lot of surprises.

EMMA KNEW she should have been more charitable, but she couldn't help the thoughts racing through her mind. Mark said he was in Sapphire Bay to see the twins start first grade. But, so far, he'd seemed more interested in studying Emma and Jack than being part of his children's morning.

As soon they arrived at the school, the twins were caught up in the excitement of talking with their friends and discovering their new classroom.

Dylan had confidently introduced them to Fred, his teacher's hairy black spider. Molly stayed far away, preferring the comfort of the reading corner to the company of the spider.

While Jack sat beside Molly, admiring the books she'd found on the reading table, Mark knelt beside Dylan, discussing Fred's eating habits.

Emma stood halfway between everyone, wanting to give each of her children a chance to show Jack and Mark what they liked about their classroom.

"It's a big day, isn't it?"

Emma pulled her gaze back to Bernadette, the twins' new teacher. "It is. Molly and Dylan haven't stopped talking about coming to school."

"I've got a feeling they'll be very happy here. Molly said you posted the message on Facebook about Sapphire Bay's Christmas events."

"That's right."

"One of the people who replied to your post asked Santa for a steamboat ride on Flathead Lake. My grandparents used to take me on the lake all the time and talk about the old steamboats. Grandma and Granddad died a long time ago, but there's a really good tour people can take that tells you about the history of steamboats in this area. Can I donate a family pass for the tour to the person who left the message?"

"That's really generous of you, but I'm not sure I'll be able to find them."

"Can you check? It would mean a great deal to me."

Emma nodded. "We made a list of all the Christmas wishes and ideas people sent us. I'll do my best to find them."

"That's wonderful, thank you. I'm sending my contact details home with each of the children. You're more than welcome to call me if you find the person."

Molly joined Emma and Bernadette. "Hi, Ms. Oliver. I've been looking at the new books."

"If you find a story you like, you could take it home with you this afternoon."

"Like a library?"

"Just like a library." Bernadette checked her watch and smiled. "I'd better remind everyone that school starts in five minutes. Otherwise, your moms and dads will be staying to learn the alphabet."

"That's okay," Molly said as she held Emma's hand. "Mommy has been showing Dylan and me how to read. She could help someone else, too."

Emma gently squeezed Molly's hand. "I'm leaving soon, but bring one of the books home. We can read it together."

"Okay. If you want to go now, I'll be all right. I can play with my friend Dorothea."

Emma was so proud of her little girl. She gave Molly a big hug. "Have a wonderful day. I'll be here after school when the bell rings."

"Bye, Mommy."

Taking a deep breath, Emma walked across to Dylan. Mark and Jack were sitting beside him, listening to something another little boy was saying.

She didn't think it would be this hard to leave the twins,

but this was the beginning of a new part of their lives. Before she knew it, they'd be going to college, spreading their wings even farther than Sapphire Bay. Was it irrational to miss them already?

When Dylan saw her, he leaped to his feet. "Guess what?"

"You're going to make a Lego spider when you get home?"

"Nope. Dad's going to spend more time with us."

Emma's gaze shot to Mark. "That's nice."

"He's going to take me and Molly fishing and stuff. You could come, too." Dylan's eyes shone with excitement.

She tried to be happy for him, she really did. But it would take a long time for her to fully trust her ex-husband. And the last thing she wanted was for Dylan and Molly to be hurt by promises Mark couldn't keep.

She hugged her son tight. "Fishing sounds like fun, but it's time for us to go."

Dylan's face dropped. If he started crying, Emma's eyes would fill will tears. Then Molly would start crying and everyone would be upset. "You'll have an amazing day. I'll be here when school ends."

Dylan sighed. "Okay." Turning to his dad, he gave him a hug, then wrapped his arms around Jack. "Thank you for coming."

"I wouldn't have missed it," Jack said with a smile. "Enjoy the day with your friends."

Dylan's solemn nod tore at Emma's heart. She gave him another quick hug, checked that Molly was happy, then glanced at Jack and Mark.

Without saying anything, Jack stood and held Emma's hand. "Bye, Dylan."

"Bye."

Silently, Emma left the classroom.

"They'll be okay," Jack reassured her.

"I know they will. But they're growing up so fast."

171

"Your mom and dad probably felt the same way when you started first grade."

"And look at me now." Emma sighed.

When they reached the parking lot, Mark took his keys out of his pocket. "Can we talk?"

"Sure. If you want to come back to my house, we could talk there. But we'll need to be finished by ten o'clock."

"It shouldn't take too long. I'll meet you there. Bye, Jack."

Jack nodded and watched Mark walk to his rental. "Will you be all right?"

She didn't need to ask what Jack meant. He was as worried about her as she was about the twins. "I'll be fine. I wanted to speak to Mark, anyway."

"Did you have any idea he was coming to Sapphire Bay?"

Emma shook her head. "What I don't understand is why he didn't call. I want him to be a part of Dylan and Molly's lives, but we'd agreed on how we would do it. Turning up out of nowhere wasn't part of our plan."

As they walked toward her truck, Emma hoped her parents weren't right. They'd warned her to be careful what she wished for.

Unfortunately, she hadn't listened.

EMMA SAT at the kitchen table with her hands wrapped around a cup of coffee. "We have an agreement, Mark. If you weren't happy with what we decided, you should have said something."

Mark didn't seem worried. "You said you wanted me to spend more time with Molly and Dylan, so here I am."

"You should have called to make sure it was okay."

"And given you an opportunity to say no? I wanted to see Dylan and Molly start first grade."

Emma took a deep breath. She'd forgotten how stubborn Mark could be. Or maybe she'd changed more than she thought. "I wouldn't have told you not to come to Sapphire Bay. But I could have let the twins know you'd be here and how long you were staying."

"They were happy to see me. I don't know what your problem is."

She felt like saying her problem was him. For some reason, Mark couldn't understand how confusing it was for the twins when he was here. "For five years, Molly and Dylan haven't had a father figure in their lives. Now they know who you are and where you live, everything has changed."

"Children are adaptable. I think you're underestimating how quickly they'll get used to having me around."

Emma's heart pounded. "What do you mean?" Mark was only supposed to see the twins once a month for the first six months. After that, they would renegotiate the time he spent with them.

"I'm thinking of moving to Sapphire Bay."

A few years ago, Emma would have been thrilled to hear those words. But a lot had changed since then. "Are you sure that's what you want?"

Mark's gaze sharpened. "I thought you would be happy to see more of me."

Did he think she'd been waiting for him? "I'm happy Jack found you for the twins' sake. But if you're implying there could be anything more than friendship between us, you're wrong. You left me with two babies, no income, and a mortgage I couldn't repay. I know you were going through a difficult time, but you never bothered to tell me where you'd gone or even if you were all right. That's not the type of person I want in my life."

"Perhaps I've changed, too."

"It's too late. You'll always be Molly and Dylan's father

and my ex-husband. But I don't want anything more from you." She saw the disappointment on Mark's face and knew her words had hurt him. "I'm sorry if that's not what you wanted to hear, but it's how I feel."

"After what I did, I'm lucky you still want me to be part of the twins' lives." He took a sip of coffee, then carefully placed his mug on the table. "Molly and Dylan like Jack."

Emma studied her ex-husband's face. If she didn't know better, she'd swear he was jealous. "We're both fortunate he came to Sapphire Bay. Without him, you wouldn't have met your children again."

Mark rubbed his hand around the back of his neck. "I'm sorry if I sound ungrateful, because I'm not. But I would like to spend more time with Molly and Dylan."

"They need time to adjust to having you back in their lives, and I need to know I can trust you."

"What do you mean?"

"I don't want the twins to get used to having you in their lives, then you leave again."

Mark flinched. "Do you really think I would do that?"

"You've done it before. If you've changed, that's great. But saying you'll be there for them doesn't mean it will happen."

"I want to be a good father."

"And you can be, just don't expect too much from Dylan and Molly. When are you going back to Evergreen?"

"My flight leaves at ten o'clock tomorrow morning. I was hoping I could stay here for the night."

Emma frowned. "I don't—"

"I know what you're going to say, but think about Molly and Dylan. It will give them a chance to get to know me. We could have dinner together by the lake, throw a ball around."

"You aren't supposed to be here."

A resigned look crossed Mark's face. "Next time I'll call first. I promise."

Emma looked him in the eyes and said, "You have to follow the guidelines we agreed on or this won't work." She took a deep, steadying breath. There weren't many places to stay in Sapphire Bay, but sleeping in her cottage would have to be a last resort. "I've got the phone number of the nearest hotel and a couple of bed-and-breakfasts that friends have used. If they don't have any rooms available, you can sleep here."

"Thank you."

"This is new for all of us," Emma said firmly. "The reason we set ground rules was to make sure Dylan and Molly adjusted to having you in their lives. I don't want to do anything to jeopardize their relationship with you, but I also want to make sure they're okay."

"That's what I want, too."

Emma hoped so. Otherwise, she would be calling her lawyer.

CHAPTER 16

*H*alf an hour later, Emma walked into Kylie's flower shop. The rainbow-colored walls of Blooming Lovely were a wonderful backdrop to shelves full of sweet-smelling flowers. It was a plant lover's paradise, the kind of store Emma could have stayed in for hours.

Kylie walked out of the workroom and smiled. "Hello. How are Molly and Dylan?"

"Enjoying every moment of first grade, I imagine."

"And how were you when you said goodbye?"

"I was okay. My bottom lip quivered, but I didn't cry."

"Thank goodness for that." Kylie added a bouquet of pale pink roses to a vase. "If you'd started, everyone would have shed a tear or two. Did Jack enjoy being there?"

"He would have enjoyed it more if Mark hadn't been there."

"Your ex-husband?"

Emma nodded. "He flew into Polson this morning."

"From your expression, I'm guessing he didn't tell you he was coming."

She pulled out a stool and sat down. "I don't know why he

thought he could change the visitation rules in our agreement."

Kylie frowned. "I could tell you, but I won't."

"He apologized."

"I'm sure he did. How long is he staying?"

"Mark goes home tomorrow."

Kylie stuck her hands on her hips. "Tell me you're not letting him stay with you."

"What was I supposed to do? He wouldn't have found anywhere else to go."

"It's summer. He could have slept under the stars."

"Now I know you're crazy." Emma pulled her laptop out of its case. "There's no way you would let anyone sleep outside."

"True, but the people I know wouldn't abandon their wife and babies."

"He said he was sorry and I believe him. Come and look at the new and improved Blooming Lovely website. I can guarantee your online orders will increase."

Kylie walked around the front counter and peered over Emma's shoulder. "That's incredible. Are they the photos Willow took?"

Emma nodded. Last month, Willow had spent a few hours taking photographs of the store, the flowers, and some of the arrangements Kylie was creating. The end result was a collection of images that were colorful, engaging, and almost whimsical. After Emma saw them, it gave her another idea for the website.

Emma moved her laptop to the right, giving Kylie easy access to the keyboard. "Move the mouse over the page."

"It's not going to zap me, is it?"

"Not today."

Kylie ran her finger over the trackpad. As soon as she moved the cursor, it changed from a blinking line to a fairy, flapping its wings as she moved around the page. "Oh, my gosh. How did you do that?"

"I made a special code that recreates a butterfly's movements as it flies from one plant to another. Then all I had to do was use my imagination and lots of Molly's favorite stories to create an animated fairy. When a customer visits the Blooming Lovely website, the fairy helps them choose what flowers they'd like. After that, she guides the customer through the ordering, delivery, and feedback processes. What do you think?"

Kylie wiggled the mouse and grinned. "It's fabulous. Everyone will want to visit my website."

"As long as they buy your flowers, I'll be happy." Emma pulled a report out of her case. "I've based my marketing suggestions around your new website branding. You could leverage off the fun element of the fairy. We could focus your campaigns on engaging new customers who want an interactive, streamlined experience when ordering flowers."

"Does the fairy have a name?"

"Not yet. If you don't have one in mind, we could have a competition to name the fairy."

Kylie smiled. "You're incredible."

"I'm glad you like what I've done."

"I *love* what you've done." Kylie opened another page and laughed. "The fairy smiled at me."

"That's because your mouse hovered over the purple bouquet for more than ten seconds. Usually when that happens, customers are considering a purchase. I'm hoping a smile from the fairy will encourage them to go to the checkout."

"How did you learn to do this?"

Emma shrugged. "My professors taught me the basics. The rest is by trial and error."

"Do you know how amazing you are?"

"I just hope your customers like what I've done."

"Are you kidding? I'll have to employ more staff to keep up with the online orders." Kylie tilted her head sideways and smiled at the screen. "It's no wonder Pastor John is getting more requests to make people's Christmas wishes come true. You're a genius at what you do."

Emma's eyes widened. "I didn't know that."

"He said he'd call you tonight. But, right now, I'm going to make you the biggest cup of hot chocolate you've ever seen."

Emma leaned her elbows on the counter. "You know the way to my heart."

A deep voice cleared his throat behind her. "If I'd known it was that easy, I would have made you a hot chocolate at my brother's wedding."

Emma's heart leaped in her chest. She turned and smiled at Jack. "You would have scared me away." His grin made her tummy do cartwheels.

"I'm glad you survived this morning."

Jack's gentle kiss made Emma sigh.

"Excuse me," Kylie said loudly. "There's a single woman in the room. Please keep your lips to yourselves."

Emma laughed. "I can't help it. I'm addicted to my boyfriend's kisses."

"I wish I could say the same," Kylie murmured. "Where have all the single, sexy men gone?"

Jack rested his arm on Emma's shoulders. "They're probably in the steamboat museum building the tiny homes. Pastor John is welcoming a new group of building apprentices onto the site."

Kylie checked her watch. "How long will they be there?" When Emma groaned, Kylie laughed. "I'm joking. But when you speak with John, tell him I'm happy to bake some muffins for his new recruits."

"He'll see straight through your plan," Emma warned.

"Not if I include a batch of huckleberry muffins. They're his favorite."

Jack shook his head. "I can't believe I'm hearing two intelligent women discuss ways to bribe a pastor into playing matchmaker."

Emma slid off the stool. "John is worse than we are *and* he's single." She sent a pointed glance at her friend.

"No way," Kylie said with a frown. "He isn't my type."

"I know I shouldn't ask," Jack said, "but what is your type?"

"I like men who are tall, handsome, rich, kind, and intelligent."

Jack's eyebrows rose. "Are you sure you haven't forgotten something?"

Kylie opened the door to the workroom. "He can't be allergic to flowers."

And that, above everything else, made Emma smile the most.

LATER THAT NIGHT, Emma packed the last of the picnic leftovers into the basket. Mark's idea to have dinner beside Flathead Lake had been just what everyone needed. It was a gorgeous evening—the kind that made you realize just how wonderful it was to live in Montana.

"Come and kick the ball with us."

She looked up as Mark jogged toward her. "I'll be there soon. I just need to—"

Mark scooped the plates and utensils into the bag she was using for the dirty dishes. "All done. The rest can wait a few minutes."

She looked at Molly and Dylan. They were laughing and kicking a ball to each other. "Okay. I'm coming."

"Thank goodness for that. I thought I'd have to sling you over my shoulder."

Emma smiled. "The last time you did that you hurt your back. And we're both a little older and heavier than we were when that happened."

Mark pulled back his shoulders and sucked in his already flat stomach. "I think we're doing pretty good for two people in their mid-thirties."

"I'm only thirty-two. My mid-thirties are a long way off."

With a theatrical bow, Mark rolled forward from his waist. "My humblest apologies, oh young one. I added a whole three years to your age."

Emma wiped her hands on her jeans. "Remember that when I'm dodging your feeble attempts to outmaneuver me with the ball."

"You'll have to be quick." Mark rushed toward Molly and Dylan.

"Hey," Emma yelled. "You're supposed to wait for me." When Mark turned around and ran backward, she sprinted after him. "Show off," she yelled.

The grin on his face reminded her of when they were first married. They'd had a lot of good times together. A lot of times that, regardless of what happened after he left, would always be imprinted on her brain.

"You're getting slow, Emma."

"Some of us don't have time to go to the gym." Were her lungs really that wheezy? She used to be able to run at least three miles without losing her breath.

"Neither do I. Look around you. All you need to do is go for a hike or swim in the lake. You'd be fit in next to no time."

Mark was right, but she wasn't willing to admit that her exercise routine was the first thing to go after she'd had the twins. "That's easier said than done."

"Here you go, Mom." Dylan kicked the ball toward her. For a six-year-old, he had a strong right foot.

"Thanks, Dylan." Before she could kick the ball to Molly, Mark rushed across the field, intercepted the pass, and flicked the ball toward his daughter.

"Someone's skills are a little rusty."

Mark was really beginning to annoy her. "You haven't seen anything yet. Molly and I could outmaneuver you any day."

"Is that right?" Mark turned to Dylan. "Should we have a game against your mom and sister?"

Dylan gave an excited nod. "We could kick the ball through the goalposts we made."

"Good idea." Mark pointed to two sticks about thirty feet away. "The last team to score three points has to buy the other team ice cream."

Emma smiled at Molly. "What do you think?"

"We can do it." And before anyone stopped her, Molly ran toward the sticks, taking the ball with her. As soon as she was close enough, she kicked the ball hard, scoring their first goal.

Emma grinned. "Yeah, Molly. That's one goal to us."

Mark high-fived his daughter. "Well done."

When Molly wrapped her arms around Mark's legs, Emma sighed. There was one major drawback to spending more time with Mark. When he left, Molly and Dylan would miss him even more than they had before.

A LAST-MINUTE PHONE call to Manhattan meant Jack didn't make it to the park in time for dinner. But that didn't mean he wanted to miss the entire night.

He parked his truck beside Emma's and checked his

watch. In New York City, he'd call this fashionably late. In Sapphire Bay, he was almost at the stage when it wasn't worth being here.

But nothing, including his latest case, would keep him from spending time with Emma. Especially when Mark was here.

The look on Mark's face when he was around Emma was exactly the way Noah looked at Cassie. It was the familiarity that came with closeness, the easy way two people could communicate when they knew each other from the inside out. And even though Mark hadn't been part of Emma's life for a long time, he still knew her.

And, if Jack's gut instinct was correct, he wanted to keep getting to know her.

"Jack!" Molly was jumping up and down, waving her hands in the air like a scarecrow stuck in the middle of a tornado.

He locked his truck and waved back. Emma and Dylan were chasing after Mark.

Mark was kicking a ball toward Molly, running fast enough to outpace his ex-wife and son, but not quick enough to totally lose them.

Emma lunged forward, grabbing the back of Mark's shirt to slow him down.

He turned, laughed at something she said, then wrapped her in a hug while Dylan kept kicking the ball across the park.

Jack's eyebrows rose. Instead of stepping out of Mark's embrace, Emma was laughing and yelling at Molly to stop her brother.

Jack walked toward Emma. Whether Dylan managed to keep the ball away from his sister didn't matter. What mattered was making sure Mark kept his hands to himself.

Mark's smile disappeared when he saw Jack.

Emma looked across the park and frowned.

Finally, Mark's arms dropped from around his ex-wife.

By the time Jack reached them, Dylan and Molly were running back to their parents telling them it was time for ice cream.

Dylan smiled at Jack. "I scored the winning goal. Now Mom and Molly have to buy everyone ice cream. Do you want to come?"

"I'd love too, but only if it's okay with your mom."

"It's more than okay," Emma said. "There's a sandwich in the picnic basket for you, too. Did you get all your work done?"

"As much as I could." Jack looked Mark in the eye. "Did you find somewhere to stay?"

"Emma was happy for me to stay with her."

"On the sofa." She scowled at Mark. "And only for one night."

As far as Jack was concerned, it was one night too many. After five years of having nothing to do with his family, Mark was taking his role of being a father far more seriously than Jack thought he would.

When no one said anything, Emma held onto Molly and Dylan's hands. "Let's get some ice cream."

"I'm going to have three scoops," Molly said excitedly.

Dylan looked around his mom's legs at his sister. "It will fall off the cone."

"I'll have it in a bowl," Molly said, undeterred by her brother's practicality. "With chocolate sauce and sprinkles."

A smile tugged at the corner of Emma's mouth. "What about you, Dylan? What would you like?"

He reached for Jack's hand. "I'll have the same ice cream as Jack."

Jack gently squeezed Dylan's hand. It was hard not to feel

a small sense of satisfaction when Mark was standing beside him. "Choose a flavor you like."

"I like them all," he whispered.

"You should ask for a little bit of everything," Molly said. "It would be like a rainbow ice cream."

Mark picked up the ball. "I know which flavor your mom will choose."

"Orange chocolate chip," Molly said.

Mark shook his head.

"Strawberry," Dylan guessed.

Another shake of Mark's head had everyone looking at Emma.

"Your mom's favorite ice cream is lemon and lime," Mark said. "Am I right?"

Emma smiled. "You remembered."

"I hope so. I don't think we bought any chocolate ice cream for the entire time we were married."

Emma made a scoffing sound. "You're exaggerating."

Molly looked up at her mom. "What does that mean?"

"It means your dad is pretending we didn't buy chocolate ice cream. He ate plenty of his favorite flavor."

Dylan's hand swung in Jack's as they walked across the grass. "What's your favorite ice cream, Jack?"

"I like all flavors of ice cream."

"Like me," Molly said with a grin.

"Just like you." And just like Dylan, he planned on getting every ice cream flavor the store sold.

He had a feeling he'd need all the comfort food he could lay his hands on tonight.

"You're being oversensitive," Noah said. "Emma and Mark were married for a long time."

Jack ran his hands through his hair and stared at the night sky. After he'd left the ice cream shop, Jack had come to see his brother. "I'm worried it's more than that. Emma is comfortable around him. She laughs at Mark's corny jokes and doesn't seem worried that he's here."

"What did you expect? She wants to give Molly and Dylan a stable home. If she ignores Mark or doesn't include him in what they're doing, the twins will be the ones who will suffer."

His brother was making perfect sense, but that didn't stop a gnawing fear from growing inside Jack. He could feel his relationship with Emma slipping away and he didn't know what to do. "I knew any relationship with Emma would have to include the twins. But now that Mark is back, I feel like I'm stuck in a three-way tug of war."

"He's only just come back into their lives. In a few months, everything could be different."

"I saw the way Mark was looking at Emma. It didn't look as though he wanted to be friends."

Noah's eyebrows rose. "Are you sure you're not seeing things that aren't there?"

"I wish I were."

"Have you talked to Emma about how you feel?"

Jack shook his head. "Between the new case I'm working on and Mark's arrival, we haven't had a lot of time on our own."

"Talk to her. She's probably feeling just as unsure about everything as you are. It can't be easy welcoming her ex-husband back into her children's lives, especially when she knows how important he is to them."

Jack's hand trembled as he picked up his cup of coffee. "I think I'm losing her."

Noah sighed. "From what I've seen, Emma adores you. If her feelings for you have changed, she would have told you."

"Maybe." Jack leaned back in his chair and closed his eyes. Even at ten o'clock at night, it was warm enough to be sitting outside in shorts and a T-shirt. Usually, the quiet evenings were like a cooling balm on his emotions. It didn't matter what happened during the day, everything seemed less stressful. But not this time.

Mark wouldn't be going away in a hurry. The twins had the rest of their lives to get to know their father, to grow a relationship that had all but disappeared. All Jack could do was support the twins and make sure Emma knew how much he cared about her.

"I know you're not going to like what I say next, but I have to say it. If your relationship with Emma continues, Mark will always be part of your life. You need to work through your differences with Mark. Otherwise, no one will be happy."

"What if he doesn't want to meet me halfway?"

"Then you've got a decision to make. And believe me, I wouldn't want to be in your shoes."

Jack dropped his chin to his chest. He loved Emma more than anyone he'd ever met. He just hoped she felt the same way about him.

CHAPTER 17

*E*mma was working on a client's website when her back door burst open.

"Drop what you're doing and come with me." Kylie's cheeks were flushed and she was almost breathless.

If Emma didn't know better, she'd swear her friend had run from Main Street to her cottage. "Why aren't you at work?"

"Mabel came in to buy some flowers. When she saw what had happened, she offered to look after the store for a couple of hours."

Closing the lid of her laptop, Emma studied the excitement on her friend's face. After a sleepless night, it was good to spend time with someone who was happy. "It must be important for you to leave the flower shop."

"It is. Do you remember the Christmas wish someone made for a new bicycle?"

Emma vaguely remembered talking about it with Kylie and Bailey. "Was it the bicycle that would replace the one that had been stolen?"

"That's it. The little boy included photos of what his dream bicycle would look like."

An image of a black frame with red stars shooting along the side made Emma smile. "I remember the wish. Did the police find his bicycle?"

"Not quite. Come outside. I've got something to show you." Kylie grabbed her hand and pulled her toward the back door. "It's not just our community that wants to make people's Christmas wishes come true. A police officer in Great Falls saw the post about the bicycle. When he was young, the same thing happened to him. He knows how the little boy is feeling. And this is what he did about it." Kylie opened the tailgate of her truck.

Emma peered inside. Pushed to the back was a shiny, black bicycle. "He donated a bicycle?"

"It's not just any old one, either. It matches the bicycle Toby wanted. I called his parents and they called his elementary school. If we're quick, we can visit Toby's classroom and give it to him before the last bell rings."

"How did you find him?"

Kylie shrugged. "I hunted through all the Facebook messages. Toby used his mom's account to tell us his Christmas wish. It only took a few minutes to send her a message. As soon as she saw it, she called me."

"What would have happened to the bicycle if you hadn't found Toby?"

"The police officer was happy for us to donate it to someone else. So, what do you think?"

Emma checked her watch. "I think we should make Toby happy. But I need to be outside Molly and Dylan's classroom by three o'clock."

"Consider it done. Let's go and make another early Christmas wish come true."

With less of a heavy heart than before Kylie arrived, Emma rushed back to the house to lock the front door.

Even though she was going through a rocky patch, Emma would gladly make someone else's life a whole lot better. And a brand-new bicycle was guaranteed to make everyone smile.

AFTER THEY'D VISITED Toby and given him his new bicycle, Emma collected Molly and Dylan from their classroom.

Kylie had offered to drive them home, but it was such a lovely day that Emma didn't want to waste another minute inside.

"Has Dad gone back to Colorado?" Molly asked.

Emma nodded. "He left Sapphire Bay a few hours ago. Did you enjoy seeing him?"

"It was fun. Can we have a picnic tonight? We could ask Jack if he wants to come."

She wasn't sure that was a good idea. Emma thought Jack and Mark would learn to like each other. But it didn't look as though that was happening.

Last night, while they were at the ice cream shop, Jack had been very quiet. When they left, he decided to go home instead of coming back to Emma's cottage for coffee. At this stage, she didn't know whether he would ever return.

"Jack's really busy with work at the moment. He might want to have dinner with us another night."

"What about tomorrow?" Dylan asked.

Emma sighed. "I'll give him a call and see if he can come."

"Okay. Do you want to know what happened at school today?"

Molly stuck her hands over her ears. "Don't say it. It was scary."

"Spiders aren't scary."

Emma looked at the twins. "What happened to the spider?"

"It got out of its cage," Dylan said. "It didn't bite anyone, but all the girls were screaming."

"That's because it's big and hairy," Molly said with a shudder. "I was worried it would land in my hair."

Dylan frowned. "Spiders don't like people's hair. They can't eat it and they don't sleep in it."

"I don't ever want a spider in my hair, 'cos they have big legs." Molly held her red curly hair in one hand and kept her gaze fixed on the shrubs they were passing.

Dylan glanced at his sister. "Spiders are clever. They make sticky webs to catch their food. I could show you one by the woodshed if you want to see it."

Molly shuddered. "I want to go to The Welcome Center. Mr. Jessop is reading some stories about Peter Rabbit. Can we go there, Mommy?"

Emma thought about the work waiting for her at home. "I don't know if we can go to story time this week. I have a lot of work to do."

"You could talk to Pastor John while we listen to Mr. Jessop. *Please*. It's only for a little while."

Emma looked into Molly's big blue eyes. She wanted to speak to John, anyway, so maybe it could work. "What about you, Dylan? Would you like to listen to Mr. Jessop read stories?"

"Yes, please. Mr. Jessop said he's bringing some carrots and beans with him. We're going to eat all the things Peter Rabbit likes to eat."

Molly grinned. "It's going to be awesome."

There was no way Emma could say no to something that was awesome. "In that case, let's go to The Welcome Center."

"Yeah! We can tell all our friends where we went," Molly said to her brother. "They might want to come next week."

Dylan looked at Emma. "Will Jack be there?"

Her heart sank. "I don't think so. He's probably at Acorn Cottage, doing some work."

"Oh."

Dylan's disappointment made her feel even worse. She'd been so worried about how the twins would react to Mark going home, that she'd forgotten how important Jack had become in their lives.

And if she didn't talk to Jack soon, the twins might see even less of him.

WHILE THE TWINS were listening to Mr. Jessop, Emma knocked on John's office door. "Can I interrupt you for a few minutes?"

"Of course you can. I was just going through the project plan for our Christmas program. You're doing a great job of keeping everything on track."

"Kylie and Bailey have been fantastic, too. I've still got a few doubts about the train ride, but we're working on it."

"If you need another pair of hands, I can help."

Emma knew John had very little spare time. Between The Welcome Center, the tiny home village, and the fundraising activities he was organizing, he had even less spare time than she did. "We should be okay. Can I talk to you about Mabel's book?"

"Sure."

"I've organized a surprise book launch for her. I reserved the church's middle meeting room, but a lot more people than I expected want to come. Could we use part of the old steamboat museum for the launch?"

John turned to his computer. "Let me check the meeting

rooms at the church, first. I might be able to move a few events around. When is the book launch?"

"Next week on the eighteenth." Emma bit her bottom lip. She'd almost left it too late to make any changes. Hopefully, John could pull a rabbit out of his magician's hat and find a solution to her problem.

After studying the screen for a few minutes, he smiled. "If you're happy to have the book launch at five o'clock, we could squeeze it in between two other events in the big meeting room. The room would have to be empty by seven o'clock, though."

"That's perfect. Are you sure it won't cause a problem for anyone else?"

"Leave it with me. The group that had booked the room will be happy to move to a smaller area. How is everything else?"

Emma gripped her bag. Somehow, John knew when she was upset. But if she told him about Mark and Jack, she might burst into tears. And that's the last thing she wanted to do. "Everything's going well. I've updated the Christmas program budget, Dylan and Molly have settled into school, and I have a lot of new clients."

"You've worked hard to create a successful business. On top of that, I don't know what the church would do without you. But that wasn't what I meant."

Emma sat on the edge of a chair. "You're talking about Jack."

John nodded. "I saw him at the steamboat museum this morning. He was a lot quieter than usual."

"My ex-husband arrived unexpectedly the other day." Emma took a deep breath. She didn't want to go into any details with John. That wouldn't be fair on Jack or her. "Starting a new relationship is a lot more complicated than Jack or I thought it would be."

"You've had a lot of change in your life over the last few months. Don't be too hard on yourself."

That in itself was almost enough to make Emma cry. "I'll remember that at three o'clock in the morning when nothing is making sense. I'd better go. Dylan and Molly are listening to this week's story time."

John smiled. "I saw the basket of vegetables Gordon took into the room. It looked as though it would be an exciting story."

"Peter Rabbit is a good choice. I'll see you in a few days."

"I'll look forward to it."

Emma waited until she was in the corridor before taking a deep, shaky breath. If she couldn't tell John how she was feeling without crying, how would she talk to Jack? And if Jack was as upset as John thought, any discussion between them would be even more difficult.

After her marriage fell apart, she'd promised herself she would be extra careful if she ever fell in love again.

But she hadn't counted on meeting Jack.

AFTER EMMA LEFT John's office, she saw Kylie in The Welcome Center's kitchen. "Hi. Something smells good."

Her friend turned and smiled. "I'm baking some cookies for the guests." Kylie's eyes narrowed. "You look worried. What's wrong?"

"Telling you won't help."

"It might. A problem shared is a problem halved, or something like that. Is there an issue with one of the Christmas events?"

Emma shook her head.

"Molly and Dylan are with Mr. Jessop, so they must be all right. If something had happened to your business, you would tell me. That only leaves two possibilities and they both love you."

"Mark doesn't love me. He loves the person I used to be."

"That's not what I saw. From the very first time he came to Sapphire Bay, he had a crush on you."

"I told him I don't want any type of relationship with him apart from friendship."

"And you think he'll listen?"

"Why wouldn't he?"

"He's a man." Kylie took a batch of cookies out of the oven.

Emma didn't know what that had to do with anything. Besides, Mark was the least of her worries. "I need to speak to Jack. I think something's wrong."

"And that takes us straight back to problem number one."

"Mark?" Emma rushed across the kitchen and moved a bowl away from where Kylie wanted to place the hot cookie sheet.

"Thanks. Jack must be feeling a little insecure. He'd only just realized he'd fallen in love with you when your ex-husband arrived and wanted to play happy families. And to make matters worse, Jack's the person who found him."

"I can't ignore Mark. He's the father of my children."

"But you can make sure he sticks to the rules of your agreement."

"It wouldn't have helped that he stayed with us."

"Probably not."

Emma sighed. She'd really made a mess of everything. "I need to talk to Jack."

"You do. And fortunately for you, I have the rest of the day available to babysit."

"Are you sure?"

Kylie hugged Emma. "My only condition is that you don't

ask me to be your bridesmaid. I refuse to walk down an aisle wearing another frilly, pink dress."

"What if I choose a sleek, sexy, midnight blue sheath that shows off your curves to perfection?"

"Then I might consider it. Good luck."

"Why do I think I'm going to need it?"

"Because you're as human as the rest of us. Loving someone means being vulnerable, and that's something no one wants to feel."

Before Emma cried, she picked up her bag and gave her friend another hug. "I'll call you when I'm on my way home."

"Don't rush. I'll take Molly and Dylan home with me and give them dinner."

"Thank you." And before she ran out of courage, Emma walked out of The Welcome Center and into the rest of her life.

CHAPTER 18

*E*mma opened her truck door and looked at the pretty cottage overlooking Flathead Lake. Named after the large oak tree growing beside the veranda, Acorn Cottage was one of the loveliest bed-and-breakfast accommodation options in Sapphire Bay.

Her mom and dad had stayed here six months ago, and they'd enjoyed every minute.

"Is that you, Emma?"

She turned around. Despite how nervous Emma felt, she smiled at the tall woman walking toward her. "Hi, Cassie. I tried calling Jack but his phone is turned off. I thought he might be at the cottage."

Cassie's smile disappeared. "He's gone away for a couple of days. I thought he would have told you."

Emma didn't know what to say. "I haven't spoken to him since the weekend. Was he okay when he left?"

"To be honest, I haven't seen very much of him. I've been working on my next jewelry collection."

"How is it going?"

"Better than last week. Do you want me to call Noah? He might know how you can contact Jack."

"No, it's okay. He'll call me when he's ready. I hope your collection works out okay."

"I'm sure it will. Would you like a cup of coffee? Noah won't be too far away."

"Thanks for the offer, but I'll go back into town. Kylie is looking after Dylan and Molly."

Cassie walked with Emma to her truck. "I spoke to Pastor John the other day. He told me about the Christmas events you're organizing. If you need more help, just ask."

"That would be wonderful. Closer to each event, we'll need all the volunteers we can find. Can I add your phone number to the list we have?"

"Sure. Add Noah's name as well. He'll want to help."

Emma smiled. "Consider it done. When are you leaving for your honeymoon?"

"We fly out of Montana at the end of October. It's so close that I can almost taste the Italian pizza and gelato we're going to eat."

"I've never been to Italy, but everything about it sounds wonderful."

Cassie opened Emma's door. "I hope you're able to talk to Jack soon."

"So do I." With a heavy heart, Emma said goodbye to Cassie and drove to Kylie's house. Speaking to Jack would have to wait until later. She had two excited children to take home and about an hour's worth of work to do.

And after that, if she were feeling brave, she would try calling Jack again.

Hopefully, by that time, he would have turned on his phone.

❄

JACK STOOD BESIDE HIS TRUCK. The last time he was at Evergreen Lodge, he didn't know if he would find Emma's husband. Now he knew where Mark lived, but that didn't make this journey any easier.

The cabin at the end of the road sat silently in the midmorning sunshine. Jack had considered calling Emma's ex-husband to let him know he was on his way. But, in the end, he'd decided to take his chances and come anyway. Clearing two days from his schedule hadn't been easy, but what he had to say couldn't be said in Sapphire Bay or over the phone.

The sound of heavy footsteps coming closer made him turn around.

"You rented a different vehicle." Mark stood a short distance away with a fishing rod in one hand and a cooler in the other.

"I took what was available. How was the fishing?"

"As good as it always is. Why are you here?"

Jack appreciated Mark's directness. From what he'd seen, he was the type of person who didn't hide who he was or how he felt. Except where his ex-wife was concerned. And that was why Jack needed to speak to him.

"I want to talk to you about Emma."

Mark rested the end of the fishing rod on the ground, holding it like a warrior's spear. "What happens between Emma and myself is no one's business except our own."

"That's where you're wrong," Jack told him. "I plan on being part of Emma and the twins' lives for a long time. That means either we get along or something has to change."

Mark's jaw tightened. "It shouldn't have surprised me that Emma is dating someone else. But I'm the twins' father. I made a mistake when I left but, from now on, I'm not going anywhere."

"I don't have an issue with you being part of Emma and

the twins' lives. In fact, I think it's the best thing for everyone. What I have an issue with is you turning up unexpectedly and thinking you can manipulate Emma into feeling sorry for you."

"Is this about me coming to Sapphire Bay to see Molly and Dylan start first grade?"

It was a whole lot more than that and Mark knew it. "You signed papers that made it clear when and how you would see your children. What made you think you could suddenly arrive and expect a warm welcome?"

"I wanted to be there for the twins."

"If that were true, you would have called Emma and asked if it was okay to visit."

Mark didn't say anything.

"I've seen too many dysfunctional families to want anything like that for Molly and Dylan. But, one day, if you keep turning up unexpectedly and pushing your way into Emma's life, she's going to snap. And believe me, you won't want to be there when that happens."

"Emma wants me to be part of the twins' lives."

"As long as you follow the rules in the parenting agreement."

"No one can stop me from seeing my children."

Jack sighed. "A judge might see things differently if you keep breaking your agreement." Jack couldn't blame Mark for wanting to spend time with Dylan and Molly. He would be exactly the same in his position.

"Did Emma tell you I've been offered a job at Flathead Lake Resort?"

"She told me you were thinking of moving to Sapphire Bay."

Mark placed the cooler on the ground. "That was the plan, but there aren't many jobs in Sapphire Bay. The resort is in Bigfork. I'd be managing the staff who look after the cabins, hotel rooms, and RV sites."

Jack looked around him. "What about these cabins?"

"I'd hire a manager to look after them. Moving to the resort would mean I was only a twenty-minute drive from Molly and Dylan."

"You realize that you'll only be able to see them a few times a year?"

"In the beginning."

Jack admired Mark's tenacity, but that didn't mean he thought he would stick to the agreement. Living closer to the twins would only make it more likely that he'd arrive unexpectedly.

Jack couldn't change what Mark decided to do, but he could change his own attitude. If they were going to make it less stressful for Emma and the twins, someone had to take the first step. "Good luck with the move. I hope the job works out."

Mark nodded and picked up his cooler. "Is there anything else you want to say before you leave?"

There was only one thing, and that was more important than anything he'd already said. "I love Emma and the twins. I want you to know that I'll look after them, no matter what happens."

Tears filled Mark's eyes. "I guess that makes two of us. I messed up my relationship with my family. Don't make the same mistakes I did." And without a backward glance, Mark walked toward his cabin.

After he left, Jack stood on the shore of Evergreen Lake, staring across the calm, blue water. He'd done what he had set out to do. But that didn't stop him from worrying about Emma or the twins.

❄

EMMA OPENED the last box of Mabel's children's books and placed them on the sales table. So far, the surprise book launch had gone really well.

Mabel was thrilled that most of the community was here to celebrate the publication of her first book. Her impromptu speech was funny and emotional and, after she'd thanked Allan and Emma, there weren't many dry eyes in the room.

"We're running out of change," Kylie said. "Do you think we could ask Pastor John for some smaller bills?"

Emma looked around the meeting room. "He said to let him know if we needed extra money. I'll ask him."

Kylie handed Emma a small bag. "Take this with you. I don't like having too much money on the stand."

"I'll ask John to leave it in the safe. Will you be all right while I'm gone?"

"I should be. If it gets too busy, I'll ask Allan to give me a hand."

"I'll be back soon." As Emma wove through the crowd, she was filled with a deep sense of pride. Mabel had worked hard to finish her book so quickly. Not only had she produced a classic, beautifully illustrated book, she'd made her dreams come true.

"I thought you might still be here."

Emma froze. Jack had been gone for five days. Even though he'd called her when he arrived in Manhattan, it didn't make the distance between them any easier to handle.

She looked into Jack's brown eyes and smiled. "I've missed you."

Jack opened his arms. "I've missed you, too."

As she hugged Jack tight, she tried to remember what her life was like before she'd met him. She had been happy, but not as happy as she was now. Even Molly and Dylan seemed more settled.

"Congratulations on the book launch. It's a huge success."

Emma kissed his cheek. "Mabel is over the moon with happiness. All the bookmarks have gone and nearly all the books are sold."

Jack held up one of Mabel's books. "I bought a signed copy. I thought Molly and Dylan would like it."

"They'll love it. With everything that's been happening, I haven't had a chance to get them a copy." She glanced across the room at the sales table. "Would you mind if I come back in a few minutes? I need to ask John if we can have some more change."

"That's fine. Granddad's standing beside the banner on the far wall. I'll wait for you there."

"I won't be long." Emma kissed Jack once more before heading toward John.

Once the book launch was over, she'd take a deep breath and prepare herself for the next few months. Because next Saturday was the beginning of the Christmas fundraising events. And from then until December 25, her life would be even more hectic than usual.

BY THE TIME Jack made it across the room, his grandfather was talking to Gordon Jessop. It never failed to amaze him how well his grandfather had slotted into life in Sapphire Bay. For a man who had always lived in large cities, his grandfather had taken to small town life as if he'd been born here.

Gordon smiled when Jack joined them. "I've been telling Patrick about Molly and Dylan. They've been helping me after school in the community garden. They're great kids."

Jack smiled. "They really enjoy your company, too."

Patrick pointed to the book under Jack's arm. "I can't

believe Mabel has published a book. It got me thinking about the stories that have been buzzing inside my head for years."

"You should write them down," Gordon said. "Mabel has inspired a lot of people. We could start our own publishing company."

"I'll think about it after the Christmas parade." Patrick sent Jack a concerned frown. "Emma told me who will be on the sleigh with me."

Jack studied his grandfather's face. "It can't be that bad." The parade was in five days. If Patrick was worried about who was playing Mrs. Claus, they didn't have a lot of time to convince him everything would be okay.

"Do you remember meeting a woman named Kathleen at Sweet Treats?"

Jack visited the candy shop so often that he knew everyone who worked there. "She's Natalie's mom. She moved to Sapphire Bay after her daughter decided to live here permanently. Is Kathleen dressing up as Mrs. Claus?"

Patrick looked over his shoulder. "I don't want her to think I asked her to sit on the sleigh with me."

"Why not?"

Gordon shook his head. "I've tried telling your grandfather it's not a big deal, but he won't listen."

"I'm eighty-one years old," Patrick whispered. "What if someone got the wrong idea?"

Jack's eyebrows rose. "Kathleen is pretending to be Mrs. Claus. No one would think…" He looked around the room, hoping Kathleen wasn't close enough to hear his next question. "Do you like Natalie's mom?"

"Of course he likes her," Gordon said. "He always visits the candy shop when she's working."

"You don't complain when I bring fresh fudge to The Welcome Center," Patrick grumbled.

Gordon crossed his arms in front of his chest. "I'd be a fool to turn down the best fudge in Montana."

Jack didn't understand why his granddad was so worried. "You're allowed to like someone, Granddad. Kathleen is a really nice lady, although she's probably a little young for you."

Gordon grinned. "I told you you're robbing the cradle."

"She's sixty-three years old," Patrick spluttered.

"My point exactly. When you were listening to the Beatles, she was a baby."

Jack had only been joking when he pointed out their age difference. "If you're really worried, why don't you talk to Emma? She could let Kathleen know that you had nothing to do with choosing Mrs. Claus."

"Emma's got more on her mind than who's wearing the costumes she bought."

"Do you want me to tell her?"

A blush streaked across Patrick's face. "No. I shouldn't have said anything."

"If you don't feel comfortable—"

Patrick rested his hand on Jack's arm. "It will be all right. Kathleen has no idea how much I like her, so don't say anything." He glanced at Gordon. "That means you, too."

"As long as you still bring me plenty of fudge from Sweet Treats, your secret is safe with me."

"What secret are you talking about?" Emma asked.

Patrick's blush returned. "It isn't important. How are the book sales?"

"I'm happy to report that Mabel has officially sold all the books we brought with us. But, if you missed out, we're taking orders. The next shipment should arrive in less than two weeks. Are you looking forward to being Santa next weekend?"

Patrick glanced at Jack. "I've been looking forward to it all week."

"That's great. Mabel invited Kathleen to the book launch. She thought it would be good for you to get to know the person who's playing Mrs. Claus."

"Well, that's, umm...very thoughtful of her."

Jack had never seen his grandfather so tongue-tied. Instead of leaving him to flounder, he offered him a lifeline. "I saw Noah by the main doors, Granddad. He wanted to see you before you go home."

With a relieved smile, Patrick picked up his glass. "I'll have the barbecue waiting for you. Don't be late for dinner." And before Gordon could invite himself for dinner, Patrick disappeared into the crowd.

"Well," Gordon said with a smile. "That's something I never thought I'd see."

Emma seemed confused. "What do you mean?"

Gordon clamped his mouth shut. "Nothing. It's just me, rambling on again. I'll leave you to enjoy something to eat and drink. I promised Mabel I'd say hello."

Emma watched Gordon leave, then turned her blue eyes toward Jack. "Did I miss something?"

"I'm not sure," he said slowly. "I'll let you know after the Santa Claus parade."

CHAPTER 19

*M*olly rushed into the kitchen "Mom, Dad wants to speak to you!"

Emma looked up from her laptop. Mark had called to speak to the twins. They enjoyed their regular catch-ups, often talking for more than an hour. Emma was pleased they were getting to know each other, even though Mark hadn't seen the twins since they started first grade.

She took the phone from Molly and held her hand over the mouthpiece. "Remember to empty the dishwasher."

"Oh, Mom. Do I have to?"

"There's no point batting those big blue eyes at me. The answer is yes."

"But Dylan hasn't done anything."

"He tidied up the kitchen."

Molly let out an agonized breath. "Can Snowflake help me?"

"As long as your kitten doesn't end up in the dishwasher, that's fine. I'll help you as soon as I've finished speaking to your dad."

As Molly raced out of the room to find Snowflake, Emma held the phone to her ear.

"Hi, Mark. How are you?"

"I'm doing okay. I wanted to let you know I've accepted the job in Bigfork."

The last time they'd spoken, Mark had told her about the job. At that stage, he didn't know whether he wanted to move so far away from his cabins in Colorado. "That's good. Did the owners send you photos of where you'll be living?"

"They arrived yesterday. The cabin is twice as big as where I am now and has a huge workshop. It will be perfect for my sculpting."

"It sounds nice. When do you move?"

"At the beginning of December. If you'd like to bring Molly and Dylan for a visit, you're more than welcome."

"They'd like that. Let me know which weekend works for you and I'll do my best to be there."

"I will."

Even though she hadn't spent a lot of time with Mark since Jack found him, she had a feeling he had something else on his mind. So instead of telling him what the twins were doing at school, she waited.

Mark took a deep breath. "I'm sorry I broke our agreement when I flew to Sapphire Bay. It won't happen again."

Emma's mouth dropped open. She hadn't expected him to apologize. "It will take time for everyone to get used to the new arrangements."

"You should be angry with me."

"To be honest, I was a bit angry. But what good would that do?" Emma said softly. "I know you love the twins. Not seeing them for five years doesn't change that. Just call me when you want to visit them outside of your scheduled visits. I'll do what I can to make it work."

"That's more generous than I deserve. Did Jack tell you he came to Evergreen?"

Emma frowned. "No. When was he there?"

"A few days ago. He reminded me about our agreement."

Jack must have stopped at Evergreen on his way to Manhattan. Emma couldn't understand why he'd want to see Mark in person. He could have easily spoken to him on the phone. And why on earth had he gone there without talking to her first?

"He also told me how much you mean to him." Mark's voice had lowered to a whisper. "I hope you have a happy life together."

Emma heard the regret in Mark's voice. It tore at her heart. Even though they were adults, they were just as emotionally fragile as Molly and Dylan. "I hope my relationship with Jack works out, too. He's an important person in our lives."

She didn't want to end their conversation there, so she forced a smile onto her face. Hopefully, it gave her voice an extra boost of positivity. "I took some photos of Dylan and Molly while they were helping me cook dinner. They looked cute with their aprons tied around their waists and big spoons in their hands. I'll email them to you."

"I'd appreciate it. I'd better go. It's getting late and you'll have things you want to do."

This time, Emma's smile was genuine. "You're saving me from helping Molly load the dishwasher. But you're right, I'd better go. She asked if Snowflake could help her."

"That sounds ominous."

"That's what I thought, too. Have a good night."

"You, too."

After Emma ended the call, she stared at the phone. She was meeting Jack tomorrow for coffee. That would be soon enough to talk about his visit to Evergreen. For now, she had a kitchen to clean and a kitten who might need rescuing.

And then she'd go and see what Dylan was doing.

"I ORDERED you a cappuccino and a lemon and honey muffin."

Emma sat in the seat opposite Jack. "Thanks. I'm sorry I'm late. I had to spend some extra time with a client."

"Don't worry about it. I checked a few emails while I was waiting. How was your morning?"

"Interesting. A man I've never met before called me about designing his website. He's a friend of Noah's."

"Does it look as though it will be an interesting job?"

Emma smiled. "It's going to be amazing. He's a talent scout for a record company. The story he wants his website to tell is different from anything else I've seen."

"When will you start?"

"In three weeks."

The waitress brought their order across to their table.

"Thank you."

"You're welcome. If you need anything else, just ask."

Emma waited until Jack's sandwich and coffee were in front of him before cutting her muffin in half. "This looks delicious."

Jack smiled. "The coffee at this café is the best in Sapphire Bay. I had lunch with Granddad yesterday. He wants you to know how much he enjoyed Mabel's book launch."

"I'm glad he could make it. It's hard to believe he's eighty-one."

"Sometimes I forget, too."

Emma took a sip of coffee. If she didn't tell Jack that she

knew he'd been to Evergreen, she'd have another sleepless night. "Mark called the twins yesterday."

Jack cleared his throat. "Is he okay?"

"He's accepted the job at the resort in Bigfork."

"Good for him. I hope it lives up to his expectations."

"I'm sure it will. He told me you saw him a few days ago."

Jack carefully placed his coffee cup on the table. "I didn't tell you I was going to Evergreen because I knew what you'd say."

"Did it sound anything like, 'I can look after myself'?"

"It sounded similar," Jack muttered.

"Just for the record, I don't need looking after."

"You've told me that before."

"You haven't been listening."

Jack sighed. "I want to make sure you're okay."

Emma broke off a piece of muffin and left it on the side of the plate. "I'm more than okay. I was surprised when Mark turned up unexpectedly, but it wasn't the end of the world."

"Not this time. What if he does it again?"

"Then that would be different. My lawyer told me to call her if Mark didn't follow the parental agreement. Having said that, I want to thank you. I don't know what else you said to Mark, but it worked. He apologized for coming to Sapphire Bay and for not telling me he wanted to see the twins. I didn't expect an apology, but it was appreciated."

"Will you let him see more of Molly and Dylan when he's living in Bigfork?"

"I don't know. We'll see how the visits go. Promise me that next time you have an overwhelming urge to protect me or the twins, you'll tell me. You might be surprised by my answer."

Jack's eyebrows rose. "Does that mean you'll let me help you?"

"Only if you catch me at a vulnerable moment." Emma grinned. "But be warned. They don't come along too often."

"I'll remember." Jack lifted his coffee cup off the table. "To friendship and love, and everything in between."

Emma tapped her cup against Jack's. "That sounds like a good toast to me. Are you looking forward to the Santa Claus parade and night market this Saturday?"

"I am. Do you still want me to look after Molly and Dylan?"

Emma nodded. "That would be great. I have to be on call to fix any problems. Hopefully, there won't be too many."

"At least you don't have to worry about the twins. After Granddad has finished playing Santa, we'll join Noah and Cassie. There will be plenty of people around them to keep Molly and Dylan amused.

Emma knew who the stallholders and food vendors were. Dylan and Molly would have no issue keeping themselves amused—especially when all their favorite foods were on one street.

She just hoped the first Christmas events went according to plan. If anything major happened, five thousand ticket holders wouldn't be amused. And neither would Emma.

"CAN you believe it's only three days until the first Christmas event?" Pastor John asked.

Emma sighed. "The time has gone by so quickly. I'm glad everything is on track for the Santa Claus parade and the night market."

Bailey placed her cup of coffee on Emma's kitchen table. "I visited each of the stores on Main Street. Everyone's displays look incredible. And I've got to say, the miniature Christmas trees outside each store are stunning."

"Wait until tonight," Kylie said. "When everyone turns on their fairy lights, the whole street will be magical."

Emma looked down at her spreadsheet. For the last hour, the entire fundraising committee had gone through each of this weekend's events line by line, double checking that every task had been completed.

"Talking about magical, the snow machine truck will be in Sapphire Bay at four o'clock on Saturday afternoon. The driver said it would take no more than an hour to fill Main Street with thick, white snow."

John turned to the next page of tasks. "It's just as well there aren't any horrible chemicals in the compound. The last thing we need is everyone getting red, itchy rashes."

"What about when it melts?" Bailey asked.

"I can answer that one," Kylie said. "It's totally biodegradable, environmentally friendly, and won't leave any stains or marks on the sidewalk. Or that's what the company told us."

"I spoke with six other event organizers who have used the artificial snow. They were all impressed and didn't have any issues with it." Emma took a quick sip of coffee before looking at the next line on the spreadsheet. "The Mothers' Motorcycle Club arrives in Sapphire Bay on Saturday afternoon. I invited them to my place for coffee and something to eat. After they've pulled Santa's sleigh down Main Street, they'll drive south until they find somewhere to stay for the night."

John looked up from reading the spreadsheet. "If they change their mind and want to stay in Sapphire Bay, let me know. The Welcome Center is usually full, but we could ask the members of our church if they could look after them."

"That would be great, thanks." Emma made a note on the side of the spreadsheet and moved to the next item. "All the stallholders and businesses along Main Street are ready for the night market. The food vendors are excited and, for everyone with a sweet tooth, Brooke has created a special limited edition fudge for the fundraiser. I've added a pre-order link to our website."

Kylie picked up her phone. "I'm on the website now. The fudge is called Christmas Hope. It looks yummy." She turned the phone around so everyone could see the photo.

The creamy white chocolate bars were filled to over-flowing with cranberries, green cherries, and soft, gooey marshmallow. Just looking at the photo made Emma's mouth water.

"My mom and sisters would love the fudge," Bailey said. "I'll order some after our meeting."

Emma had a feeling Bailey wouldn't be the only person in the room making sure they didn't miss out. "Well, that covers this weekend's events. Does anyone have anything else they want to talk about?"

"I do." John opened a large folder he'd brought with him. "We've collected more than a thousand Christmas wishes from people who responded to the Facebook post. What do we want to do with them?"

Kylie read the sheets of paper John handed to her. "Can we help some more people?"

"We could, but it takes a lot of time," Emma said.

Bailey looked up from the list she was reading. "You've already helped some people. But this number of requests would be a full-time job for a team of people, not just one or two. We almost need a separate Christmas wish committee."

John sighed. "I was hoping you wouldn't say that. I'm trying to limit the number of committees we have in the church. Administering them is a big job."

Kylie glanced at Bailey. "John's right. It's the behind-the-scenes work that takes a lot of time. But the committee doesn't need to be associated with the church."

"The same group of people who manage the Christmas

events could look after the Christmas wishes." John pointed to their spreadsheet. "Next year's program will be less time-consuming to organize because we already have the project plans and we'll know what works and what doesn't."

Kylie nodded. "If everyone's happy to combine the Christmas program with the Christmas wishes, what do you think about making more wishes come true this year? Even if we only help a few more people, it would be better than nothing."

Emma smiled at the excitement on her friends' faces. "I'd like to keep going. Toby was so overwhelmed with the bicycle that it made me want to help someone else."

"I'm in," Bailey said.

John gathered the papers in front of him. "I can't do a lot of hours, but I'd like to help, too."

Emma smiled. "It's a unanimous decision—we're going to make more Christmas wishes come true. The only other thing we need is a name for our group. Does anyone have a suggestion that doesn't include the word, committee?"

Kylie tapped her pen on the table. "What about Santa's Elves? They make gifts and give them to the children who have asked for them. It ties in with the wishes theme."

"It's better than Rudolph's Secret Helpers," Bailey said with a grin.

"I know," Emma exclaimed. "Why don't we combine Kylie and Bailey's ideas? We could call ourselves Santa's Secret Helpers."

John stared thoughtfully across the table. "I like it. As long as you don't expect me to wear red tights and a short green tunic, I vote for the combined suggestion."

Emma looked at Bailey. "Are you happy to call our group, Santa's Secret Helpers?"

"Absolutely. But how secret are we talking? Can we tell our families and friends what we're doing?"

John frowned. "We could tell everyone we're organizing the Christmas events, but I wouldn't mention the wishes. We'd be inundated with requests for help."

"If someone realizes what we're doing, we could say we're delivering the wishes on behalf of someone else," Emma said.

Bailey leaned forward. "Or let people's wishes come true without them knowing who helped them."

John smiled. "Now that we have a name, why do I feel more excited about what we're doing?"

"Because it's a secret," Kylie said. "And everyone loves a good secret."

And this one, Emma knew, was one of the best secrets of all.

CHAPTER 20

*J*ack grinned at his Granddad. "If I didn't know better, I'd swear you were the real Santa Claus."

Patrick stroked his long, white beard. "Cassie did a good job of getting me ready."

"The pillows helped, too," Noah added as he patted his grandfather's stomach. "As long as you don't move too quickly, everything should stay in place."

With a hip wiggle that would have impressed any dancer, Patrick jiggled his stomach. "The extra padding isn't going anywhere."

Emma hurried toward them. "The Mothers' Motorcycle Club is ready. How's Santa?"

"I've got my royal wave sorted and my ho-ho-ho's are ready to go."

"All we need is Mrs. Claus." Emma frowned as she searched the street where they were waiting. "Has anyone seen Kathleen?"

A tall woman with dark brown hair strode toward them. "Mom's coming. We had a problem with her dress."

Mrs. Claus followed her daughter around the edge of the building.

Jack looked at the two women and smiled. Apart from what they were wearing, Kathleen and her daughter were like two peas in a pod. They had the same oval face, startling blue eyes, and pixie nose.

"I'm sorry I'm late," Kathleen said as she caught her breath. "The zipper in my dress broke and we had to buy some safety pins from the general store."

Patrick cleared his throat. "You look lovely, Kathleen."

If Jack weren't mistaken, a blush filled Mrs. Claus's cheeks. "Thank you, Patrick. You look handsome in your suit, too."

From beneath his bushy beard, Patrick smiled. "Shall we find our sleigh?"

Kathleen grinned. "We shall."

Patrick held out his hand and Kathleen placed her white-gloved fingers in his.

Emma checked her watch. With a relieved smile she looked at Jack. "We're still on time. I need to go, but I'll send you a text when I'm finished."

"Don't rush. Molly and Dylan will have a good time with us."

Emma looked over her shoulder at Patrick and Kathleen. "I know they will. I'll see you later."

Jack watched Mr. and Mrs. Claus make their way toward the sleigh. "Why do I feel like I'm in a Hallmark movie?" he murmured to his brother.

"Because love is in the air," Noah whispered back.

Jack's eyebrows rose. "I thought I was the only person who knew Granddad liked Kathleen."

"Are you kidding? He goes to the candy shop at least three times a week. Granddad has a sweet tooth, but no one needs that much fudge."

"We give him a big discount," Natalie said. "Patrick is our favorite customer."

Jack turned to Kathleen's daughter and shook her hand. "We haven't met. I'm Jack."

"It's nice to meet you. I'm Natalie."

"Do you think we need to chaperone Mr. and Mrs. Claus?"

Natalie grinned. "They'll be okay. Mom promised me she'd be on her best behavior."

Jack almost groaned. It sounded as though her mom had the same sense of humor as his grandfather. It was no wonder Patrick enjoyed seeing Kathleen so much.

"Mom always has a coffee with Patrick when he comes into the store. They're good friends."

Jack knew it was more than that, but he wasn't going to tell Natalie.

When Patrick was halfway down the street, he turned around. "Are you boys coming? Cassie and the twins will wonder where you've gone."

"We're coming." Jack knew for a fact the twins wouldn't be worried. The last time he'd checked, they were in their favorite store, choosing a new toy with Cassie.

Deciding to follow his grandfather's lead, Jack held out his arm to Natalie. "Shall we follow Mr. and Mrs. Claus into the sunset?"

"I don't mind if we do." And with her other hand wrapped around Noah's arm, Natalie grinned. "Do you think Patrick will ask Mom to go on a date with him?"

Jack almost tripped over his feet. "You know?"

"The whole of Sapphire Bay knows they like each other. They just need a little push."

Noah smiled. "You're in the right company. Jack's really good at telling other people how to run their lives."

Even though what Noah said was true, Jack felt a moral

obligation to stand up for himself. "I might have ideas about how to tweak a relationship, but that doesn't mean I'm perfect."

But he was working on it. And later tonight, he would know for sure whether the major tweak he was about to make would work.

EMMA HELD her breath as the marching band strutted down Main Street. The crowd clapped and cheered as trombones, trumpets, and drums provided a musical backdrop to the costume-clad children skipping down the street.

Next came the special floats that different groups had been working on for the last few weeks. The Christmas theme had been twisted and turned into a modern-day feast of color and light.

With a thick layer of snow lining the sidewalk and Christmas elves handing gifts to the eager crowd, there was something here for everyone.

"You did good, Emma Lewis." Jack wrapped his arm around her waist and kissed the side of her face.

Emma leaned into him and smiled. Molly and Dylan were beside him, sucking on the biggest lollipops she'd ever seen. "Thank you. I've got my fingers crossed that nothing happens. It looks as though the twins are enjoying themselves."

"The lollipops are sugar-free."

"Really? Did Molly tell you that?"

"Do I look that gullible?" Jack asked with a smile. When Emma didn't reply he laughed. "Okay. I'll admit that Dylan told me the lollipops are sugar-free. But in my defense, I did check with the stallholder. They assured me they had the lowest sugar content of any candy they sold."

"I guess that's better than nothing."

"And it's not as if they eat lollipops each week."

"True." Emma glanced at a text message on her cell phone. John was having trouble starting the vintage fire truck that would follow Santa down Main Street.

"Bad news?"

"I hope not. John can't get the fire truck to start."

"Does he need a hand? I'm freakishly good at spotting engine issues."

Emma had always assumed that, apart from fishing, Jack was a city boy at heart. "I thought the nearest you came to engine oil is when your car goes into the garage for a service."

Jack held his hand over his heart. "I'm wounded. I'll have you know that I single-handedly fixed Noah's old truck before his first ever date. I deserved a gold medal for that save."

"Let me guess. You've never let Noah forget what a miracle worker you are."

"That's true. You must know me better than I thought."

Emma's phone vibrated again. "Disaster averted. The engine is working." The low hum of motorcycle engines rumbled along the street. "Santa is on his way."

"I hope Granddad doesn't stand up inside the sleigh."

Emma bit her bottom lip. "So do I. Kathleen assured me she wouldn't let him do anything foolish."

As the first motorcycles slowly drove along Main Street, Emma held Molly and Dylan's hands. Attached to the last bikes by thick rope, was Santa's sleigh. Emma sighed. Now that it was in the parade, the sleigh was every bit as spectacular as she'd imagined. With its shiny, bright red exterior and plush velvet seats, it was the perfect setting for Mr. and Mrs. Claus.

Molly jumped up and down. "I can't see."

Jack knelt down. "Do you want to sit on my shoulders?"

"Yes, please."

Before Santa got much closer, Jack scooped Molly up and onto his shoulders.

"I can see everything," she yelled.

Noah whispered something in Dylan's ear and moments later, he was sitting on top of Noah's shoulders, looking proudly above the heads of the crowd.

"Look at me, Mom," Dylan said. "I'm taller than Jack."

Emma held out her hand. "I'll hold your lollipop before it gets tangled in Noah's hair."

Jack reached up and took Molly's. "Here's another one."

"Can we stay here forever?" Molly asked.

Emma almost felt sorry for Jack. Molly's hands were wrapped so tightly around his neck that it looked as though he was being strangled. "Only for the parade. Otherwise, you'll bang your head on all the doorframes."

Molly pointed at something down the street. "Look at the reindeer!" she squealed. "They look amazing."

Emma agreed. When the riders had shown her the antlers and flashing red noses they'd brought for the motorcycles, she'd thought they were cute. But, with the last rays of sunlight dipping below the horizon, the red noses shone like miniature lighthouses from between each set of handlebars.

"Here comes Santa." Dylan pointed down the street.

People all around them eagerly waited for the arrival of the merry man in red.

"Mrs. Claus looks beautiful," Molly said with a sigh.

Emma kept checking her cell phone. There were no texts, no emergency phone calls, nothing to make her think the parade was anything other than perfect.

"Relax," Jack croaked. "Everything will be all right." He unlatched Molly's hands from around his neck and took a deep breath. "That's better."

Emma's phone vibrated and she read the text. Her shoulders sagged in relief. "The fire truck is moving and the marching band has made it to the end of the street."

Molly frantically waved at the sleigh. "Santa Claus saw me and Mrs. Claus blew me a kiss."

Emma looked up at her daughter. "You're awfully lucky."

Whistles and applause broke out around them.

Emma's gaze shot back to the parade.

"What happened?"

Jack groaned. "Santa just kissed Mrs. Claus."

"On the mouth!" Molly added.

Emma didn't know who was more surprised—Jack, Noah, or Molly. But either way, Mr. and Mrs. Claus looked as though they'd enjoyed it.

AFTER THE PARADE, Jack stomped through the artificial snow beside his grandfather. "I can't believe you kissed her."

"It was a spontaneous gesture of affection."

"You kissed Kathleen. In the middle of Main Street. With almost everyone in Sapphire Bay watching."

Patrick's eyebrows rose. "And your point is?"

"The parade is a family event. Mr. and Mrs. Claus aren't supposed to kiss each other. They're supposed to wave to the crowd and look happy."

"We *are* happy."

Jack walked around a family looking at a Christmas craft stall. The night market was another huge success. With Main Street open only to the five thousand ticket holders, people had been good-natured about waiting in line to buy the Christmas-themed arts and crafts, or sample the delicious food.

He waited for his granddad to wish someone a merry

Christmas before continuing down the street. "When Kathleen agreed to be Mrs. Claus, you were worried what people would think."

Patrick cleared his throat. "I'm not worried anymore. Kathleen and I had dinner last night. We've decided to spend more time together."

Jack froze. "You had a date? And you didn't tell me?"

The people waiting in another line looked at them and smiled. It probably had something to do with his granddad still wearing the Santa costume.

"You don't need to yell," Patrick grumbled. "I might be in my eighties, but I'm not deaf."

"I wasn't yelling. I was surprised."

Patrick pulled Jack under the awning of a jewelry store. "I don't know how many years I've got ahead of me, but life is too short for regrets. I loved your grandma beyond measure. After she died, I was devastated. I never thought I'd find someone I'd enjoy spending my time with. When I met Kathleen, I knew she was special. We talk and laugh and share parts of our lives that mean a great deal to us. I care about her and she feels the same about me."

A lump formed in Jack's throat. "Do you love her?"

When Patrick looked at him, there were tears in his eyes. "I do. Despite our age difference, despite the things that brought us to Sapphire Bay, I love her so much that it scares me."

Jack hugged his granddad. As he held him close, he felt his grandma's presence, wrapping them in her love. "I'm happy for you, Granddad."

Patrick wiped his eyes. "I've had more than a few sleepless nights worrying about what your grandma would have said."

Through his own tears, Jack smiled. "Grandma would tell you to make each day of your life count. She'd be happy that you're happy."

"I hope so." Patrick took a deep breath. "But we're not here to talk about my life. Did you check the snowmen?"

Jack nodded. "They're still there. I was worried they might have melted, but whatever's in the artificial snow is almost indestructible."

"That's modern technology for you. Where's Emma?"

"She's in Sweet Treats with everyone else. When we're ready, Noah will bring her outside."

"You're about to take a big step. Are you sure you're ready?"

Jack nodded. "I've been waiting for her my entire life. I'm more than ready."

Patrick wiped more tears from his eyes. "In that case, we'd better move fast. I don't know how much longer the snowmen will last."

As they walked into the parking lot behind Sweet Treats, Jack sighed. Decorating the empty lot had been easy.

Now all he had to do was ask Emma to spend the rest of her life with him.

EMMA HANDED Molly a container of white chocolate buttons. For most of the evening, the fundraising committee had been coming and going from the kitchen at Sweet Treats, the designated meeting point for tonight's events.

When they weren't on duty, it was great to have somewhere they could go to get away from the people lining the sidewalk. With the night market closing in half an hour, all Emma had to do was wait here, then help secure everything until the morning.

Brooke had provided cakes and cookies for everyone to enjoy. And, when Molly and Dylan arrived, she created a cookie decorating table to keep them amused.

Emma added chocolate frosting to the cookie she was decorating. "What do you think, Dylan? Does he need a mouth?"

Dylan studied the round cookie. "If you want him to look like an elf, I think you should."

Molly picked up her cookie. "Does this look like Snowflake?"

Using lots of white frosting and adding pale gray whiskers and white chocolate eyes, Molly had done a good job of decorating her cookie. "It looks lovely," Emma said with a smile. "I can almost hear Snowflake purring."

"That's because Snowflake likes eating cookies," Molly said proudly.

Emma raised her eyebrows.

"But she only gets little crumbs," Molly added.

"That's good."

With a happy smile, Molly started decorating another cookie.

Emma handed her friend, Brooke, a piping bag full of frosting. "Thank you for letting us stay here."

"I'm glad John called. It's not often a candy shop becomes the headquarters for a Christmas fundraising committee."

Noah's cell phone beeped. He checked the screen before looking at Emma. "Can you do me a favor?"

"Sure. What is it?"

"I ordered a special Christmas present for Jack. The stall-holder has left it outside. Can you give me a hand to put it inside my truck before he arrives?"

Emma wiped her hands on her apron. "Of course I can. But don't tell me what you bought. If Jack asks, I can plead ignorance."

Noah took his keys out of his pocket. "It won't take long."

Emma made sure Molly and Dylan were okay before she

followed Noah outside. "We were lucky with the weather. I was worried it might rain and melt the snow."

"You should be proud of what you've achieved. After tonight, people will be rushing to get tickets for the rest of the events."

Emma started to say something, then stopped. The parking lot wasn't the same drab gray area she'd seen earlier in the day. Someone had transformed it into a snow-covered Christmas wonderland. Jack stood in front of four snowmen who were dressed in colorful hats and scarves. Fairy lights decorated a huge tree and Christmas carols played from a nearby speaker.

"This is amazing." She turned to Noah. "Do you think Jack found the box?" she whispered.

"There isn't one," he whispered back.

"But you..." she looked at Jack and frowned. "Why are you standing in front of four snowmen?"

He stepped forward and Emma's frown deepened. She'd never seen him look so serious. "Is everything all right?"

"It's more than all right. I wanted to ask you something."

"You did?" Emma was even more confused.

Jack held her hands. "I love you, Emma. I can't imagine spending the rest of my life without you by my side."

Her heart pounded as Jack got down on one knee.

"Emma Lewis. Will you marry me?"

Tears filled her eyes. She took a deep breath and tried to think rationally, to weigh up everything she knew and didn't know about Jack. Agreeing to marry someone was a big commitment. It would change her life, change Molly and Dylan's lives, too.

"I don't know what to say."

"You could say, yes."

The gentleness in Jack's voice calmed her nerves. "I love

you Jack, but I need to talk to Molly and Dylan. Whatever we decide will—"

"Say yes!" Molly yelled from somewhere behind Emma.

She turned around and stared at the empty doorway.

"We're up here, Mommy."

Emma looked above the candy store to Brooke's apartment. Molly and Dylan were standing in front of an open window. Brooke waved from behind them.

"Jack asked us if he could marry you. We said yes, but only if you want him to be our daddy."

Emma's gaze shifted to Dylan.

"I want Jack to be my dad, too," he said shyly. "He knows about the stars, and frogs, and he likes fishing. We made a snowman family. It's me, Molly, you and Jack."

Emma wiped the tears from her eyes. When she turned around, she got the fright of her life. Jack's granddad, still dressed as Santa, stood beside the Christmas tree.

"I'm sorry. The snow muffled my footsteps. I didn't mean to scare you."

"It's okay," Emma said quickly. "I'm just feeling a little overwhelmed."

Patrick gave her a hug. "If it makes any difference, it would be wonderful if you and the twins joined our family. I'd have two of the loveliest granddaughters in Montana."

"Thank you."

"You're welcome. I've also got something my grandson asked me to look after." Patrick took a little black box from one of his pockets and handed it to Jack. "Good luck."

Jack opened the lid and stood close to Emma.

Her mouth dropped open when she saw the sparkling sapphire and diamond engagement ring. "It's beautiful."

"I asked Cassie to make it for you."

"She knew?"

"She's known how I feel about you for weeks. Will you marry me?"

Emma looked into Jack's eyes and sighed. "I never thought I'd fall in love again, but I have. I love you and I'd like to be your wife."

Jack's eyes filled with tears. With trembling hands, he slid the ring onto her finger, then wrapped her in a hug. "I love you so much. Thank you for saying yes."

"Does that mean Jack is going to be our daddy?" Molly asked.

Emma laughed before looking up at her daughter. "Yes, Molly. Jack is going to be your daddy."

The smile on her children's faces touched something deep inside Emma. "We're getting married," she whispered to Jack.

"I hope so. Is next Saturday too early?"

Emma smiled. "Maybe a little."

"Okay. How does two months from today sound?"

"It sounds perfect." And before Dylan and Molly ran outside, she wrapped her arms around Jack and kissed him until they were both breathless.

Today was the beginning of their new life together, and she couldn't have been happier.

THE END

THANK YOU

Thank you for reading *Christmas On Main Street* I hope you enjoyed it! If you did…

1. Help other people find this book by **writing a review.**
2. Sign up for my **new releases e-mail**, so you can find out about the next book as soon as it's available.
3. Come like my **Facebook** page.
4. Visit my website: **leeannamorgan.com**

Keep reading to enjoy an excerpt from **Mistletoe Madness**, Kylie and Ben's story, the second book in the *Santa's Secret Helpers* series!

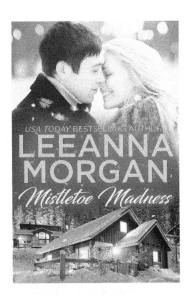

Mistletoe Madness
Santa's Secret Helpers, Book 2

This Christmas, something magical is happening in Sapphire Bay.

Kylie loves everything about Christmas. The lights, the carols, the snow-covered streets and, most of all, the smiles on the faces of everyone she meets. Well, almost everyone. When her friends ask her to organize the biggest fundraising Christmas party Sapphire Bay has ever seen, the florist inside of her is itching to get started. But that means talking to Ben Thompson, the closest thing to the Christmas Grinch she's ever met.

Ben owns the only Christmas tree farm in Sapphire Bay, but that doesn't mean he's full of the Christmas spirit. He came to Montana searching for peace and quiet, but pesky Kylie

Bryant, with her addiction to all things Christmassy, is driving him insane.

When Kylie helps him save his business, everything about her begins to make sense. She's getting under Ben's skin and making him feel alive. But a letter from his lawyer changes everything. Will a secret from Ben's past tear them apart or will they finally get everything they've ever wanted?

Mistletoe Madness is the second book in the Santa's Secret Helpers series and can easily be read as a standalone. Each of Leeanna's series are linked so you can find out what happens to your favorite characters in other books. For news of my latest releases, please visit leeannamorgan.com and sign up for my newsletter. Happy reading!

Turn the page to read the first chapter of
Mistletoe Madness
Santa's Secret Helpers, Book 2

CHAPTER 1

*K*ylie hurried across the parking lot and stepped inside The Welcome Center. With a quick wave at the receptionist, she headed toward Pastor John's office.

She was late. Again.

It wasn't as if this was one of the fundraising group's usual catch-up meetings. She had an emergency and only her friends could help her.

With a quick knock, she opened the office door. John, Emma, and Bailey sat around the desk with spreadsheets, laptops, and cups of coffee in front of them.

"Sorry I'm late."

"Don't worry." Emma's smile did nothing to calm Kylie's nerves. "Bailey was telling us about the Christmas carol competition."

For the last three months, they'd been organizing events to raise money for Sapphire Bay's tiny home village. As well as adding some early Christmas cheer to the community, the events were bringing more tourists to the small Montana town. Last weekend they'd held the Main Street Santa Claus

Parade and the Night Market. Both events were a huge success—which made her news even harder to share.

Pastor John handed her a cup of coffee. "Have a seat. You looked stressed."

"I am." Kylie took off her jacket and sat beside Emma. "I'm sorry I called an emergency meeting, but I didn't know what else to do."

Bailey leaned forward. "What's happened?"

"We can't use the community center for the Christmas party. The water pipes burst and no one can use any of the rooms for at least four weeks."

Emma's eyes widened. "When did that happen?"

"Last night. I've called all the venues that can seat two hundred guests, but they're booked for weddings and other events."

Kylie loved living in the small town but, sometimes, when you needed something at the last minute, your choices were severely limited. Like now. If she were still living in San Francisco, she could have easily found a hotel or conference facility. But this wasn't California. This was a small town on the edge of Flathead Lake.

"Have you asked the McGraw's?" Emma asked. "Jack and I were looking at wedding venues last weekend and their barn is amazing."

"It's booked. I even called the Cozy Inn, but their conference room is too small." Kylie pulled a list out of her bag. "These are the places I've tried. If you can think of another venue, I'd really appreciate it."

John studied the sheet of paper. "Do the caterers need a commercial kitchen?"

"Probably not. They have a mobile kitchen they can use to keep the food hot. Have you thought of somewhere we could use?"

"Maybe. I'd have to talk to the foreman, but what about

the old steamboat museum? We'd have to move the half-finished tiny homes into the yard, and our tools and supplies would need to be stored somewhere else, but it could work."

The old steamboat museum was on the outskirts of town. When John was looking for somewhere to build relocatable tiny homes, he saw the abandoned building's potential. With its incredibly high ceilings, arched windows, and large foyer, it could also be a stunning venue for a Christmas party.

Emma tapped her pen against her chin. "It could work. The kitchen is too small, but if the catering company can bring a mobile kitchen, it won't matter."

Bailey frowned. "The main hall is huge. Do we have the time and the budget to make it look amazing?"

"Maybe not." Kylie pulled another file from her bag. "Most of the Christmas decorations we were going to use were damaged in the flood. Renting more decorations would be expensive. And with our limited budget, buying new ones isn't an option, either."

Emma wrote something down on a piece of paper. "I'm heading into town tonight to speak to the Business Association about last weekend's events. I'll ask them if they know anyone who could help."

"That would be great."

"What about Ben? Has he decided to donate the Christmas trees?"

Kylie sighed. "Not yet, but he's still happy to provide the mistletoe." Of all the people who lived in Sapphire Bay, Ben was the hardest to figure out. "He's stopped answering my phone calls. I don't know what his problem is. Anyone would think he doesn't like Christmas."

"We all have issues we're dealing with," John said softly. "If you tell him about the community center, he might be more willing to help."

"I don't think that will make a difference." Over the last

few weeks, she'd tried everything she could think of to show Ben how important the trees were to their events. She'd even resorted to bribery. But no amount of gingerbread men, Christmas cookies, or shortbread made a difference. For someone who owned a Christmas tree farm, he was the most "unchristmassy" person she knew.

"As a last resort, we could use the artificial trees on Main Street," Emma suggested. "The store owners won't mind if they aren't there for a couple of nights."

Kylie shook her head. "The whole point of having our events start a few months before Christmas was to encourage tourists to come here. If we take away the trees, Main Street won't look the same."

"Kylie's right," Bailey said. "Try Ben one more time. You never know, he might change his mind when he hears what's happened."

Kylie looked around the table. "Regardless of what he says, I don't think we have any choice but to use the old museum. The profit we make from the Christmas party will pay for at least one tiny home. I don't want to give that up."

"I agree," Emma said. "Apart from not being able to build another tiny home, we'll have two hundred disappointed ticket holders calling us."

"I'll talk to the foreman at the museum," Kylie said quickly before John could offer. He already worked long hours in the church and didn't need the added pressure of organizing the venue for the party. "If there are any issues, I'll send everyone an email."

"Are you sure?" John asked. "I don't mind—"

"I'm sure."

When Emma asked about the music for the party, Kylie had good news. "Willow can perform with her band. Her wedding is the following weekend, so the timing is perfect."

Bailey rubbed Kylie's arm. "At least that's one less thing to organize. If you need someone to help in your flower shop, I have Wednesdays available."

"And our youth employment program is always looking for job opportunities," John said. "There are a couple of students who would be more than capable of helping in your store."

"Thank you." Kylie appreciated her friends' support. Juggling the Christmas events, their Christmas wish program, and her business was becoming more difficult.

If one more thing went wrong, Ben wouldn't be the only person in Sapphire Bay who wasn't looking forward to Christmas.

ON HIS WAY THROUGH TOWN, Ben stopped at the traffic lights and glanced at Blooming Lovely, the flower shop Kylie Bryant owned. His eyes narrowed as he took in the fairy lights decorating the front window, the Christmas tree standing outside, and the baskets of red and white flowers filling the veranda with color.

Blooming Lovely wasn't the only store to break out the tinsel and bring the holiday season forward three months. The sleepy little Montana town had caught a serious case of "Christmasitis". And, judging by the amount of traffic on the road, it was increasing the number of people coming into town.

He just hoped the Christmas program raised enough money to build more tiny homes. He knew better than most how hard it was to start over, especially for the most vulnerable in a community.

Two years ago, he'd arrived in Sapphire Bay to begin a new life. Unlike most of the people who came here, he had savings and skills he could put to good use. Even so, he wondered what he'd been thinking. What did a builder know about growing Christmas trees?

His family and friends thought he was crazy. He'd never owned a garden. Even the indoor plants his mom insisted on bringing him wilted on the windowsill. But through sheer stubbornness, his business was making a small profit. It wouldn't make him rich, but it kept food in the pantry and gave him an excuse to work outside.

The traffic lights turned green and he joined the vehicles cruising down Main Street.

He hoped Kylie wasn't anywhere near The Welcome Center. The tree he'd loaded into the back of his truck might give her the wrong impression. If she saw it, she'd think all her prayers had been answered, but this was a special gift for the church. One tree he could donate. Twenty was out of the question.

He might not be an expert at growing Christmas trees, but he knew about budgeting. The modest salary he earned would disappear if twenty of his best trees ended up decorating a party—even if it was for a good cause. He had bills to pay and a mortgage that would keep him in Montana for a few more years.

Turning right, he headed toward the church. The sooner he saw Pastor John, the sooner he could return to the farm. And the sooner he would be away from the Christmas cheer that made his stomach churn.

JOHN STRODE across the parking lot toward Ben. "You made it here in good time."

"I'm glad I left when I did. It looks as though the Christmas events are bringing more people into Sapphire Bay."

"They are. Quite a few newspapers have run stories about what we're doing. Emma even gave an interview to a TV reporter yesterday."

Ben opened the tailgate of his truck. "The fundraising committee must be happy."

"They are. Thanks for bringing the tree into town."

"You're welcome. I can't supply the trees the fundraising committee want, but I'm hoping this one will brighten someone's day."

John grabbed one side of the tree as Ben pulled it out of the truck. "I'm sure it will. Can you do me a favor?"

"Sure."

"Next time you see Kylie, talk to her."

"It won't do any—" Ben followed John's gaze. Coming out of The Welcome Center was the woman he'd been dodging for the last week.

John cleared his throat. "Just so you know, I didn't plan this. Kylie called an emergency meeting."

"Can pastors tell white lies?"

"Only if they're very careful."

Ben ignored John's smile. His gaze traveled back to Kylie, absorbing everything about her in one earth-shattering sweep. She was, without a doubt, the most attractive woman he'd ever met.

She was also obsessed with everything Christmassy. Today, the fabric of her red knee-length dress had pictures of candy canes all over it. Her blond hair, normally caught in a ponytail, fell around her shoulders in soft, silky waves.

His eyes narrowed. She'd even dyed two wide strands of her hair, green. All she needed was pointy ears and she could have been one of Santa's elves.

She stopped in the middle of the sidewalk and frowned. It didn't look as though she wanted to see him, either. For someone who loved Christmas, it must be daunting to realize there was one person who didn't share her enthusiasm.

"Hi, Ben. I didn't expect to see you here." Kylie's gaze shifted to the tree. "Did you change your mind about supplying the Christmas trees for the party?"

Ben shook his head. The hopeful note in Kylie's voice made him feel bad. He knew how much the trees meant to her, but there had to be other decorations she could use. "This one is for The Welcome Center's living room."

She sighed. "It will look beautiful."

Ben gripped the string he'd wrapped around the branches. "I'm sorry I can't supply the trees."

Kylie walked toward him, the skirt of her dress swishing around her legs. "You've never told me why you can't donate them."

And he didn't want to. Admitting his business was going through a difficult time was like telling his family and friends they were right. Everyone had expected his business to fail, but he was still here. Just.

John adjusted his hands on the tree. "I need to leave for another meeting soon. Would you mind if we took this inside?"

"I'll help." Kylie stood beside the tree, her hands gripping the string that held everything tight.

Ben glanced at John, hoping he'd intervene and tell Kylie they could manage without her.

"That would be great," John said. "If you carry the top, we'll hold the sides."

Ben studied the innocent expression on John's face. If you didn't know him very well, you'd think he was being friendly. But John had an ulterior motive, and that motive involved Ben talking to Kylie.

With no excuse left, Ben repositioned his hands. When everyone was ready, they carefully carried the tree inside.

John nudged open the door to the living room. "We thought we'd put the tree between the piano and the sleigh."

Ben looked around the room. Someone had moved the sofas and chairs, creating a large open space in front of the glossy black piano.

His eyes widened when he saw the ornate wooden sleigh. With its high back, curved sides, and plush velvet seat, it was the perfect size for most of the children who stayed at the center.

Ben smiled when Mr. Whiskers, The Welcome Center's resident gray-haired cat, peeked his head out from under one of the runners. The children weren't the only ones who were enjoying the new piece of furniture.

John moved toward a bright red Christmas tree stand. "Mabel made sure everything was ready. She even mixed some of Kylie's special powder in the container beside the piano."

Ben frowned at the old juice bottle sitting on the floor.

"It's not illegal," Kylie muttered.

She was scowling so hard that Ben almost smiled. "I didn't think it would be."

"It's the same powder I use to keep my flowers fresh. I thought it might stop the tree from drying out too quickly."

Ben lowered the trunk of the tree into the container. "If it drops too many needles, I'll bring the center another one."

When the tree was secure, Kylie stepped back and lifted her gaze to the ceiling. "It's the perfect height for this room."

"Let's see what it looks like out of its wrapping." Ben pulled out a knife and quickly cut through the string. As the branches fell into place, he walked around the ten-foot tree, making a few adjustments as he went. Thankfully, none of the branches had been damaged on the journey here.

"Oh, my," Mabel said from the living room entrance. "That's one of the prettiest trees I've ever seen." As well as co-owning the town's general store, Mabel Terry spent many hours volunteering at The Welcome Center.

Ben's eyes widened. A red tinsel wreath sat on top of her hair and gold bells dangled from her ears. "You can thank the previous owners of the Christmas tree farm for that," he said. "It was planted more than fourteen years ago."

"Well, it sure is a beauty." Mabel picked up a remote control and pointed it toward the far wall. "We need some music. It will make it feel more like Christmas if we play some carols."

Stuffing the string into his pocket, Ben prepared to leave. After living with profound hearing loss in one ear, he knew when he was better off at home. The background noise would confuse his brain and make it impossible to hear what everyone said.

Kylie turned away and opened a box of decorations.

When she looked over her shoulder at him, he frowned. She was waiting for something, but he had no idea what it was.

"Kylie asked if you're selling many Christmas trees at the moment," John said.

Heat scorched Ben's face. He should be used to missing parts of conversations. But he wasn't, not by a long shot. He hated not being able to hear what everyone said. Hated feeling as though he was damaged. That he was different.

He glanced at Kylie, hoping she didn't realize he was partially deaf. "It's too early for most people to buy a Christmas tree. Sales don't usually pick up until the end of November."

"I must order one for us," Mabel said with a smile. "Allan loves the smell of a real Christmas tree."

Ben picked up his gloves and looked over Mabel's shoulder. At least six children were walking into the room. "I'd better leave you to decorate the tree."

John beckoned the children forward. "This will bring a lot of joy to our guests. Thank you."

The children's eyes were wide with excitement.

"That's okay. With all the events happening around town, it would have been a shame not to make the center a little more festive." His gaze connected with Kylie's. She might think he was the Grinch, but be wanted everyone at the center to enjoy Christmas. "Good luck with the events you're organizing."

"Thanks. Would you mind if I walked back to your truck with you?"

That was the last thing he wanted. "I don't—"

John cleared his throat.

"Fine," Ben muttered. "But I have a lot of work to do."

Kylie took a piece of tinsel out of the box of decorations. "It will only take a few minutes."

And before he knew what she was doing, Kylie twisted the tinsel into a necklace and lifted it over his head. "Merry Christmas, Ben."

KYLIE KNEW Ben didn't want to talk to her, but she needed his trees more than ever. Without them, the old steamboat museum would look bare and uninviting—the last thing their guests would expect at a Christmas party.

She glanced at Ben. He hadn't said much since they'd left the living room. "How did you learn to grow Christmas trees?"

He opened the front doors and followed her into the parking lot. "When I was a teenager, I worked on a Christmas tree farm. The rest I've learned from the previous owners."

"You must be proud of what you've achieved."

Ben shrugged and Kylie sighed. Most of the time, when she tried talking to him, he either changed the subject or didn't seem to hear her. He was one of the most frustrating people she knew, but that didn't mean she was giving up.

"We have to find another venue for the Christmas party."

Ben's footsteps slowed. "Why aren't you having it at the community center?"

"One of the water pipes burst. It will take a few weeks to fix everything."

"Where will you go?"

"John suggested the old steamboat museum. It has the space we need and it's close to town."

"It's also full of half-finished tiny homes and all the tools and building materials the construction crews need."

"We don't have a lot of choice. Everything else is booked."

"There must be somewhere."

"Not that I've found." Kylie looked across the parking lot. The first stage of the tiny home village was well underway. Ten houses sat tall and proud on the large lot, each of them built by volunteers.

On the hardest days, when juggling her business and volunteering at The Welcome Center was too much, Kylie thought of the people waiting for a house. The tiny home village was their last chance to feel a sense of belonging, of being part of a community that cared about them. And for some people, it was the first time they'd had anywhere to call home.

Ben pulled up the zipper on his jacket. "The steamboat museum is huge. How are you going to decorate it?"

"We'll have to rely on other organizations to help us. Emma is talking to the local business association tonight and Mabel will approach some of her suppliers. Hopefully, we'll be able to borrow or buy enough decorations to make the museum look less like a spaceship."

Ben grunted.

Did he just smile?

"You'll need a cherry picker to reach the high ceilings."

She'd need more than that to help fill the enormous space. "I spoke to Willow after my meeting with the fundraising committee. A friend of hers designs the lighting for her concerts. She thinks we can use some kind of laser system to create a holiday feel without spending thousands of dollars on decorations."

"So you don't need the Christmas trees?"

"We do. The trees will give a real Christmas feel to the party, especially if we don't have a lot of other decorations." Kylie bit her bottom lip. She was so excited when her friends had asked her to organize the Christmas fundraising party. She'd walked through the community center, imagined a winter wonderland, and begged and borrowed what she could to make the dream a reality.

But most of that was gone.

She took a deep breath. "I know you said you can't donate the trees. Would you change your mind if I helped recover the cost of them?"

"Each tree sells for seventy-five dollars. Multiply that by twenty and you have a whole lot of money I can't find anywhere else."

Kylie looked into his serious brown eyes. "I looked at your website. It needs a little work."

Ben frowned. "I'm not a web designer."

"You don't need to be," she said quickly. The last thing she wanted to do was offend him, but this was important. "I can't pay for the trees, but I can do something even better."

Kylie crossed her fingers, hoping Ben could see the benefit in what she was about to say. "I talked to my friend, Emma. She can update your website using mine as a template. All we need to do is take different photos and replace the text."

"That won't pay for the trees."

"No, but it will make it easier for customers to place online orders for your trees. I had some other ideas, too. What about selling a range of Christmas products? You could have wreaths, garlands, table centerpieces, and lots of other Christmas accessories for your customers to buy."

Ben's frown turned into a scowl. "I have no idea how to make any of those things and I can't afford to buy them. And even if I could, I don't have the staff to organize everything."

Kylie held onto Ben's arm. "I know it could work. No one else in Sapphire Bay sells Christmas trees, let alone locally made decorations. With all the visitors arriving for our events, it's the perfect opportunity to capture another market."

Ben's gaze focused on her fingers clutching his jacket.

She dropped her hand. "Sorry. I get carried away where Christmas is concerned."

"I hadn't noticed."

A sinking feeling hit Kylie's chest. She'd said too much, tried too hard to make Ben see other ways he could earn money. "I need to get back to work. Thanks for listening to me." She had been so sure Ben would jump at the chance to have a new website and sell decorations, but she was wrong. Imagining the Christmas party without twenty glittering trees was difficult, but what choice did she have?

With a heavy heart, she opened the door to her truck. If she were lucky, Mabel might know someone who could—

"Do you know how to make wreaths and garlands?"

Kylie turned around. Ben was standing where she'd left him, scowling so hard that the end of the world could have been coming. "I do."

"Could you bring some samples out to the farm?"

Kylie's mouth dropped open. "Okay."

"Call me first. If I'm working outside, I won't hear you arrive."

And before she said anything, Ben turned around and walked across the parking lot.

"Thank you!" she yelled.

He kept his head bowed, acting for all the world as if he hadn't heard her.

Kylie sighed. At least he was open to selling different products to make up for the cost of the trees.

And maybe, if she tried really hard to forget all the other times she'd talked to him, he wasn't so bad after all.

AVAILABLE NOW!
Mistletoe Madness
Santa's Secret Helpers, Book 2

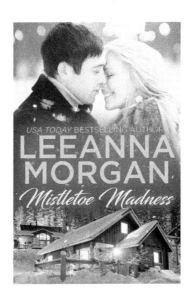

ENJOY MORE BOOKS BY LEEANNA MORGAN

Montana Brides:

Book 1: Forever Dreams (Gracie and Trent)

Book 2: Forever in Love (Amy and Nathan)

Book 3: Forever After (Nicky and Sam)

Book 4: Forever Wishes (Erin and Jake)

Book 5: Forever Santa (A Montana Brides Christmas Novella)

Book 6: Forever Cowboy (Emily and Alex)

Book 7: Forever Together (Kate and Dan)

Book 8: Forever and a Day (Sarah and Jordan)

Montana Brides Boxed Set: Books 1-3

Montana Brides Boxed Set: Books 4-6

The Bridesmaids Club:

Book 1: All of Me (Tess and Logan)

Book 2: Loving You (Annie and Dylan)

Book 3: Head Over Heels (Sally and Todd)

Book 4: Sweet on You (Molly and Jacob)

The Bridesmaids Club: Books 1-3

Emerald Lake Billionaires:

Book 1: Sealed with a Kiss (Rachel and John)

Book 2: Playing for Keeps (Sophie and Ryan)

Book 3: Crazy Love (Holly and Daniel)

Book 4: One And Only (Elizabeth and Blake)

Emerald Lake Billionaires: Books 1-3

The Protectors:

Book 1: Safe Haven (Hayley and Tank)

Book 2: Just Breathe (Kelly and Tanner)

Book 3: Always (Mallory and Grant)

Book 4: The Promise (Ashley and Matthew)

The Protectors Boxed Set: Books 1-3

Montana Promises:

Book 1: Coming Home (Mia and Stan)

Book 2: The Gift (Hannah and Brett)

Book 3: The Wish (Claire and Jason)

Book 4: Country Love (Becky and Sean)

Montana Promises Boxed Set: Books 1-3

Sapphire Bay:

Book 1: Falling For You (Natalie and Gabe)

Book 2: Once In A Lifetime (Sam and Caleb)

Book 3: A Christmas Wish (Megan and William)

Book 4: Before Today (Brooke and Levi)

Book 5: The Sweetest Thing (Cassie and Noah)

Book 6: Sweet Surrender (Willow and Zac)

Sapphire Bay Boxed Set: Books 1-3

Sapphire Bay Boxed Set: Books 4-6

Santa's Secret Helpers:

Book 1: Christmas On Main Street (Emma and Jack)

Book 2: Mistletoe Madness (Kylie and Ben)

Book 3: Silver Bells (Bailey and Steven)

Book 4: The Santa Express (Shelley and John)

Book 5: Endless Love (The Jones Family)

Santa's Secret Helpers Boxed Set: Books 1-3

Return To Sapphire Bay:

Book 1: The Lakeside Inn (Penny and Wyatt)

Book 2: Summer At Lakeside (Diana and Ethan)

Book 3: A Lakeside Thanksgiving (Barbara and Theo)

Book 4: Christmas At Lakeside (Katie and Peter)

The Cottages on Anchor Lane:

Book 1: The Flower Cottage (Jackie and Richard)

Book 2: The Starlight Café (Andrea and David)

Book 3: The Cozy Quilt Shop (Shona and Greg)

Book 4: A Stitch in Time (Laura and Joseph)